DAUGHTER
OF THE
DAWN

BOOKS BY MARION KUMMEROW

DAUGHTER OF THE DAWN

MARION KUMMEROW

bookouture

Published by Bookouture in 2022

An imprint of Storyfire Ltd.
Carmelite House
50 Victoria Embankment
London EC4Y 0DZ

www.bookouture.com

ISBN: 978-1-80314-388-0
eBook ISBN: 978-1-80314-387-3

1

Margarete Rosenbaum, in her guise as Annegret Huber, left the mansion where she lived and asked her handyman Nils to take her with him into the nearby town of Plau am See.

As they reached the market square she said, "I'll meet with a few of the ladies, while you run your errands. Can you pick me up here three hours from now?"

"Sure, Fräulein Annegret." The man approaching sixty years of age nodded his head. With most able-bodied men having been drafted, he was one of the few old staff who still worked for her.

Three hours would give her enough time to sip a coffee at the small bakery that had become the meeting spot for the non-working women in town. But first she needed to see someone else: the man she loved. Who she hoped would help her with a pressing issue in the munitions factory she owned. She had fallen in love with Stefan last summer, and ever since he'd rescued her from a sinister attempted murder, she also confided in him.

Along with Oliver, her estate manager, and Dora, Oliver's new wife and her personal maid, he was the third person who knew her real identity. Margarete Rosenbaum, a Jewish woman impersonating a rich Nazi heiress named Annegret Huber.

After living for more than two years under this false identity she often forgot who she really was, so she relished the moments with Stefan, where she could just be herself.

Obviously nobody could know about their blossoming love, because the town elite would be shocked that Fräulein Annegret was interested in a lowly fisherman, while the political elite would be even more scandalized to find out that staunch Nazi Annegret was attracted to a man accused of sabotage and deemed politically unreliable.

If only they knew that she wasn't who she seemed to be! She nervously giggled, but sobered almost immediately again. She'd gotten a rather unpleasant taste of what it meant if someone found out.

She cast the thought aside and quickened her steps, as she headed toward the wharf. Anxious to see Stefan, she still kept a careful eye out for anyone who might see her and wonder where she was going.

He was on his boat, cleaning the early morning catch. After a quick glance to check that there was no one else lingering on the dock, she stopped to talk with him. As always when she saw him, a warmth spread from her heart throughout her body. It wasn't only his rugged appearance with the flaxen hair, blue eyes and broad shoulders she loved, but also his stunningly kind personality. But above all she loved him for being one of the few good men in the world who wouldn't stand by and look the other way when Jews and other unfortunate citizens were mistreated by the Nazi government.

"Good morning, Herr Stober," she called to gain his attention, making sure she was speaking on his left side, since he was deaf in his right ear after the explosion in a factory he'd worked in. That explosion had not only cost him his hearing, but also his job, since the Nazis had accused him of sabotage and ultimately prohibited him from working in his studied profession as a chemical engineer. Instead, he earned his keep by taking over his grandfather's fishing boat.

Stefan looked up, the brightest smile appearing on his face. To keep up appearances they addressed each other formally in public. "Good morning, Fräulein Annegret. What brings you here this early in the morning?"

Her heart palpitated while she wondered how to best broach the subject. "Good fishing this morning?"

"Good enough," he replied, putting down the knife he'd been using to gut and clean the fish. He walked to the side of the boat and leaned over the railing, rinsing his hands clean with a bucket of water, before he wiped them on a towel. Holding out a hand, he invited her onboard the deck.

Margarete shook her head and took a half-step back. "No, I'll stay right here," she said as bad memories befell her, transporting her back in time to the ledge of the bluff that overlooked the lake. Her body stiffened with fear as she stared into the abyss. The black, icy water held her in a spell, wanting to pull her down beneath the surface, devour her and suck the very life out of her.

"… alright?" Stefan's sonorous voice reached her, helping to shake off the deathly fear immobilizing her.

"Yes. I was just… for a moment." She didn't have to tell him, because she knew he understood. It had been him who'd pulled her out of the deathly water, mere seconds before she had drowned. Regaining her composure, she said, "I came to ask for your help."

Stefan gave her a considering look. By the way his eyebrow twitched she could tell that he knew what kind of help she needed. As if to prove her assessment of the situation, he said, "Wouldn't it be better to have this discussion on the boat where there are no prying ears?"

She nodded reluctantly, gathering all her courage to take a step forward, muttering, "I hope I don't regret this."

Stefan reached up a hand and she gingerly placed hers in it. As soon as she touched him, he tightened his grip on her fingers saying, "Easy does it now," before he reached with his free hand to guide her onto the deck of his boat.

Margarete gave an audible sigh of relief when both her feet were firmly planted on the wooden deck, evoking a soft chuckle from Stefan. The scolding glare she gave him silenced the chuckle within an instant. As much as she realized the absurdity of her fear she couldn't let go of it. Being a Jew, who had been pretending to be a German heiress for what felt like several lifetimes, having faced more dangers than she cared to remember, and yet water was what truly scared her now.

"Come and sit down while I finish cleaning this morning's catch," Stefan invited her.

Despite being alone on the boat, her voice was barely above a whisper. "I want you to work for me in the factory."

Stefan's eyebrows disappeared beneath his hair. "Me? Why?"

"I need someone working on the inside to sabotage the production."

Picking up another fish he nodded, before he slipped the knife down the belly and Margarete watched as he expertly cleaned the fish and set it aside reaching for another.

"You still want to go through with that idea, after everything that has happened?"

"Now more than ever."

"It's incredibly risky. I don't want to see you hurt," he said with a voice full of love.

"That's why I need you. You have the expertise to make it subtle. Things that can't easily be identified or traced back to the factory."

Stefan shook his head. "I don't know."

"You promised! Remember? Last fall after we went to that dance at your friend's house. You said you would help me with this."

He grimaced. "I do remember very well. But back then I didn't know what I know now."

She looked at him with the sternest expression she could muster. "Why is that such a game-changer that you don't want to keep your promise?"

"Ach, Gretchen." He wiped one hand on a rag and traced a finger down the back of her hand, causing ripples of delight to spread through her body. "I have fallen in love with you and can't imagine ever again living without you."

In spite of being moved by his words, she insisted, "There are bigger things at stake here than my personal safety. We need to do everything we can to shorten this war. And who would be better equipped to do this than you?"

He sighed. "You're right, but I still think it's a bad idea for me to work for you."

"Why's that? Because you don't want to take orders from me?" She couldn't help give him a smirk.

"You know you can give me orders all day long and I wouldn't mind." Mischief glinted in his eyes. "This is different though. Wouldn't the authorities be suspicious if you employed me? A known critic of the regime?"

She had already pondered this aspect for several days and had come up with a satisfying solution. "They might, although since most able-bodied men are drafted left and right I don't really have that many options for the empty position as my head of quality control."

"Have you thought of everything?" he said with a smile.

"I have. And before you find more stumbling blocks, here's the short version: I need you. The prisoners need you. Our country needs you."

"Well, that's quite the burden you're loading onto my shoulders."

"I wouldn't if it weren't necessary." She took a deep breath before she spoke again. "Believe me, I hate the idea as much as you do, because it's dangerous. It doesn't bear contemplating what happens if you get caught... and contrary to popular opinion, I'm not the cold-hearted heiress playing chess with her pawns. I don't want to lose you either." Her voice began to tremble. It had seemed such an easy task to convince Stefan to sabotage her factory, but now that she realized what that entailed, she felt the cold hand of fear grip her heart.

"Shush." He looked furtively around to make sure nobody could see them, before he took her hand into his. "I'll do it."

"Thank you." She was relieved and horrified in equal parts.

"Before you thank me, this will be done on my terms." Stefan looked at her with love and determination in his eyes.

"And those are?"

"First, I'm not going to be an employee." She opened her mouth to protest, but he gestured her to keep quiet. "Instead, I'll consult with the factory, advising the production managers. Not more and not less."

Margarete reluctantly nodded.

"Second, I'll report to your estate manager exclusively."

"But—"

"This point is non-negotiable. I'll not endanger your life by getting caught discussing sabotage. After today, you and I will never speak of this matter again." The stern set of Stefan's jaw told her he wasn't going to give on this point. Not even a tiny inch.

She considered his conditions for a minute and then agreed. "Fine. We'll do it the way you propose. You can discuss whatever you're doing with Oliver."

"And you won't ask me about what's happening?" Stefan added.

"Fine. I won't ask you about what's happening," she groused. When Stefan smiled and rubbed his thumb across the back of her hand, she added, "You drive a hard bargain, Herr Stober. Let's hope you're just as clever in your new position."

"Yes. Let's hope so," Stefan agreed with a chuckle before releasing her hand.

With his assistance she stepped back onto the dock, already missing being close to him.

"We'll need the delivery at the manor by tomorrow afternoon," she said loudly for the benefit of another fisherman who'd just docked his boat next to Stefan's.

"It'll be done to your satisfaction, Fräulein Annegret," Stefan responded.

"Good day," she greeted the other fisherman, as she walked away from the man she loved, wondering whether she'd done the right thing in asking for his assistance. She knew he was the best person for the job, although she hated to put him in jeopardy. Sabotage of war-critical production was a severe crime, punishable by death.

Yet, what wasn't punishable by death these days?

2

Stefan watched his beloved Gretchen, as he called her, leave the wharf, shaking his head at how easily he'd been convinced to help her. "I should have refused," he murmured as he cleaned up the deck of his boat, before he made sure it was tethered securely to the dock. "Why did I agree to do this?"

Because you know it's the right thing to do. You want to help her and those who are unable to help themselves. Also, because you've fallen head over heels in love with her and would do anything to put a smile upon her face.

Stefan hated when his inner voice made sense. It wouldn't be the first time his conscience had gotten him into severe trouble with the Nazis.

He packaged up the morning's catch and delivered the fish to the official buyer from the *Reichsstelle für Fische*, since the fishermen were obliged to sell their entire catch, except for a small personal allowance to this department of the Agricultural Ministry.

When his work was done, he headed home, the fish allowance for his own needs packed into waxed paper.

His grandfather was sitting on the front porch of the tiny

house tucked beneath a copse of fir trees. Stefan took a moment to observe him quietly without his knowledge. The old man was getting frail. Yet, his mind was still very sharp, even as he pretended to be suffering from dementia. *If only his physical body wasn't falling apart.*

Stefan had looked up to his grandfather since he was a child and valued the old man's advice. After being deemed politically-unreliable by the Nazis, he'd moved from the city of Cologne to the countryside and had taken over his grandfather's fishing boat.

After musing about how much this man meant to him, he finally entered the small gate and joined his grandfather on the porch, taking a seat in the empty chair.

"Morning, Opa," he greeted him.

"Good morning, Stefan. You're late. Something happened?"

Stefan knew his grandfather constantly worried about his well-being, especially after the explosion and subsequent investigation where he'd only escaped being sent to prison as a traitor by a hair's breadth. "Fräulein Annegret came down to the wharf."

"The Huber heiress?"

"Yes." Stefan felt his ears burning under his grandfather's scrutinizing gaze.

Opa nodded and then met Stefan's eyes. "You need to be careful, Stefan. She is from a different social class. Her kind don't socialize with our kind."

"I know." Stefan heard the familiar warning his grandfather had given at other times in the past and wished he could tell him the truth about her. But it was much too dangerous, and he would never put his grandfather in such a position.

It wasn't that he distrusted the old man, because he'd never willingly endanger his grandson, which was exactly the problem: willingly. Everyone, and especially those in the resistance, knew the Gestapo had ways to wrest a secret from anyone in their care. What his grandfather didn't know he couldn't be forced to divulge, should—God forbid—he be asked. Keeping him in the dark was for his own safety.

"What did she want?" Opa asked.

"Who?"

"Fräulein Annegret. You're not going to tell me she came to the wharf personally because she wanted to buy some fish, are you?"

That was exactly what he'd been planning to tell everyone who asked. "What's so outrageous about that?"

Opa smirked, showing several tooth gaps. "Don't take me for a fool. She's the lady of the manor, she has servants to do the grocery shopping for her."

Stefan pondered telling Opa that even rich people had to tighten their belts because of the war restrictions, then thought better of it. The old man was much too smart to fall for that ruse. "She asked me to work in her factory."

"Whyever would she want you to do that?"

Stefan squirmed under his grandfather's scrutinizing gaze. "It seems most of her skilled workers have been drafted and she urgently needs a Head of Quality Control."

"Aha." Opa stuffed his pipe with deliberate movements, before he squinted his blue eyes at his grandson. "Doesn't she know you're considered politically unreliable?"

"I got the impression that my prior experience in Cologne was the very reason she asked me." Stefan didn't dare to speak out loud that she had asked him to sabotage her own factory. Yet, he knew his grandfather would understand the hint.

"I see." Opa lit up the pipe and took a long smoke. "Everyone of us has to do whatever we can to end this war." He knocked on his thigh. "These old bones are skipping out on me, or I'd go fighting myself."

"Opa. You have done enough. Without you I'd probably be in some work camp. They let me go, because they were confident I couldn't do much harm out here in the middle of nowhere, and because they needed someone to take over your boat. War effort and all, feeding the population."

"You be careful, Stefan. I surely don't want you to leave this earth before me." With this warning, Opa took another drag of his pipe. Just minutes later, his chin fell to his chest, because he'd fallen asleep.

Stefan took the pipe from his grandfather's lips and extinguished it. Then he entered the small house they shared, bringing a blanket to cover the old man. After his parents had died not long ago in the horrible bombings of Cologne, Opa was his only family left. He loved him dearly, always had.

3

Ernst Rosenbaum, Margarete's uncle, took a careful breath, closing his eyes against the wave of pain that accompanied the task. After being tortured by Oberscharführer Thomas Kallfass, he'd been incarcerated in a small cell that he assumed to be in a prison hospital. Where it was, he didn't have the slightest idea, because he hadn't seen a single soul except for the nurse and the doctor who attended to him. They could as well have been mute because they refused to speak to him, other than barking commands.

During the first pain-filled days, he'd barely noticed them and definitely hadn't cared, since he'd needed every ounce of energy to stay alive, which he had, despite the severe wounds inflicted by the torture and the agonizing pain he constantly felt.

Then, he'd tried to worm some information out of them. Where was he? Why was he here? Normally a Jew like him, a prisoner forced to hard labor in the Nazis camps, wasn't treated in a hospital but hauled away like a piece of trash. Instead, they'd kept him in the hospital and continued to treat his injuries to help him recover.

So why were they going to such lengths trying to make sure he survived the ordeal he'd received at their hands? Or was it just another cruel twist in their morbid game? To extend the suffering of their victims, when a quick death was what they desired most? Nobody was willing to tell him.

As a professor of philosophy at the University in Leipzig he'd spent most of his life pondering questions about the purpose of life. Why did people do the things they did? What greater sense propelled their actions?

During the past weeks he'd realized that none of that actually carried any importance whatsoever. In the end, faced with one's own mortality, even the most compassionate and altruistic individuals fought for themselves alone. Perhaps stronger men than him might prevail, but he'd been willing to sacrifice everything, and everyone, to prevent one more moment of excruciating pain.

And what had he received in exchange? More pain.

Admittedly, it was a lower intensity hurt, yet it was incessant, caused by the slightest movement in his body, such as breathing. It was more bearable than what Oberscharführer Kallfass had done to him—short, excruciating bursts of agony. Wave after wave of torment, until he'd succumbed and told the man what he wanted to know.

The guilt of having betrayed his own flesh and blood, his favorite niece Margarete, tugged at his soul like a freshly opened wound. The emotional pain might even surpass the physical one. A Jew by birth, married to a Christian, he'd become an atheist in his later years, not believing in the existence of a God anymore after he saw what the Nazis were doing.

In the end, he himself had chosen his own life over that of his niece. Because after he'd betrayed her secret, there was no hope that the Oberscharführer would have left her alive. Tears of shame filled his eyes as he relived the moment he'd revealed her true identity, his voice hoarse from screams of torment.

In his desperation, he prayed for forgiveness. If not by a God he didn't believe in, then at least by his sweet niece Gretchen, should they ever meet again—in this life or the next.

He was still wallowing in guilt when the door opened and a man he'd hoped never to see again walked into the room. Kallfass' subordinate, a cruel and sadistic man called Lothar Katze.

Katze had personally whipped that poor escaped and re-captured prisoner Lena to death, and had taken great joy in assisting torturing Ernst, since his boss hadn't wanted to dirty his own hands. Just like his last name Katze might suggest, he enjoyed playing, cat-like, with his victims before he finally ate them alive.

Ernst tried to sit up straight as the man approached his bedside, but fresh pain racing across his body defeated his efforts and he ended up sagging back on the mattress. "Herr Unterscharführer."

"Oberscharführer!" Katze said, proudly pointing toward his shining new shoulder straps. "I was promoted after turning in my superior for treason."

Ernst did not show his contempt for the man who so willingly admitted to betraying his own kind. Perhaps he even envied the brute for not having to experience the agonizing moral pangs that tormented the conscience of less corrupted men. Somehow he pulled himself together and came to sit, albeit leaning against the wall. "Congratulations are in order then, Herr Oberscharführer?"

"They definitely are." Katze looked at him with an expression Ernst couldn't quite read. "But I didn't come here to claim praise from a Jewish swine."

"Of course you didn't," Ernst said because he sensed an answer was required.

"You see, I couldn't care less about you and your ilk. All this ideological talk is for more sophisticated men than I am. Where I'm concerned I divide humans, or subhumans for that matter,"

Katze gave a derisive hooting, "into two classes: useful and not useful. You are a lucky man, Jew, because you acquired the status of useful for me." Katze looked at him expectantly.

"Well, thank you, Herr Oberscharführer." Ernst hoped it was the answer Katze had been looking for. Indeed, he was rewarded with a big smile.

"Not stupid, are you?"

This time Ernst preferred not to answer and simply bowed his head, because he had a feeling that self-praise wouldn't please Katze. He still wondered why the man had bothered to come and visit him.

"As I was saying, today is your lucky day, because I'm going to have you transferred to a regular prison instead of sending you to the east." Katze paused, before adding his reasoning for such an unusual action, "I despise the cruelty of the camps."

Ernst barely contained his revulsion at the blatant lie. The man who had personally tortured him suddenly wanted to convince Ernst that he was looking out for his best interests? That whole thing stank to high heaven.

"It really is my lucky day, Herr Oberscharführer. To what do I owe your generosity?" Ernst asked.

"I trust you'll remember whom to thank when the time comes." With these words Katze clicked his heels and took off, leaving a very pensive Ernst behind.

It was clear that Katze was making an effort to cover his ass for the not-so-unlikely situation that the Allies would win the war and the Nazis would be held accountable for their crimes.

Apparently he believed he could evade justice by helping one Jew in need. But Ernst would be damned if he ever put in a good word for a Nazi. He could not and he would not dirty the sacrifice of so many.

4

"Fräulein Annegret, there's a message for you," Frau Mertens, the housekeeper, announced as she stood at the door of Margarete's suite of rooms. It wasn't yet nine o'clock in the morning—barely a decent hour for visitors.

"Who is it from?" Margarete asked, putting down the book she'd been perusing.

"From the district office in Parchim. The driver is waiting for your answer downstairs."

Margarete arched a brow to hide her nervousness and held out her hand for the missive. When she read it, anguish rose in her chest. *Oberscharführer Katze requests your immediate presence in his office.*

She felt herself blanch under Frau Mertens' worried gaze, doing her best to hide her nerves, while gathering up all her strength to keep her limbs from trembling. "It seems my presence is needed in Parchim. Oberscharführer Katze even had the thoughtfulness to send his car for my convenience. Please tell the driver I'll be ready to accompany him within ten minutes."

Frau Mertens raised an eyebrow. "He would never have dared to treat you this way if your father were still alive."

"I assume it must be urgent. With the war and everything the usual rules of politeness don't apply anymore," Margarete answered. Social rules still did apply, but certainly not where a Jew in hiding was concerned, and she had every reason to believe that Katze was privy to her true identity.

"Dora is in town to see the midwife, so I'll send Gloria to help you get dressed."

As soon as Frau Mertens had left, Margarete sagged against the doorjamb. There was still a slight chance that Katze didn't know about her dark secret. *Yes, it must be something about the factory*, she tried to convince herself. In any case, whatever the reason the new SS district leader wanted to see her, she had to follow the order summoning her, since anything else would only raise suspicions and possibly lead to disaster.

Gloria, the Polish girl they'd employed to help Margarete's trusted maid Dora with her chores, showed up a few minutes later. She still spoke only rudimentary German, and usually worked in the kitchen helping cook prepare the food for the several dozen farm and stable hands, while Dora catered for Margarete's personal needs.

"Hand me the black one to the very left," Margarete advised her, pointing to the huge wardrobe occupying one entire wall in her bedroom. She would have managed on her own, but tradition apparently required that the lady of the manor got help in getting dressed.

Today, though, she was grateful for the aid, because her fingers trembled terribly as she slipped into the elegant, yet modest, black costume consisting of a slim skirt ending about mid-calf and a slightly tailored jacket. She paired this outfit with a black hat and black gloves, since she was pretending to be grieving the tragic death of her fatherly mentor, Reichskriminaldirektor of the Gestapo, Horst Richter.

Perhaps Katze wanted to express his condolences for her loss? She shook her head, since in that case he'd have sent a card, instead of summoning her to his office. The more she thought about it, the more she came to the conclusion that this action was a show of power. Whatever he wanted from her, he was intent on proving to her that he held all the cards in his hands.

She climbed down the stairs, bid goodbye to Frau Mertens and then stepped outside to greet the SS driver.

"Please, have a seat." The man in his fifties held the back door open for her and closed it once she was seated.

Yes, sending a driver was definitely a power play, while at the same time showing appreciation for her. For the moment she had nothing to fear, at least that's what she tried to convince herself of.

During the drive she did her best to calm her nerves and wrap Annegret's personality around her. Haughty. Self-confident. Assured.

When they arrived at the headquarters in Parchim, the driver exited the vehicle to open the passenger door for her. She took it as a good omen, because he'd surely not treat her like royalty if Katze was about to have her arrested or worse.

"The Oberscharführer is waiting for you in his office," the driver said, gesturing toward the front doors of the building.

Margarete inclined her head and then walked briskly toward the building. She dreaded going inside, because of all the memories it held of Thomas Kallfass: the Nazi who'd amorously pursued her relentlessly—and but for a lucky escape, would have had her sent to Auschwitz.

She assumed Lothar Katze was now occupying Thomas' office. Even the notion of entering that room raised her hackles. Instead of slowing down her steps as her fear tried to demand, she sped them up. Whatever was about to transpire, delaying it certainly wouldn't benefit her.

Plastering a pleasant expression on her face, she greeted the receptionist behind the dark-brown oak desk. "Good morning, Oberscharführer Katze wanted to see me."

The young woman asked, "Are you Annegret Huber?"

"I certainly am," she bristled, as the real Annegret would have done.

"The Oberscharführer is expecting you."

Margarete inclined her head and passed the disrespectful woman without another word. When she entered the huge corner office, a dreadful sense of foreboding attacked her. She shrugged it off as Thomas' lingering ghost. After all the dreadful events of the past months it was no wonder that she'd feel haunted in his former office.

Lothar Katze looked up from his desk. "Oh, there you are, Fräulein Annegret. Thank you for arriving so promptly."

Was it just her imagination or had he drawn out her name into the syllables, making it sound like An-na-gre-te? She pulled herself together to answer in a matter-of-fact tone. "I'm always eager to serve Führer and Fatherland."

He looked somewhat surprised, then got up to shake her hand, which was, if not inappropriate, at least unusual. "Please have a seat." He gestured toward the chair in front of his immense desk.

While she took a seat, he walked to the door and shouted at the receptionist, "I don't want to be disturbed while Fräulein Annegret is here." Then he closed the door firmly and returned to his desk, settling into his oversized chair, looking down at her with his cat-like grin that she had learned to fear. The gleam in his eyes increased her anxiety tenfold.

After a lengthy pause, he steepled his hands on the desk and said without further ado, "I know who you are."

Margarete's heart missed a beat. When she regained control over her senses, she answered, "Of course you do."

"Well, most people believe they know who you are, but I actually know your true name." He rubbed his chin, giving her a once-over, leaving hot anguish in the wake of his stare. "Unlike my predecessor, though, I'm rather sympathetic to your plight."

She breathed again, though she didn't believe a single word. Katze was infamous for his exceptional brutality, which she herself had witnessed on various occasions. It was only surpassed by his greed.

If he claimed sympathy, he obviously wanted something from her. Since she didn't know yet what it was, she decided to play for time, not answering, and most importantly, not showing her fear.

Fortunately Katze was too absorbed in his own importance to take much notice of her body language like an experienced interrogator would have done. Unable to bear her silence any longer he continued, "You are wondering how I found out, aren't you? Well, let me tell you one thing: I'm as clever as my predecessor was, actually even more so, because he's now toiling in a concentration camp, whereas I, the notoriously underestimated Lothar Katze, have been promoted to Oberscharführer and am sitting in his chair. All because he was too stupid to see the signs on the wall."

Margarete chose to give a silent nod. Should the fool want to drone on about his own greatness, she'd patiently sit here and find out as much information as she could.

"And before you think how to get away a second time, let me tell you this: I'm not your enemy. I can protect you and keep you alive, as long as you play by my rules."

Despite cold sweat running down her spine, she kept still, graciously bestowing a smile on him. He was cruel and greedy, but also quite dumb. Therefore she decided to wait and see what he wanted, perhaps she could talk herself out of this.

He cast her a confused stare. "You're not even denying your crime. Why's that?"

Margarete put on her most innocent mien, opening her eyes

wide, as she answered, "Herr Oberscharführer, you have yet to accuse me of anything."

He pressed his lips into a thin line, apparently trying to come up with a witty response. "You think you're too clever for me, don't you? But it's me who holds all the trump cards. With one phone call I can expose you as the horrible person you are: a ghastly Jew posing as one of the most esteemed women in our area."

Raising an eyebrow, Margarete reminded herself that Horst Richter had burnt the treacherous identification card exposing her as a Jew. "There's no proof of your outrageous accusation."

"Oh, my dear Fräulein, there is plenty of proof. I took the liberty of photographing your original *Kennkarte*." He pushed a rather grainy picture across his desk. Despite the bad quality, both her image and the big "J" stamped across her name and data were clearly visible. "Just so you don't get any ideas, this isn't the only copy I have."

"Nothing would be further from my mind," she lied. "Why are you telling me this? What do you want?"

"You really are as astute as they say you are. Never one to beat around the bush." Katze broke out into a satisfied grin. "Before I tell you, I want to make sure you know what's at stake here. It's not only your own life, but your uncle's as well."

She flinched as if he'd physically hit her.

"He is as well as can be expected after his ordeal. To prove my sincerity I have taken the liberty of putting him under my protection. As we speak he's being transferred to a prison for political prisoners instead of being herded onto a train to Auschwitz." His eyes bore into her. "You and I both know what happens to the old and frail who arrive there. The man you pretended was your father, Standartenführer Wolfgang Huber, I hear, was one of the masterminds behind the Final Solution for the Jews. So I'm sure this warning isn't needed, but I'll issue it anyway: your uncle will remain safe only as long as you fully cooperate."

That was it. There was no way out. The news about her uncle's whereabouts had shaken her to the core. She'd sworn to protect him and failed. It was her fault he'd been deported to the transit camp and it had been through another mistake of hers that Thomas had been able to make the connections. She'd thoroughly and completely messed up. Guilt ate at her, because she hadn't taken better care of her father's youngest brother.

Whatever Katze wanted in exchange for Uncle Ernst's life, she'd give it to him. She'd never be able to undo what Uncle Ernst had endured because of her, but as God was her witness, she'd make it up to him.

"I appreciate your kindness. Please tell me your demands." Margarete kept her voice neutral as if she were negotiating with him about a business deal, which it intrinsically was.

"Ah, I had hoped you'd be pliable. My demands are not unreasonable as you'll see for yourself. Giving protection to subjects considered enemies of the Reich is rather, shall I say, costly?"

Now she knew he was solely after money, and a huge burden fell from her shoulders. She'd feared that he'd want herself as part of the bargain. "I assume it is."

"It's a relief to know you understand my position. While I personally have nothing against Jews, I do obey the laws and rules our omniscient Führer has seen fit to issue."

Margarete hoped he'd finally come to the point. Now that she knew what he was after, she simply wanted to get it over with. *Tell me the sum. Let me get on with my life.*

"I was thinking about a monthly allowance to help cover my expenses." Then he mentioned an amount that took Margarete's breath away. It was about the same number she spent every month to feed the several dozen employees at Gut Plaun.

"That is an outrageous amount, which I certainly don't have handy. It will take me quite a while to get it," she hedged.

"I'll leave it to your ingenuity to come up with the required money." He looked at her for a while, before he added, "Just to show my goodwill, I'm also willing to include exemptions for all Jewish workers in your factory in the deal."

She carefully hid her elation at hearing this. Around four hundred Jewish prisoners worked in her factory, and they were always in peril of being deported on a whim. If Katze issued fresh exemptions, at least one problem was taken off her plate.

Even though she didn't trust him an inch, she nodded in agreement. "It's a deal then."

"Somehow I knew you would make the right decision." Katze grinned. "Shall I visit the manor let's say in two weeks from now? I'd love for us to chat some more over a nice dinner and I trust you'll have my first monthly payment ready by then."

"Very well. I will see you at the manor." Margarete stood up and let herself out of his office. Since she didn't want to use the official SS driver, she gave a wide berth to his car and walked toward the train station, hoping she'd be able to catch a train to Plau am See without having to wait for too long. These days the trains never ran on schedule and one simply had to show up on the platform to see whether a train was expected or not.

A million worries whirled in her head, starting with Uncle Ernst, the factory workers and how she was going to come up with Katze's monthly bribe. Soon enough she heard a locomotive wheezing and deliberately pushed the thoughts away.

She'd take it one step at the time.

5

Oliver set the glass of water down on the table next to his wife Dora. After lunch, with Frau Mertens' approval, she had taken a rest to prop up her swollen feet.

He kissed her cheek, worrying about the dark circles beneath her eyes. "You look tired, darling."

Dora leaned into his touch, before she stretched out her hand to reach for the glass of water. "I'm fine. It's just that the baby kicked me so hard I woke up several times last night and couldn't get back to sleep."

"If the baby is playing football already, it must be a boy." Pride at the new life inside his wife's belly warmed his heart. He'd be a father soon. And, like so many fathers, he wished for a son to carry on his name. On the other hand he feared for the future of the little one. If Hitler wasn't defeated soon, it wouldn't be a good place for a child to grow up.

"I don't know about that." Dora laughed.

"Rest for a while, will you?"

"Just for a bit, since I have so much work to do. Fräulein Annegret asked me to rearrange her closet for the warm season."

"Where is she, by the way? Haven't seen her all morning." Oliver took the glass from Dora's hands and returned it to the table.

"I was ironing when a black Mercedes drove into the yard. Frau Mertens said the district office in Parchim had sent for her urgently."

"That's rather strange," Oliver murmured, instantly worried about the reason behind such an action.

"Probably the new boss wanting to show his importance."

Both Dora and Oliver had met Lothar Katze several times. Oliver considered him an unintelligent man whose brutality was only topped by his greed. Not a good combination during normal times, but for the purposes of Gut Plaun his openness to bribery had been beneficial.

Dealing with Katze was so much easier than with Thomas Kallfass, a self-proclaimed honest and upright man who unfortunately had been seriously deluded by Nazi propaganda and wouldn't deviate an inch from the official party line. Especially not where Jews were concerned.

Oliver gave a small sigh. For better or worse, Kallfass was history. After the tumultuous events during which Fräulein Annegret's true identity had almost been exposed, the SS man had been sent to the Mauthausen concentration camp. He'd never bother them again.

They heard clopping in the yard, indicating Nils had arrived with the coach. Soon after Frau Mertens entered the kitchen, eyeing the two of them. She'd initially been very skeptical about their marriage, since Oliver came from a local family, and had worked himself up from stable hand to estate manager, whereas Dora was merely a Ukrainian national, who'd only recently been Germanized. But after the announcement of them expecting their first child, her stance had softened.

She never said as much, but it was clear that she relished the prospect of a baby in the house. If not the offspring of her mistress, then at least the estate manager's. Oliver remembered how strict she'd been with all the children on Gut Plaun, including him, and wondered whether she was getting sentimental.

Approaching sixty years of age, both of her sons had fallen in the war so she'd never have grandchildren of her own.

"Here you are, Oliver," she said. "Fräulein Annegret wants to see you urgently. She's waiting in your office."

"Thank you, Frau Mertens, I'll go there right away." On the way to his office he mused that it could as well be Annegret's office, but since she was only a woman and not supposed to run the family estate, she preferred to keep up appearances and let him be the face to the outside. Which didn't mean that she hadn't clear expectations about the way Oliver should manage her estate, and most importantly the nitropenta factory. The factory was considered essential for the war, producing explosives and ammunition, for which it employed forced workers from the prison camps.

Before her arrival at Gut Plaun the conditions for the prisoners had been deplorable. As soon as she'd found out about her ownership over this badly disguised extermination camp, she'd begun to make small improvements to the inmates' living conditions, as well as protecting the Jewish workers from being deported elsewhere.

Annegret never spoke of the horrors she knew happened in camps like Auschwitz, and he didn't ask, since some things were better left unsaid.

"You wanted to see me?" he asked as he entered his office, where Annegret was busy scribbling some things on a notepad.

"Yes. Sit." She stood to let him settle in his chair and began to pace the room, stopping at the door to lock it. "Or better, stand. Or... I don't know."

"What's wrong, Annegret?"

She gave a huge sigh, looking as if she'd break out into tears any moment, which was highly worrisome, since she usually was absolutely composed.

"We have a problem."

"What kind of problem?" Their life engaging in underground activities against the Reich was a constant succession of headaches.

"A very bad one. Perhaps you should remain seated." She walked around his chair and flopped down onto the guest chair in front of his desk. "Katze summoned me to the SS headquarters this morning."

"So I heard."

"He knows."

"Knows what?" Oliver normally wasn't a fool, but that day his brain couldn't make sense of what she told him.

"Everything. About me. He even has a copy of that darned *Kennkarte*."

Oliver's heart stopped beating. That was indeed bad news. Although, if Katze hadn't arrested her right away, there might be a silver lining somewhere. "What does he want?"

"Money. He asked for a monthly allowance that's higher than the amount I spend on food for all the house and stable employees."

Now he was glad that she'd urged him to sit down. "That *is* a lot. What did you say?"

"I agreed." She buried her head between her hands. "He has my uncle Ernst. He's holding him hostage to make sure I 'cooperate', as he called it."

Oliver hadn't pegged Katze to be clever enough to arrange for leverage. Perhaps he needed to revisit his judgment of the man as purely dumb and greedy. In an effort to calm Annegret, he said, "It could have been worse. We'll come up with the money somehow."

She suddenly raised her head, looking at him with her hazel eyes, revealing a world of vulnerability within them. "We desperately need the money to feed the prisoners. I'm not worth it."

"What?"

"One life, or even two counting my uncle, is not worth paying such an extortionate sum for God knows how long." She sprung up and walked toward the door. "I'm going to Parchim to tell Katze that he can hang me if he wants, he'll never get a single *Pfennig* from us."

"Wait!" He charged after her, grabbing her by the shoulder, just as she was about to unlock the door.

"No." She turned around to stare at him. "This is the right thing to do. I'm just one person, the money is better spent feeding the prisoners."

Oliver forced his brain into overdrive. Somehow he had to talk her out of sacrificing her life—for the benefit of everyone, including himself, Dora and the unborn baby.

"Please hear me out." Finally, phrases formed in his mind to express what he knew to be true. "It's not only your life at stake."

"My uncle's life is forfeit either way. I don't trust Katze to keep his word and spare him."

"It's not only your uncle, it's all of us. Me, Dora, Nils, Frau Mertens. If you're exposed as a Jew, suspicion will fall on all of us to have helped you."

She shrugged, but he'd seen the twinkle of doubt in her eyes. "The risk is low. Not even Reichskriminaldirektor Richter knew. That will count in your favor, won't it?"

"It may or may not. But do you think they'll let us continue business as usual? What will happen to the prison workers if you're gone? Who will be the new owner of Gut Plaun? Will the Reich take possession of it and send an estate manager who closely toes the party line? Do you think he would agree to spend all his personal money to buy food and clothing for the prisoners? Do you really believe they'll be safe without you?

Who's going to ask for exemptions for the Jewish workers? Or are they going to be deported before your corpse is even disposed of?"

He noticed a shiver running down her spine, hoping his drastic words had made her reconsider. It wasn't only her life he was worried about, or his... hundreds of people depended on her protection.

"Annegret?"

She blinked several times, before she finally nodded. "I'm afraid you're right. I was being selfish."

If the situation hadn't been so dire, he'd have laughed out loud. How could wanting to sacrifice herself for the well-being of others be selfish?

"No, you are not. You just didn't realize the stakes. Without you, nobody is safe. Whether we want it or not, we'll have to agree to Katze's blackmail. At least for the time being, I don't see any way out."

6

Stefan entered the main building of the factory where the workers stuffed nitropenta into cases to make bullets, grenades and other kinds of ammunition. He walked from one workstation to the next, closely observing the processes and jotting notes on his pad.

He already had several ideas in mind on how best to sabotage the production, however he wanted to get a feel for the procedures before making a decision. It was of utmost importance that no worker was harmed due to his interventions and that all results would appear to be caused by low-quality raw material, rather than by negligence.

Oliver had introduced him to the factory manager Franz Volkmer as a contractor who'd come to work on quality assurance. Despite his official role, he had chosen the timing for his inspection during Volkmer's day off.

The man was innocuous enough, since he wasn't one of the staunch Nazis in town. Nevertheless, despite his apparent sympathy for the plight of the prisoners, Stefan didn't trust him. Certain that Volkmer would race to denounce him to the

Gestapo if he as much as suspected any wrongdoings, Stefan preferred to keep out of his way.

He walked into the yard and toward one of the small bunkers scattered across the vast area belonging to the factory complex. On a site of around one and a half square miles, seemingly countless concrete bunkers were separated from each other by earth walls and trenches. Sprawling trees hid the entire complex from enemy airplanes. Should the Allied reconnaissance ever get this far, they wouldn't see anything but greenery.

Absorbed observing the women lugging heavy sacks with raw materials to the individual bunkers, where the explosive nitropenta was cooked, he all but ran into one of the foremen.

"Hey, you. What's your business here?" the man asked in a belligerent tone.

"I'm sorry. My name is Stefan Stober. I've been contracted to act as the quality supervisor."

"Never seen you here before," the man murmured, slightly mollified.

"That's because I'm new. Had my first meeting with Franz Volkmer earlier this week."

The foreman nodded, apparently content with the answer. Stefan took to his heels, trailing the women lugging the heavy sacks. As soon as he caught up with them, he called, "Wait a moment."

The two prisoners stopped abruptly, turning around to look at him with anguish in their eyes. His gaze was drawn to the yellow stars on their prisoner garb. Even after Annegret had changed the entire management of the factory it continued to be a place filled with fear and hardship, especially for Jews.

"There is no problem, I just want to have a look at the sacks."

"*Ja, mein Herr*," the older woman answered, while the other one kept her eyes on her feet.

He wanted to reassure them that he wasn't out to harm

them, but couldn't risk one of the German workers overhearing him and possibly denouncing him for being too friendly to a Jew. After all, it was his first day at the factory, and he had yet to find out whom he could trust.

"Open the sack," he barked.

The woman obeyed instantly, showing him the contents. It was a white, crystalline powder called pentaerythritol, one of the main ingredients for nitropenta. He knew it to taste sweetish, be flammable, not soluble in cold water, alcohol or benzene, but easily soluble in hot water. Which was the reason why the process of nitriding it into an explosive was called *cooking*.

He put his hand into the bag, letting the powder trickle through his fingers, while an idea formed in his mind. If he added flour to the pentaerythritol, the resulting end product would not explode properly. Then he scrapped the idea, since this staple was desperately needed to ensure the townsfolk had bread to eat. White powder sand from one of the beaches of Lake Plau might be harder to get, but would serve the same effect.

He'd just need to experiment with quantity and texture of the sand to make sure nobody noticed the difference upon inspections. He made a note on his pad and then told the women to continue on their way.

After his round he returned to the administration building to let Volkmer's secretary know that he was finished with his perusal of the production process and would send in a report with recommendations within the next few days.

Then he picked up his bicycle to pass by the manor and report to Oliver about his visit. Once he'd left the factory fence behind, he felt a strong sense of relief settling into his bones. It had been sheer luck for him not to end on the wrong side of such a fence, after the explosion in the factory where he used to work.

Cycling through the forest his mind returned to the factory

on the outskirts of Cologne, where he'd worked as a chemical engineer after receiving his degree in January 1939. He had never been happy with his job, assigned by the labor office, because he'd have far rather worked on making products for daily life for the population made from the versatile PVC and its many derivatives, than using that same material to isolate the cables for naval vessels.

Not even his love for the water and all things to do with boats alleviated his disgust. Once the war broke out, he couldn't stand by any longer and do nothing. It didn't take long until an opportunity presented itself.

At the factory he met several foremen who, while seemingly toeing the Nazi party line, were in fact old communists. After some initial suspicion, they began to trust him and invited him to gatherings and beers after work. These blue-collar men opened his eyes to so many things that he, while studying hard through university, had never consciously perceived.

From then on it had only been a matter of time before he'd actively participated in sabotaging the production in the factory. But due to his lack of experience, he'd accidentally caused a severe explosion, during which two of his communist friends had been killed and several dozen workers injured.

The Gestapo had been called in to investigate and it had soon become apparent which department was to blame for the incident. Stefan remembered well the secret meeting of the remaining people in their group.

"It's all my fault, I should have tested this more thoroughly," Stefan admitted, riddled with guilt.

"Now's not the time to feel bad. We have worse problems to take care of," their group leader said.

"Worse than the death of two of our comrades?"

"Much worse. Because if the Gestapo finds out about our group, we'll soon all be hanging from the gallows," another man added.

Stefan looked from one to the next, all of them easily twenty years older than him. He might be the only one with studied expertise in chemical engineering, but each one of them owned a much more valuable skill: life experience.

"We must save what can be saved," their group leader decided. "Karl, you arrange for all the evidence to point at the dead comrades."

"How can you!" Stefan protested, aghast that their leader wanted to besmirch their reputation.

"Would you rather the Gestapo come and torture the survivors than vent their anger on the dead?"

"No..." It felt all wrong, yet he had to admit that it probably was the best solution for everyone involved.

In the following days and weeks he realized how much truth the group leader had spoken. Every single worker in the factory was interrogated by the Gestapo. The few in the know all said more or less the same thing, which pointed to the two dead men being traitors and saboteurs. Their families were given a bit of a hard time. Stefan was sacked from his job and given the verdict "politically unreliable", which prevented him from working in the industry and that was it.

The other group members took up their lives again, laying low until everything was water under the bridge, while Stefan himself moved to Plau am See and became a fisherman.

He spied Oliver walking toward the stables.

"Oliver, do you have a moment?" he called out. The two of them had known each other since their childhoods when Stefan had spent the summers with his grandfather.

"Sure." Oliver was wearing jodhpurs and riding boots. Despite having ascended from stable master to estate manager, he still spent plenty of time with his beloved horses.

"I just finished my first appraisal of the production process-es," Stefan said, deliberately keeping it vague. "Do you want to discuss my findings in your office?"

Oliver gazed at him. "Care for a ride instead?"

"God no!" He pointed at his bicycle. "I much prefer the two-wheeled steed." As a city boy he'd never learned how to ride a horse.

"Well then, let's go for a walk. You can leave your metal steed at the stables, it'll be in good company."

Stefan did as he was told and then joined Oliver for a walk along the paddock fence. They walked in silence until they were a fair distance away from the stables, before Oliver explained. "It seems the walls and floors have ears these days and we wouldn't want anyone to listen in."

"Ah, I apologize."

"No harm was done. Now, tell me, what did you observe?" Oliver asked.

Stefan outlined several of the areas where he believed the materials could be sabotaged, without going into detail. Even though he trusted the other man implicitly, in their clandestine business, talk was silver, whereas silence was golden.

What Oliver didn't know the Gestapo couldn't torture out of him, should it ever go that far. It was one of the lessons he had learned from the utter fiasco in his first job.

"But won't someone notice?" Oliver asked.

"In the improbable case a quality control shows deficiencies, it will merely look as if subordinate materials have been supplied to the factory."

"You're sure nobody will notice? Doesn't it look suspicious when entire charges of ammunition don't explode?"

Stefan nodded. That was the point he'd spent most time thinking about. He couldn't interfere with the metal casing without it becoming obvious that the bullets were not up to specifications, but once the gunpowder was sealed inside, no one would realize that there was a problem until it was too late.

"That might indeed be a problem. In fact there's no way around it, so we have to bank on the fact that the ammo will be

utilized many, many miles away from here under a lot of stress."
Stefan paused to looked at Oliver. "Those cursed with malfunc-
tioning ammunition most probably won't live long enough to
tell the tale."

Oliver bit his lip, his face becoming a shade paler. It was an
agonizing moral dilemma he had to face. Both ways they were
accessories to murder. Either the ammunition produced by
them killed the enemy, or their own soldiers.

It sounded easy enough. War is war. Choose friend over foe.
In this case though, the lines were blurred, since the soldiers
supposedly on their side fought an unjust war of attack against
most everyone else, including part of their own citizens, like
Margarete and her fellow Jews.

Stefan watched Oliver's face as he worked through the
same inner conflict Stefan had gone through himself. It was
easy enough to pinpoint the exact moment when Oliver realized that there was no way around it: doing the right thing
required harm to his own compatriots, because his expression
hardened and he gave a pensive nod. "What do you need
from me?"

"Best you don't know anything. I have what I need and will
do everything myself. This way nobody else gets implicated."

"That is rather noble of you."

"Just as well if only one of us has to suffer the consequences," Stefan said nonchalantly, since Oliver didn't have to
know that he acted out of guilt rather than bravery. This time he
wouldn't let others take the fall for his own failures. If the sabotage was discovered, he'd be the only one punished. "If there's
nothing else, I'll send you and Volkmer my report mentioning
quality issues with the purchased raw materials within the next
few days."

"Good idea. Let's return now, I have to attend to a million
other problems."

"Me too." For a second Stefan wished to return to his quiet

life as a fisherman, before his friend Sandra had recruited him to hide illegals on their journey to ultimately be smuggled out of Germany, and before Annegret had thrust him into sabotaging her factory's production.

His moment of weakness passed. A life without fighting evil was a wasted life.

Since Oliver headed for the stables, there was no good reason for Stefan to take the detour passing by the manor on his way home to exchange a few words with Annegret or at least catch a glimpse of her beautiful face. Heavy-hearted he mounted his bicycle and pedaled through the forest without having seen her.

When they met privately, which wasn't often because they had agreed to meet only if circumstances necessitated it so as not to raise suspicion, he called her Gretchen. But to keep her guise guarded and not accidentally blurt out her real name, he always, always referred to her as Annegret, even in the presence of Oliver or just in his own mind.

Once back at home, he spent most of the afternoon writing up his inspection report. In it, he outlined that some raw materials had proven to be of low quality or even defective. He suggested to implement a thorough inspection of any and all materials in store, and offered himself to take on the tricky task of finding and removing the defective supplies.

With that done he settled in a chair on the porch, sipping a cup of *Ersatzkaffee*, pondering further ways of effective sabotage. He scribbled random words onto a piece of paper to get his thought process flowing.

He'd already identified several machines that could easily be brought to a standstill by adding sand to the greasing oil. Machines needed maintenance all the time and the foremen would chalk it up to age and wear.

A shadow fell over his paper, and he looked up to see his grandfather leaning over his shoulder.

"Trying to solve a problem?" Opa asked, nodding at the paper.

"I went to the nitropenta factory this morning."

His grandfather had known him long enough to realize Stefan was hiding something and said, "It smells like trouble."

Never one to lie, Stefan nodded slowly. "It does have that potential."

"I don't suppose I need to remind you that what you're doing is extremely dangerous?"

"No, Opa. I'm acutely aware of the risk. But this is something I have to do."

"You're a good boy. I wish I could help. But look at me: my old body is about to abandon me."

Grief constricted Stefan's thoughts, since his Opa echoed his own worries. "Don't talk like that. You can live many more years if you take it easy and let me do the hard work."

His grandfather grinned sheepishly. "Sometimes I thank fate for sending you my way. I wouldn't know what to do if you still lived in Cologne."

"Don't worry, I'll always be here for you."

7

A wave of excruciating pain shot through Dora's midriff.

"Breathe through the contraction," the midwife told her. Dora had met the older woman with graying hair and wrinkled, weathered skin twice before when she had examined her. She might be brusque, but everyone in town had assured her she knew her profession and had brought countless babies into this world without a problem.

"I... I... can't!" Thankfully the contractions didn't last longer than a few breaths before they subsided and left her a minute or two to recover her strength. Never in her life could she have believed childbirth would be so painful.

The next contraction hit her more forcefully than all the ones before, making her scream out loud, gripping her hands at the sheets until her knuckles turned white.

"You need to push!" the midwife demanded, completely unaffected. "Harder!"

When the wave had washed over her, Dora asked, "How do you expect me to push?"

"Breathe through the contraction and your muscles will do

the rest. A woman's body knows what to do. You just need to relax."

Relax? How was she supposed to do this, while her insides felt as if an oversized football was being pushed through? Another horrible contraction announced itself, ripping through Dora's sweaty body. It began bearably, yet increased in intensity with every passing second, until Dora screamed so loud she feared it could be heard all the way into town.

"Scream all you want, but for the love of God, push!" the midwife ordered.

Finally, Dora's body, if not her mind, listened to the midwife's demands and somehow her stomach muscles seemed to draw upon an ancient wisdom and did exactly what they were supposed to do.

Another push through the pain and the midwife called out, "One more. The head is coming out."

The next seconds or minutes passed in a complete haze and with one final push, Dora felt something slip out of her. Moments later, the midwife said, "It's a girl."

Covered from head to toe in sweat, Dora sank exhausted onto the mattress, while the midwife held a slimy, bloody baby up to check if it was healthy and had all its limbs. Then she cut the umbilical cord and briskly wiped the baby off. The wiggly little infant didn't appreciate the rough handling, though. An indignant cry emerged, a mere hiccup, before a full-scale cry filled the room.

"And a healthy one at that," the midwife commented unmoved, before she wrapped it in a blanket and deposited the package on Dora's chest.

Mother Nature flooded her with love for her new daughter and within seconds she had forgotten about the horrible pain. Without Dora realizing it, the midwife must have alerted the people waiting outside, because suddenly Oliver stood by her side, beaming from ear to ear.

"It's a girl," Dora whispered.

"She's beautiful." Oliver's eyes shone with pride and love. Once more Dora realized what a good man he was. Other men might have berated her for birthing a mere girl, while he didn't seem to mind in the slightest and traced a finger across his daughter's cheek.

For a moment Dora held her breath, afraid he might break something. His strong, calloused hand was almost as big as the entire infant lying in her arms.

"Congratulations," another voice said.

Dora looked up and for the first time realized, that as well as Oliver, Fräulein Annegret, Frau Mertens and even Gloria, the new maid, had entered the room to welcome the new child into the world.

"Thank you, Fräulein Annegret. Also for everything you have done for us." Without her mistress' help in the Germanization process Dora and Oliver would never have been able to marry.

"No need to thank me." When all the women had admired the baby, Dora spied Nils, the handyman and longtime employee at Gut Plaun, lingering in the doorway, his eyes shining suspiciously. As far as she knew, he'd lost his wife and son many years ago during childbirth and had never married again.

"Come in, Nils," she called out.

He entered hesitantly, his cap in his hands. It took several attempts for him to speak. "Congratulations to you too."

Dora suddenly had an idea and whispered it into Oliver's ear, who nodded.

"What will you call her?" Fräulein Annegret asked after a while.

They had considered several names and had ultimately settled on one that was a common name both in Germany and in the Ukraine.

Oliver raised his voice. "She'll be Julia Gundelmann."

"A beautiful name and a wise choice," Fräulein Annegret, who'd been privy to their quest, said.

"Such a fitting name, Yulia," Gloria, the Polish maid pronounced the name the way a native Slavic speaker would.

Dora smiled, since she was too exhausted to do anything else.

Oliver cleared his throat and announced, "It might be unusual, but since we are at war, we want to baptize the baby as soon as possible." He paused slightly, and everyone in the room understood. Despite living far away from the actual war events, one could never be too sure they'd live to see another day. "And... it would be an honor for us, if you, Nils, agreed to become our daughter's godfather."

Nils was at a complete loss for words, although the joy was written all over his weather-beaten face. After several seconds, he won the war against his emotions and nodded. "I'd love to. Thanks for trusting me to do this."

Dora anxiously looked over to Fräulein Annegret, fearing she might feel bypassed, but her mistress gave her a secret wink of approval. Nils was the better choice, not only because he'd be a wonderful substitute grandfather, but also because Annegret herself was in a tenuous position, not being herself and all that.

"I think we should give the new mother some time to rest," Frau Mertens said, ushering everyone, including Oliver, out of the room, for which Dora was thankful, as she was utterly exhausted.

Frau Mertens turned around in the doorjamb and added, "I'll send Gloria with hot chicken soup in a bit. It'll help you regain your strength."

"Thank you, Frau Mertens," Dora whispered, before she laid back on her pillows. But she wasn't allowed to sleep just yet. As soon as everyone had left, the midwife approached to show her how to nurse the baby.

"I'll return tomorrow to check on you. You'll be back to work in no time at all." With these words the older woman left Dora with a tiny infant suckling at her breast.

Both of them must have fallen asleep, because she woke with a start when Gloria put a steaming bowl of soup on her nightstand.

"I'm sorry, but Frau Mertens insisted..." Gloria muttered.

"Don't worry." Just now Dora realized how famished she was. "Could you please also get me a cup of water?"

"Yes. Fräulein Annegret said to tell you she expects you to stay in bed for the next three days. She even had an argument with Frau Mertens over this, who said when Frau Huber was still alive the married farmhands always went back to work the next day, or even on the same day."

"Please give Fräulein Annegret my thanks." Dora couldn't imagine dragging herself out of bed to walk over to the manor and attend to her chores right now. She was truly blessed with her mistress.

8

Several weeks later Oliver stalked up to the manor, irritated and angry at the latest turn of events. Piet, the stable manager, had just dropped the bomb that he, along with all the remaining German grooms, had been drafted.

The letter from the Wehrmacht required them to report for training the coming Monday. From experience Oliver knew there was nothing he could do. Every single one of the men had previously been categorized "UK", which deferred them from military service due to the war-importance of their work.

If the powers that be had decided caring for the horses that would be sold to the Wehrmacht wasn't war-important any longer, any objection would make no difference, except to raise the suspicion that Gut Plaun might not be as loyal to Hitler's cause as it pretended to be.

Obviously the detail of being left without employees wouldn't be a valid excuse for Oliver when the next delivery date came around and he was supposed to sell more horses to the Wehrmacht. Either, the left hand didn't know what the right hand was doing, or they somehow assumed he had miracle powers and the horses would train themselves.

The disregard of the well-being of his charges—the horses that was—was a constant thorn in his side, but he'd reluctantly agreed to whatever his clients wanted, since he had no desire to get on the bad side of the authorities.

As he reached the manor, the worst of his wrath had subsided and he could think a bit more clearly. Not clearly enough, though, to come up with a solution. It wasn't that there was an abundance of able-bodied men in the surrounding towns either, since most everyone had been shipped off to the front, leaving only the very young and very old men behind.

Even the young and old were being pressed into forced work: at the harbors on the Baltic, into anti-flak service, or whatever else the Reich needed.

He entered the kitchen hoping to catch a glimpse of Julia and to talk for a few minutes with Dora. But she wasn't there. Gloria, though, was peeling potatoes and asked him, "Are you looking for Dora?"

"Actually, yes."

"She is with Fräulein Annegret. Has been up there all morning."

"Thank you." He wouldn't dare disturb the two women, so he walked into his office on the ground floor of the manor. From the window he observed a horse-drawn coach drive into the yard, the trailer full of potato sacks.

Almost immediately several men in striped uniforms jumped down from the trailer, unloading the heavy sacks with amazing speed and carrying them down into the storage cellars.

He worried his lip. It wouldn't be his preferred solution, but he might have to use prisoners to care for the horses. So far he'd only used them for menial labor, like mucking out the boxes. His stomach churned, since every single one of the grooms had been hand-selected for their ability to work with horses.

It bothered him to leave his beloved animals in unskilled hands. Contrary to what the Wehrmacht might believe, training a horse for battle deployment was a difficult task and plenty of damage could be done by rushing it.

Therefore he decided to discuss it with Annegret. She didn't actually require him to do this, but he liked to run important decisions by her. After all, it was her property. So, he returned to the kitchen. Dora still wasn't there, but Frau Mertens was.

"Good morning," he greeted the housekeeper. "Is Fräulein Annegret still upstairs? I need to consult with her."

Frau Mertens pressed her lips together, clearly indicating her disapproval. The old-fashioned woman believed the lady of the manor should leave any and all business to the men, just as her mother had done. "She's in her rooms with Dora and the seamstress, since she has set her mind on mending the prisoners' clothing."

"I'll ask if she has a minute for me," Oliver said and walked away. On the second floor, he knocked on Annegret's door.

Dora opened it, a smile of happy surprise spreading across her face, emboldening him to steal a quick kiss before he asked, "Does Fräulein Annegret have a moment for me?"

"Sure. Come in. We're almost done anyway."

He entered Annegret's antechamber, where she was bent over the table together with the seamstress.

"Good morning," he said.

"Oh, Oliver, it's you. Not bad news, I hope?"

He calculated what to tell her in the presence of an outsider. "Not at all. It's a minor inconvenience for us, but no doubt a gain for the Wehrmacht. Piet just told me that he and all the grooms have been drafted as of next Monday."

The seamstress gave a small shriek, before she clapped a hand over her mouth and apologized. "Please excuse my improper behavior. I was caught by surprise, because my Werner is one of the grooms."

Oliver sympathized with the woman who'd felt safe with

her husband's exempted status and would now have to worry day and night about his safety.

Annegret clapped her hands. "I think we're done here. Dora, will you see the seamstress out?"

Dora nodded and the two women disappeared. Once the door closed behind them, Annegret invited Oliver to take a seat. "The notice came this morning?"

"Yes. Piet got his own along with the note telling him that the Gut had to do without its grooms. I assume the men will find their letters when they return home in the afternoon."

"I thought we'd gotten them exemptions?"

"We did, but apparently that was changed. And you know it doesn't help to object." He harrumphed. "I wanted to run an idea by you."

"Would you like some coffee?"

"Yes, please."

She picked up the phone and asked for two cups of coffee with bread rolls.

The two of them had become a good team, him being the official face to the outside, while in fact she was the one holding Gut Plaun's strings in her hands, at least where the clandestine operations were concerned.

Normally he wouldn't bother her with personnel decisions in the stables, but the new situation was too severe. "We need to replace about a dozen skilled grooms within the week."

She nodded pensively. "That'll be difficult with the Wehrmacht drafting all able-bodied men left and right."

A knock on the door indicated that Dora had arrived with the coffee. Oliver saw no reason to stop talking while she served them. "How am I supposed to run the stud without men to perform the work?"

"Aren't there any left? Older ones maybe?" Annegret offered.

"Not really. Most have been assigned some kind of war-critical work. Even if there were, we can't just use anyone to train the horses. We need experienced men."

"May I offer a suggestion?" Dora said, which earned her surprised gazes from both her mistress and her husband.

"By all means," Annegret invited her.

"There are quite a few women in town who are keen riders. Why not use them?"

Oliver immediately shook his head. "No way. Women aren't cut out for such strenuous work."

Annegret laughed at him. "You've been brainwashed by the Nazis. Who do you think has been doing all the hard work since most of the men were sent to war? Women. What the German women won't do, is done by prisoners, even female prisoners."

Oliver wrinkled his nose and drank his coffee. He hated the idea of using women around the big horses. Not everyone was a gifted horse whisperer like the real Annegret had been. Most women wouldn't even know how to saddle their own mount. It was a ridiculous suggestion.

"If you don't need me for anything else, I'll help in the kitchen to prepare lunch," Dora said.

"You can go. I'll phone if I need you," Annegret dismissed her maid. As the door closed behind Dora she said, "Is it really such a bad idea?"

Oliver pondered the situation once more and shook his head. "I came here to discuss another approach, which I still think is the better one."

"Now you're making me curious."

"We've been using a few prisoners for the menial work in the stables. One of them, his name is Ladislaus, is a master at dealing with the horses. He used to work on the biggest stud in Poland, overseeing a dozen men and training race horses."

"He sounds like he has exactly the experience we need," Annegret said.

"Yes. Currently, he and the others are officially working and living at the factory, but have been loaned to the stables."

"So you want to employ them full-time as stable hands?" Her face lit up. "Then we can request more prisoners for the factory!"

He knew she had made it her mission in life to save as many people as possible from being deported eastward into one of the extermination camps. At least in her factory, the prisoners were treated like humans and didn't suffer too badly with hunger or the cold, though they were still forced to work hard.

"Yes, that would be possible." He smiled at her. "I could ask Ladislaus to identify another dozen prisoners at the factory who have experience with horses and then transfer them to the stables. I'd make him their boss, unofficial stable manager, if you will. His German is pretty good, furthermore he speaks Polish and Russian, which will be useful, since most of our new workers seem to be Poles or Soviet prisoners of war."

"But can we trust him?" Annegret asked.

"Trust him to treat the animals well? I would say yes. He loves them."

"Like you." She giggled. "I often believe that you love horses more than humans."

"A horse will never betray you."

"Anyhow, back to our problem. Can we trust Ladislaus not to stab us in the back?"

"What would he gain from it? He's got an easy job at the stables, compared to what he's gone through in the camps. Why would he risk it?"

"Because he's greedy, perhaps?"

Oliver shook his head. "He's not Katze."

"Speaking of the devil, after enduring the ordeal of entertaining him over dinner when he came to collect his first monthly payment, I fear we are going to need to buy less food next month in order to continue to pay his bribe."

He saw it written on her face how much she detested depriving prisoners of food, even if it was to be done to save their lives, but he had no words of comfort to offer.

"Where are the new stable hands going to live? It won't be feasible to have them traveling back and forth from the factory. Besides, we will need the room for the new workers we are going to request," Annegret asked.

"I haven't thought about this yet. In the servant quarters?"

Annegret shook her head. "No. Frau Mertens would never agree to that, not even if I ordered her to. But, more importantly, we don't have that much space, and it wouldn't look good to have prisoners living in the manor, with all the strangers coming and going on a daily basis."

He sighed, because she had a point there. "I could convert some of the empty stalls into living quarters. It won't be ideal—"

"—but certainly not worse than their current conditions at the factory," she completed his sentence. "Let's do it. I'm sure the prisoners won't mind, as long as they stay dry and warm."

"There's never a shortage of warmth with all the horses around," Oliver agreed. Back during his childhood he'd often snuck away from home and spent the night at the stable with his favorite mare. He took a last sip of his coffee and excused himself. "I'd better get down to the stables to find Ladislaus and arrange everything."

When Oliver found Ladislaus, he waved him over.

"Yes, Herr Gundelmann?" The Pole stood in a submissive position, his cap in hand, the eyes looking to the ground. Despite having told them many times that they had nothing to fear, the prisoners were so conditioned from years of captivity it seemed they simply couldn't behave otherwise.

Oliver began to doubt this was a clever idea. Perhaps a woman from town, even an inept one, might be better suited to commanding a group of anguished prisoners. It wasn't without reason that the Nazis had installed mostly hard-core, sadistic criminals as kapos in the camps. They knew how to enforce law and order among the other inmates.

"Ladislaus, I've been watching your work for a while now." The Pole seemed to shrink even further, as if he feared he'd done something wrong. "You have a gift for dealing with horses."

"Thank you, sir." Ladislaus' voice was but a murmur.

"I'll be frank with you, because I need your help."

The man's head shot up, his entire being forming a question mark. "Me, sir?"

"Yes, all my grooms have been drafted and I need men with experience to care for the horses."

"Sir, I appreciate all you do for us and I will certainly give you all the help I can."

"I know that, but I need more. So, if you could come to the factory with me—"

"No, please, don't. I'll do everything you want!" Ladislaus begged miserably, apparently mistaking the request and fearing he'd be sent back to the dangerous work of cooking explosives.

"Don't worry. You're not going to be transferred back there. I just want you to help me identify and choose about a dozen men with a history of working with horses, just like you. They'll train and care for the horses, and you'll oversee their work."

"Me?" Ladislaus still seemed to have his doubts.

"I promise, this isn't a trap or anything. By now you should have noticed that we treat the people differently here than in the other places."

The Pole stepped uncomfortably from one foot to the other. When Oliver didn't speak, he finally looked up and said, "Yes, I have noticed. But it is hard for me to trust a German."

The admission hurt, although it was understandable. At a loss for the proper words to say, Oliver simply nodded. "Not everyone agrees with the cruelty of the Nazis, but we can only do so much. Will you come with me to the factory and choose a dozen men to work under your tutelage?"

"Yes, sir."

"Then, let's go." Since they had only a few days until all his experienced grooms were gone, there was no time to lose getting the new crew up to speed. Franz Volkmer wouldn't be pleased, but he could always request replacements for the factory. The one thing in the war-ridden country that wasn't in short supply was prisoners.

9

The new baby was such a joy for everyone at Gut Plaun, taking their minds off the grim realities whenever she was around. Ever since Dora had returned to work again, Julia spent most of the time in the kitchen, where at all times someone would look after her as she lay in her bed made of a box that normally was used to transport supplies.

Margarete had arranged everything for the speedy baptism of the little girl. It would be a very small event, only for Dora, Oliver, his parents and Nils. But Margarete insisted on celebrating the occasion with an extra hearty meal for all farm or stable workers who lived at the manor, because good news was such a rare event these days.

"Fräulein Annegret, I'm afraid the numbers for dinner don't add up," Frau Mertens waylaid her in the morning.

"Don't you have enough supplies?" Margarete was instantly worried, calculating in her mind whether she could use some of the assets of the last resort they had in the storage cellars.

"No, no. On the contrary, there's too much."

Margarete looked at her in disbelief. Ever since the

rationing had begun, Frau Mertens complained about the shortage of one staple or the other. "Are you sure?"

"Well, yes. The supplies Nils brought last night will easily suffice for forty people."

"That's right." Margarete didn't understand the problem. There were exactly forty-one people living in the manor as well as the recently arranged living quarters in the stables for the former factory workers turned grooms.

Frau Mertens gave her a confused look. "We're only seventeen, and that's including some seasonal workers who live inhouse."

Margarete furrowed her brows as she re-counted the employees in her head. "Oh, you have forgotten to count in the stable workers."

Frau Mertens tore her eyes wide open. "But, Fräulein Annegret, they are prisoners. Did you actually wish to include *them*?"

Normally the foreign workers assigned to the manor or stud took their meals after the German workers, for the sole reason that the kitchen wasn't big enough to host all of them at once. Nevertheless, they received the same food as everyone else, both in quality and quantity. It had never occurred to Margarete that someone might see fit to exclude them from this little celebration.

"Are you saying I should only give the German employees extra food?"

Frau Mertens pursed her lips and fixed her jaw before answering. "Your mother would have never—"

Margarete had heard enough and for once she decided to cut Frau Mertens short. "I'm not my mother!"

"You certainly aren't," Frau Mertens said with pursed lips.

Just like her daughter, Annegret's mother had been a cold-hearted woman, only interested in her own advantage. When Margarete had been her maid, she'd been forced to live off the scraps the family left on their plates. One day Frau Huber had found Margarete cutting herself a piece from the bread loaf. She'd been livid and had accused her of stealing, with the result that Herr Huber had given Margarete a sound flogging when he'd returned home in the evening—much to the real Annegret's delight.

The vicious girl had taken pleasure in witnessing the castigation and had let Margarete know for weeks that this is what she thought the maid deserved for being a cunning, thieving, subhuman Jew.

Margarete stared at the old housekeeper who'd served the Huber family for more than thirty years. It was time to state without the slightest room for interpretation, who was the lady of the manor, and who had to obey. "I am the mistress of Gut Plaun and you would be better served to do exactly as I say, because I've had enough of being constantly compared to my mother. I do things my way and if you don't agree, you can always look for another job."

Frau Mertens stood there, her mouth hanging agape at the unprecedented lecture from the woman thirty years her junior, before she quickly regained her composure. "Of course not, Fräulein Annegret. If this is your wish, I'll attend to it immediately."

"Thank you. Is there anything else?"

"No, Fräulein Annegret. That would be all."

Margarete turned on her heel, inwardly shaking. She hadn't planned such an outburst and was surprised at herself. Truth be told, the housekeeper certainly deserved to be put in her place, since she always seemed to believe she knew better than her employer.

In a desperate need to calm her nerves, she changed into jodhpurs and strode toward the stables. The usual groom wasn't around, so she approached a man mucking out the horse boxes.

"Hello? Do you know where Hans is?"

The man, whom she'd never seen before, answered in broken German. "I'm sorry, miss, no."

She cocked her head, realizing he must be one of the prisoners Oliver had recently transferred to the stables to replace the drafted grooms. "What's your name?"

"Ladislaus, miss."

"Good morning, Fräulein Annegret," Piet the stud manager strode toward her. As he reached them, he said, "Bow your head, she's the lady of the manor."

Ladislaus seemed to shrink several inches, anxiously looking at the riding crop in her hand. With his head ducked in a posture of servitude, he murmured, "Please, forgive me, Fräulein. I had no idea."

"Stupid bloke," Piet murmured, while the prisoner seemed to have turned into a pillar of salt. Then he addressed her again. "Are you wanting your horse saddled for you?"

"Yes, please."

"I'll do it myself, since Hans is on anti-aircraft duty on the coast."

"Thank you."

Even as Piet strode off with long strides, the prisoner remained immobile with his head bowed, apparently waiting for her to give him leave. He was incredibly thin. Almost everyone they requested for the factory had a long history of different labor camps behind them—one worse than the next one. And, despite her best efforts to create tolerable living conditions for her prisoners, none of them managed to put on fat on the meagre rations.

"Where are you from, Ladislaus?" she asked him.

His head shot up, just to immediately lower his gaze again, as if he were afraid to even look at her. "Poland, Fräulein."

So, he was one of the many Slavs abducted into slave labor to keep Hitler's war machine going. The Slavs were the second lowest only to the Jews in the Nazis' hierarchy of races, while the Nordic, Aryan master race topped the pyramid, destined to subdue the worthless rest of humanity.

"You don't have to be afraid of me," she said. She wanted to say so much more, since Oliver had spoken very highly of the skills and work ethics of the newly transferred stable hands, but didn't dare to. It wouldn't do well to see the lady of the manor chatting amiably with one of the prisoners.

He still didn't move.

"You may now get back to your duties."

The moment she'd spoken the words she witnessed the transformation in his stance, as relief washed over him and he scurried away to continue his work.

When Piet returned with Pegasus, she thanked him and mounted the good-natured gelding. Since taking up riding classes with Oliver for the benefit of impersonating Annegret, she'd actually started to look forward to being out in nature on horseback.

It gave her the much-needed calm and serenity that she so much craved amidst the near-constant terror of being found out.

10

Dora walked into town holding Julia on her hip and a basket in the other hand. It had become a habit for her to visit Olga, another foreign worker from Ukraine, and her employer, Frau Gusen, with a basketful of food. Since spring had sprung, it included self-grown vegetables from the Gut, in addition to staples like bread and potatoes.

Frau Gusen was so frail she couldn't leave her house anymore, but that wasn't the reason for the charity. The elderly lady might not be able to walk, but she was still a warrior at heart and had become part of a small network of people hiding illegals.

Dora and Olga had become fast friends over the past year. It felt good to speak her native tongue with someone and reminisce about the good old times back in Ukraine. Despite not having known each other before coming to Germany, they shared a similar background: they both came from a rural area, one of many children from hard-working families. Both their parents had jumped with both feet at the opportunity to send their daughters away to earn their keep with the allied Germans.

Dora sighed. So much had happened since. Germany and Ukraine weren't Allies anymore. And she was caught between two worlds. No longer a Ukrainian after her Germanization, but not considered a real German either. She just hoped the war would soon be over and she'd somehow muddle through.

Olga greeted her at the door. "Oh, Julia is getting so big!"

Smiling, Dora responded, "Yes, she's almost two months old now and getting very heavy." The baby, used to being passed from person to person, gave a happy smile that could be considered a laugh.

"She likes you," Dora said.

"She should, if she knows what's good for her."

As a foreign worker Olga was considered too lowly to become an official godmother to a German child, but Dora had made her promise to take care of Julia and make sure she was delivered to Dora's parents after the war, should anything happen to her and Oliver.

"Want to come in?" Olga asked.

"No, I need to run some errands, but perhaps we could meet later after I've been to the haberdashery and you can accompany me a bit along the way home?"

Olga cocked her head, understanding without words that Dora needed to talk without prying ears nearby. The danger of anyone understanding them when they talked in Ukrainian was next to zero, nevertheless, they'd made it a habit to only talk German in public, since there was no need to remind the villagers of Dora's foreign background.

After putting up with some vile comments from the owner of the haberdashery, a great gossip, Dora finally reached the edge of town, where Olga was already waiting for her.

"What took you so long?"

"There was a queue for most everything I needed," Dora complained.

"Welcome to the reality of us lowly villagers." Olga laughed good-naturedly. Most supplies were delivered directly to Gut Plaun, but Frau Mertens often sent Dora into town for some last-minute purchases she needed to satisfy Fräulein Annegret's fancy needs.

Dora knew that her mistress would gladly do without, but appearances had to be kept up at all cost—and it gave her a perfect excuse to deliver the foodstuffs to Frau Gusen, which was a secret she and Fräulein Annegret had never shared with Frau Mertens. The old woman might have her heart in the right place, but she also adhered to traditions; going up against the government, even in such a small way, was out of the question for the conservative woman.

"How are things at your place?" Dora asked.

"Lili is still with us."

"What? You should have moved her on a long time ago!"

Olga looked guilty. "I know, but Frau Gusen has grown so fond of the girl. She's her only joy these days."

"It's still irresponsible," Dora chided her.

"Maybe or maybe not. She's as safe with us as she is elsewhere. And for a girl her age it's good to have a grandmother figure. She'd be so afraid all on her own."

That was undoubtedly true, but Dora still believed it would have been better to send her away. In general, the illegals never stayed longer than a couple of days in the same place.

"It won't be long now," Olga said. "With the Western Allies landing in Normandy and everything."

"We can only hope..." Dora didn't dare to pronounce her fears.

"What's wrong?" Olga stopped to look her in the eyes.

"It's just... I'm afraid... the Russians."

"Oh. You don't have to be afraid of them. We're Ukrainians, they consider us their brothers and sisters. They came here to liberate us."

"You think they have forgiven us for siding with the

Germans against them at the beginning of the war?" Dora wasn't so sure.

"Perhaps not. I heard it's official Soviet policy to consider this as a foolish mistake that we made. As long as we wholeheartedly exult over them as our saviors they won't harm us."

"That might be true for you, but for me?"

Olga put a hand on Dora's arm. "Nobody needs to know you've been Germanized. When push comes to shove, you throw away your new papers, talk to them in Russian and everything will work out just fine. You know it will. Just look at yourself in the mirror and you'll see a Ukrainian girl."

Dora hoped her friend was right. "What about Oliver? If he doesn't look like a German, then I don't know who does. What do you think the Russians will do to him?"

"Look, Dora. We don't know what will happen. They might let him go because he's with you, or they might not. But you need to keep one thing in mind: in the end, you have to do what's best for yourself and the baby. Yulia needs you more than Oliver does."

Dora shrugged her shoulders, hating the idea that she might have to choose between the man she loved with all her heart and her newborn daughter. Deep down in her soul, though, she knew that she'd choose her daughter every time.

11

Margarete watched Stefan steer them out into open water, her insides tensing. Ever since she'd almost drowned, because Horst Richter had forced her to jump off a cliff, she was deathly afraid of water.

Before all of this happened Stefan had promised to teach her how to swim and now she wondered whether he'd deluded himself into believing she was courageous enough to stick to that plan. Because she wasn't. Not by a long shot. Wild horses couldn't drag her into the water.

Even being on a boat was nerve wracking. She couldn't stop remembering the feeling of being dragged beneath the surface of the water by her sodden clothing, and...

"Gretchen." Stefan's voice brought her back to the present. When he arched a brow in her direction, silently asking if she was fine, she relaxed her shoulders, took a deep breath, and nodded.

"Where exactly are we going?"

"There's a small cove a few miles away. It's very secluded and hardly anyone goes there. My grandfather showed it to me when I was but a small boy."

"It sounds lovely." She concentrated on not looking at the gurgling black water, but focused on his wonderful blue eyes instead.

"A lovely place to spend time with a lovely woman," Stefan added with a broad grin, holding out his hand for her to take. Like always, he seemed to sense what she needed.

Margarete scooted closer to him, secretly letting out a breath when his arm came around her shoulders and pulled her close. With him by her side she wouldn't drown. He'd saved her before and would do so again.

She pushed the thoughts away, since she wasn't willing to let her fear get the better of her. Although sometimes she wondered how acutely the drowning mirrored the situation of her life. She was constantly treading water, barely well enough to keep her nose above the water while heavy weights were tugging at her feet pulling her down. One of those weights was Lothar Katze. Within the week he'd visit for the fourth time with an open hand and she didn't yet have the money to satisfy his greed.

Contrary to what he believed, she wasn't swimming in cash, because most of her assets were tied up in the Gut or in the factory.

"Relax, sweetheart. Let's forget all our problems for just a few hours, shall we?"

"Believe me, I'm trying."

"Then try harder!" Stefan grinned at her.

Tempted to tell him about her sorrow, she imperceptibly shook her head and promised herself to follow his advice and make an attempt to enjoy the beautiful afternoon together with him.

After a while they passed through the water lock at Lenz. The channel narrowed, the trees and vegetation grew thicker until they passed the impressive turning bridge in Malchow into the next lake called Fleesensee. The boat crossed the entire length of it, before Stefan steered them through a very narrow waterway into a tiny lake where the shore was completely overgrown with lush greenery.

Behind a curve, she gasped at the beauty before her. Trees, flowering bushes, a small sandy beach area, and large boulders on one side created a little paradise for visitors.

"Do you like it?" Stefan asked.

"I absolutely love it. Such a piece of paradise."

"And the best thing: it's inaccessible by land, so we'll be completely alone here."

"Except if another fisherman decides to take the afternoon off to enjoy the sunshine," she teased him.

"I should hope my colleagues have better ethics and are busy with work." The grin he flashed her made her insides hum with delight. Stefan killed the motor, and let the boat slide toward the beach, before he jumped out, not caring that the water went up to his thighs, making slurping sounds as it filled his rubber boots.

"It's warm and wonderful," he exclaimed. "Want to join me?"

"I'd rather not."

"Well then, sit and wait a minute while your devout servant makes sure you reach land without getting your feet wet."

She laughed at the exaggerated bow he gave her, before he moored the boat to a tree and then walked through the water again to swoop her up in his arms and carry her to the beach. Once he'd put her safely onto the sand, he returned for the blanket and picnic basket Dora had prepared for them.

Margarete settled on the blanket, admiring the magnificent landscape and leaned her head against Stefan's shoulder. "You know what? In this moment I'm absolutely, totally and deliriously happy."

He tipped her chin upwards to press a soft kiss on her lips, before he asked with a twinkle in his eyes, "May I ask the reason for your utter, complete and mind-boggling happiness?"

"You." She wrapped her arms around his neck, pulling him toward her while she let herself fall on her back. Just in time, he used his elbows to soften the fall so as not to crush her under his weight.

"Is that the proper behavior for the lady of Gut Plaun?" he teased her.

"This afternoon, I'm not her. I'm just Gretchen. A simple girl wildly in love with you."

After long minutes of passionate kissing, they sat up, devoured the prepared picnic and stared out onto the lake. It was such a peaceful calmness that it eased away her constant worries. Even the birds seemed to be lazy in this hot summer afternoon, because it was completely silent. The only sound were soft waves lapping onto the sand every now and then.

"I wish we could stay here forever," she mused.

"It would get rather cold in winter with no roof over our heads, don't you think?"

She elbowed him amicably. "At least for the summer then."

"I used to come here to be alone," he admitted.

"I gather it's an honor for you to show me your secret spot then?"

He looked at her with warmth in his gaze. "It is. I've never been here with a woman. But then I've never loved someone the way I love you." He rubbed his thumb across the back of her hand.

"I love you too." She felt a pang of guilt, because she kept him at arm's length to keep up appearances. "When the war is over, I hope we can finally be together."

"It won't be long now. The Western Allies are marching through France and the Red Army is doing the same in the east."

She didn't respond, hoping they'd both still be alive by the time the Allies reached them. It itched in her throat to ask him about the sabotage he was doing in her factory. Stefan seemed to be able to read her mind, because he placed a finger over her lips. "Shush. We agreed to forget reality for a while."

After spending some lazy hours in the secluded bay, they gathered their things to prepare for the trip back home. Once they were on his boat, she couldn't suppress her worries any longer. "Katze is coming for his bribe next week. I don't know how much longer I can meet his demands, since I'm running out of cash."

"How many months' worth of cash do you have?"

"I don't even have the amount he's demanding this month. I've been juggling with the payment of bills, but that won't do it for much longer. If I don't find another solution, it'll be all over in three months, maybe four." Margarete wanted to scream with frustration, since most of her fortune was tied up in non-liquid assets.

"Can't you sell something?"

"Indeed, I thought about selling some of the classic paintings in the big dining room, but there seems to be no market for art. Furthermore, Oliver convinced me that it would cast suspicion on my finances, and we don't need that."

He nodded with a serene expression. "Would Katze accept a painting as payment?"

She snorted. "That uncultured lout wouldn't know a Rembrandt from a child's drawing. No, he insisted on cash only."

"Don't you have anything that can be sold without causing too much furor? Like silverware?"

"Frau Mertens would notice, and I don't trust her to keep her mouth shut." She wrinkled her nose to think hard. "I do have some jewelry from Frau Huber that I never wear. It's in a secret vault in my room and nobody would miss it, at least not in a long while."

"Jewelry is good. It can easily be sold, especially smaller pieces. You'd have to be discreet, though. Best to do it in Berlin and not around here," he suggested.

Margarete violently shook her head. "No. I can't possibly go there. Someone might recognize me. It's too much of a risk."

"I could go for you," Stefan offered.

"But then people would want to know where you got the jewelry. What if they assume you're a thief and call the police? No, it's much too dangerous and I won't risk your life. We have to think of something else."

A heavy silence settled over them as he steered the boat across the lake toward home. Deep in her heart Margarete knew that Berlin was the best place to sell the jewelry, but she couldn't go there by herself. It was much too risky...unless—

"We could go together," she suggested.

Stefan gazed up at her stupefied, before a lazy grin appeared on his lips. "That's indeed a fantastic idea."

She chided him. "This is about business, not going to have fun."

"We can actually do both. Although," he said, his smile spreading into a promising gaze full of love, "we'd have to pretend to be a married couple."

Shivers of delight ran down Margarete's spine. "It would make things easier, indeed. Nobody will question the motives of a young couple selling jewelry. And if somebody asks, we can say we want to buy furniture."

Stefan tapped her on the nose and slid his hand behind her head, tilting her face up for a kiss. When he let her go again, he murmured, "We could perhaps act like a married couple, too."

She'd wanted to give herself to him for such a long time now, yet had always refused. Not for moral reasons, but because she was afraid she might be caught red-handed in a relationship that was improper for her social status. A trip to Berlin pretending to be married would be the perfect occasion to take their love for each other to the next level.

A little voice in her head reminded her of the teachings of her mother. *Don't let a man kiss you. Don't let him see you naked. Don't engage in uncouth thoughts before you are married.* Despite having adhered to all her mother's advice, she had still been brutally raped by her former employer's son many times. So, what good had it done?

Now, she could vanquish this dark chapter of her life by giving herself voluntarily to the man she loved, experiencing joy and kindness instead of fear and pain. The lives they led were perilous on the best of days. They might never get another chance to act on the deep love they felt for each other.

12

Stefan made another annotation on the blueprints of the factory, before he paused for a moment to stretch his arms over his head. He'd been working nonstop for the past few days fine-tuning his sabotage activities.

He'd already implemented several small actions like pouring sand into the motor oil and refusing to accept raw material that was supposedly defective. But those were mere drops in the ocean. His bold scheme was not to slow down production, but in fact to speed it up with the ultimate goal of making explosive material that wouldn't explode.

A brilliant move he hoped that nobody would be able to trace back to their factory, and if they did; he had already put security measures in place. Rejecting the supposedly defective material served not only to slow down production due to raw material shortages, but also to leave a paper trail of low quality supplies that might later be needed to blame the malfunction.

A few more tests to assure that none of the workers would be harmed in the process was all he needed to start the sabotage work in earnest. This time he wanted to get everything right, because even though the final product would turn out nonexplosive, the cooking process used different additives, which might cause an unwanted reaction and kill people through smoke, or cause nasty injuries if spilled drops burned through protective clothing.

Back in his days in the laboratory he'd learned never to underestimate a chemical reaction. If the slightest detail was changed, catastrophes could happen. At the university, under test conditions, such a catastrophe usually involved receiving a bad grade and having to do the experiment all over, but here it could mean the death of innocents, which he had to prevent.

The two dead comrades at the cable factory still weighed heavily on his conscience. If only he'd been more careful, had tested the chemical reaction one more time... It was futile to ponder the what-ifs... but he certainly wouldn't commit the same mistake twice. This time there would be no casualties on his watch.

He was almost finished preparing a test charge, when he realized that he needed the exact specification of the grenades that were filled with the finished nitropenta, or he wouldn't be able to properly calculate the amount of sand needed.

Unfortunately, these papers were stored in the factory manager's office, and he'd rather not explain to Herr Volkmer why he needed the grenade specifications. The man was unhappy enough with Stefan's presence, since he saw it as an effort to supervise his own work. Perhaps he even suspected that Oliver wasn't pleased with the factory productivity, which obviously bothered Volkmer's pride.

Stefan glanced at his watch. Oliver had assured him that Volkmer left the factory every day at the same time, because his wife hated it when he arrived late for dinner. He waited fifteen minutes and then stepped to the window, satisfied when he saw Volkmer pass through the front gate, leaving the fenced-in factory grounds behind.

He had to grin when he saw that even the factory manager

arrived at his workplace by bicycle, since that was such a step-down from even a year ago, when there was enough fuel to go by car.

Stefan turned around and hurried across the yard toward the administration building and into Volkmer's office.

Oliver had also advised him where to find the keys to the file cabinet. Thankfully security inside the factory wasn't a priority, because there was nothing classified there. Not even an industrial spy for the Allies would bother to steal the recipes for cooking explosives or the exact specifications of ammunition, since that was common knowledge in the scientific world.

For his purpose though, a millimeter of steel would make a world of difference. He quickly found the papers he needed and jotted the key figures into his notebook, when suddenly the door opened and Franz Volkmer stood in the frame.

"What are you doing in my office?" He glared at Stefan.

Stefan closed his notebook, inwardly cursing, while outwardly adopting an air of authority. "Herr Volkmer, I'm working on an experiment to do more effective quality control tests."

"The production was fine before you arrived. Does Fräulein Annegret think we're fools?" Franz Volkmer clearly felt that installing a new head of quality control was a direct sign that she didn't trust his expertise.

"I apologize for the inconvenience," Stefan tried to mollify the other man. "As far as I know Fräulein Annegret holds you in the highest esteem and appreciates all the hard work you've done. She told me that the production has soared to unbeliev-able heights since you took over."

"Well, yes."

For a moment Stefan hoped the danger was over, but he was disabused.

"But that doesn't explain your presence in my office!"

"I'm sorry."

"What do you have in your hand?"

"Just my notebook."

"Give it to me!" Volkmer jumped forward stretching out his hand.

Stefan jumped the same distance backward, pressing the notebook against his chest, since he couldn't risk the other man having a look inside. There wasn't anything illegal in there, but if Volkmer had his wits about him, he might be able to decipher the intention behind Stefan's annotations. It was best not to go there.

While he was still thinking how to hang on to his notebook, Volkmer's gaze fell on the papers on his desk.

"What's this? What have you been doing?"

"I needed to look up some specifications."

"Sneaking into my office behind my back!" The vein in Volkmer's temple was pulsating vigorously.

"I'm sorry, you had already left for the day." Stefan did his best to stay calm. If the factory manager hadn't returned for whatever reason, nobody would have been the wiser.

"You... could... have asked my secretary! Or waited! Or telephoned! Or whatever! There was no reason to violate my office and steal classified papers!"

Stefan inwardly groaned, since the last thing he needed was the police investigating an alleged stealing. "Look, Herr Volkmer, I'm very sorry. It won't happen again. I was being stupid not to ask you for permission because I was in a hurry and didn't want to wait until tomorrow."

Herr Volkmer looked slightly mollified, but his suspicions hadn't vanished altogether. "From this instant on you're only allowed on the factory grounds when I'm present, and I'll assign someone to accompany you at all times—even to the bathroom."

That was a serious determent for his subversive plans, but there was nothing he could do for the moment, so Stefan said, "Whatever you wish, I'll gladly oblige."

"And now get out of my sight! Guards!" Volkmer hollered.

Two guards arrived and Volkmer directed, "Escort Herr Stober out of the factory. Effective immediately he needs to be accompanied by one of the guards whenever he sets foot on factory grounds." He smirked and added, "For security reasons, since we don't want anything bad to happen to our quality supervisor."

Stefan followed the guards, the tension gripping him tightly. Only when he pushed his bicycle through the factory gates did his anxiety begin to fade. The incident had ended well, although Volkmer's order to give him a watchdog complicated his work.

Somehow he needed to come up with a solution. Given that the guards weren't studied in chemistry he didn't doubt it was possible, but it certainly posed a nuisance. Briefly he considered asking Oliver or Annegret to revoke the order, then thought better of it. If one of them got involved on his behalf it would only raise Volkmer's suspicions—and aggrieve him. As much as Stefan hated the situation, it would become so much worse if the factory manager became his enemy.

Instead of pedaling directly home, he took a detour into town, where he stopped at the tavern for a beer. Reasonably surprised he spotted Sandra, an old friend of his, sitting at one of the tables.

"Hello, Sandra, what are you doing in Plau am See?"

"Stefan! What a surprise. It's been too long since we last met."

Despite living in a town close by, he hadn't seen his friends since starting to work for Annegret. Being a fisherman at night, and a saboteur during the day simply didn't leave much time to hang out with friends. "Yes, I've been very busy," Stefan said, walking around her, so that his good ear was toward her.

"Doing what? And where's that cute brunette? She is your girlfriend, right?" Sandra teased him.

"Yes. Gretchen is my girlfriend." He'd invited Annegret last year to an illegal dance in Sandra's house, where he had introduced her as Gretchen, without mentioning who she really was, since for once she hadn't wanted to be the lady of Gut Plaun, whom everyone revered, but a simple girl like everyone else. Back then he hadn't even known that her real name was Margarete, but had seen immediately that she had much more in common with him and his friends, than with the snobby financial aristocracy she impersonated.

"You've made yourself pretty scarce," Sandra chided him.

"I know and I'm sorry, but there never seem to be enough hours in the day to do everything that has to be done."

Sandra cocked her head. "Sure it's fishing that takes up all your time? Or what else are you doing?"

"This and that. Nothing of importance," Stefan hedged. He implicitly trusted Sandra with his life, yet it was better not to make her privy to the sabotage or Annegret's charade.

"Very mysterious." Sandra lowered her voice and moved closer to him. "In fact, it's serendipitous to have met you, since I could use your help." Her hand snuck onto his shoulder and she pressed her cheek against his as she whispered into his good ear. "We had a delay in getting a package out of the country and urgently need a place to store it for a few days."

Stefan tensed, understanding perfectly what she was implying since this wasn't the first time he had helped her out moving illegals from one place to another. "Shall we meet tomorrow night for a drink to the good old times?"

"That would be wonderful," Sandra said, putting some space between them and taking a gulp from her beer. "I can't wait. Pick me up at the wharf."

"I'm looking forward to it," Stefan said. After some chit-chat, Sandra air-kissed his cheek and left the tavern, making sure everyone who might have overheard them knew without a shadow of a doubt that he had designs on her. In the past they'd found that this ruse made everything so much easier, because nobody suspected a horny man to conspire against his fatherland.

The next day he would clear out the storage closet in the hull of the boat and set about preparing his nets for some night fishing. If anyone happened to stop him, all they would see was a hardworking fisherman trying to catch enough food to sustain the starving population.

13

Oliver was bent over the books, wondering how he was supposed to pay the due invoices, since Margarete had made another huge withdrawal from the bank to pay Lothar Katze's bribe.

He could juggle the payments a bit, but these days most suppliers, and especially the small farmers providing food, demanded immediate payment or they'd simply sell their produce elsewhere. Still, the situation was untenable.

A knock on the door interrupted him. "*Herein.*"

Franz Volkmer marched into the office. He was a massive man. Tall and large, with hands big as shovels. Despite this exterior, he was normally a quiet man. Today though, his face was red from exertion and Oliver could almost see the steam coming from his ears.

"How can I help you, Franz?"

The other man took several seconds to catch his breath, before he answered. "We have a problem."

Not another problem! Oliver's desk was inundated with them, with no hope of ever getting to the bottom of the huge pile. "Tell me about it. I'm sure we can find a solution." Or perhaps not, at least not if it involved money.

"This new quality control manager—I want him gone!" Franz demanded.

Now, that was a problem, indeed. "What has happened?"

"He's been snooping around the factory!"

Oliver inwardly smiled, while making a grave face. "Fräulein Annegret hired him to investigate whether the production process can be more efficient, while at the same time adhering to the strictest quality requirements. I would assume he has to look at everything."

"Does that include my office?" Franz looked as if he was about to fly off the handle.

"Of course not, he's only to oversee production, mostly the chemical part of it." Oliver had a vague suspicion why Stefan might have been in Franz's office. He'd have to warn him to be more careful.

"I found him sneaking around in the filing cabinet with the Wehrmacht contracts. I'm sure he's up to something shady."

"Damn!" Oliver faked outrage. "That's grave! Perhaps we should ask him, before condemning his actions? He might have had a reason for this?"

Franz scoffed. "That slimy thief pretended to need the specifications for a grenade."

"It does sound reasonable."

"It's an excuse. He knew I caught him red-handed and he looked the part. Why couldn't he wait until the next morning? Why did he have to sneak into my office after I was gone? Don't you think there's something fishy going on?"

Oliver swallowed down a witty remark about a fisherman doing fishy things for a living, since it would only aggravate Franz's ire. "I agree. But I'd still want to question him before taking a decision. After all, he was contracted at the explicit wish of Fräulein Annegret."

Franz rolled his eyes. Obviously he would never contradict

his employer and had never shown anything but respect toward her, but Oliver knew that Franz believed she should focus on finding herself a husband instead of sticking her nose into the men's world. "I want him gone. Meanwhile, question him all you want, but, effective immediately, he won't take a single step in the factory without a guard by his side."

"That's a good compromise while I get the ball rolling, isn't it?" Oliver said, hoping to mollify Franz. He needed some time to come up with a probable excuse or some other solution. Getting rid of Stefan was out of the question, since he was the only person with enough expertise to pull off sabotaging the production without leaving a trace for the SS to find. But that, he obviously couldn't tell Franz.

Franz nodded. "There's another thing."

"Yes?"

"We're running short on some of the raw materials. I've called the supplier and he said he's waiting for his last invoice to be paid before he sends us more."

Oliver groaned, as he had feared this might happen for several weeks now. Wracking his brain for a solution, he hedged. "That's impossible. But let me check the books. What was the name again?"

When Franz left his office, Oliver sank bank into his chair, a deep furrow on his forehead. He'd have to talk to Annegret, since their cash problem couldn't impact the factory production —or they'd soon get a visit from the SS, and risk exposing their clandestine operations.

First though, he'd take Stefan to task for being reckless enough to snoop around Franz's office. On the way out he passed by the kitchen, kissed Dora during an unobserved second and cast a glimpse toward baby Julia in her sleeping box.

"Don't wait for me for lunch, I have to go into town," he told his wife.

"Problems?"

"Nothing serious, just the usual." Dora had become increasingly anxious during the past months since Julia's birth, even though he tried to keep all worries away from her.

He saddled Sabrina, his favorite mare, and galloped into the forest. After a few minutes, the tension fell from his shoulders and he breathed freely again. The calm beneath the big trees, the rays of sunshine dancing on the ground, always helped him to relax.

"Good girl." He patted Sabrina's neck and let her fall into a slower pace, feeling completely at ease with her and the nature surrounding them. If only all of his problems could be solved as easily.

About half an hour later he arrived at the wharf, where Stefan was coiling his nets. "Getting ready to do some night fishing?" he asked.

Stefan looked up, his wary expression relaxing when he recognized Oliver. "Yes. Even the fish are too lazy to move in the sweltering heat."

"I had a visit from Franz Volkmer."

Stefan chuckled. "Did you now?"

"Yes. He demanded I sack you, because he caught you snooping around his office."

Stefan shrugged. "I'm not going to apologize."

"You should have known better than to take such an unnecessary risk!" Oliver scolded him. "He thinks you're trying to steal information about the Wehrmacht contracts."

"He's a fool."

Oliver sensed impatience rising inside of him. "He might be, but we have enough trouble already, I don't need him being suspicious of you."

"Alright. It won't happen again." Stefan put up his hands in an apologetic gesture.

"You're right, it won't. Because he told me he's ordered the guards to follow your every step on the factory grounds. What were you *thinking*, breaking into his office?"

"Calm down, Oliver. I didn't break in, the door was open. And I couldn't wait until morning. What would you suggest? That I ask Franz, 'Excuse me, but can you give me the specifications for the grenade shells so I can calculate how much I need to dilute the explosive to prevent the damn thing from going off?'" Stefan's voice grew angrier with every word.

Oliver looked over his shoulder to make sure nobody was within earshot. "Don't be stupid, of course not. How are you going to do your work with a watchdog on your heels at all times?"

"I'm not going to tell you," Stefan brusquely said.

"Gosh, you're such a stubborn piece of—"

"I've heard that before," Stefan interrupted him. Then he shrugged and turned around to the work he was doing, effectively ignoring Oliver, who sincerely wondered what Annegret saw in this annoying man.

14

Margarete was in the library, finalizing her plans for the trip to Berlin. Since her afternoon spent with Stefan at the secluded beach, almost two months had passed. Lothar Katze had visited again last week for more cash, which she had barely scraped together.

Oliver had warned her that several suppliers had complained about late payments and wouldn't deliver more materials without receiving their owed money first. But there was nothing left. Not a single penny in the bank account, not the emergency fund, nothing.

It was high time to convert some of Frau Huber's jewelry to cash. A discomfort settled in her stomach at the prospect of finally tackling the trip to Berlin. If she was being honest with herself, she had to admit that the majority of the problems impeding her from going to Berlin had been excuses, because she was too anguished to face her past.

Trouble at the stables. Trouble at the factory. Trouble with the trains. The list of reasons was long and varied, although none of them would actually hinder her if she absolutely wanted to go.

With sudden clarity she realized that her entire ploy would fall to pieces next month, when Katze held out his hand again and she had nothing to put into it. The deadline was approaching fast and since she would be doomed either way, she might as well travel to Berlin. It was the only way out— dangers and worries aside; this was the only solution to her problems.

Not only for herself, but for all the people who depended on her.

"Fräulein Annegret?" Stefan's voice caused her heart to jump with joy. When she turned around, he was standing in the doorway, looking as handsome as ever, but with a quizzical look upon his face.

"I didn't hear Frau Mertens announce you," she said, getting up and walking toward him. Her entire being yearned to hug him, yet she resisted and kept a ladylike distance, treating him like any other employee of hers, perhaps a bit more haughtily to dispel any rumors that might otherwise spring up.

"I'm sorry if I scared you," he answered, with a wink that was only meant for her. "Normally I wouldn't have bothered you, but Oliver asked me to get your approval on these," he said much louder than was necessary, holding a bunch of papers in the air.

"Well then, if Oliver needs me to sign them." She sighed exaggeratedly, before she turned around and picked up the phone to dial the kitchen. "Frau Mertens, would you be so kind and send Dora with coffee and biscuits into the library. Oliver wants me to go through some contracts with Herr Stober."

"Of course, Fräulein Annegret." Despite Frau Mertens' ready acquiescence, Margarete could *see* the disapproval on her face. *A woman in your position should not concern herself with business. When your mother was still alive, she would never...*

In one of their many exchanges of words, Margarete had told the housekeeper, "But my father did. And he's dead now, so someone has to step up to the job. Or have you forgotten about Gustav?" The former estate manager had robbed them blind because he'd been given too much authority. Margarete shuddered at the memory of the man's brutality, shown toward those he considered inferior to him.

Frau Mertens had sucked in a deep breath, perhaps ashamed about her own, albeit unintentional, role in the fraud.

Margarete had taken the opportunity to clarify the new distribution of roles in the household. "I appreciate your concern, Frau Mertens, since you have served my family well throughout all these years. But things have changed. I'm no longer a child you need to chastise. Now, I'm the lady of the manor and I do as I wish. I don't have to ask permission of anyone, and I certainly don't appreciate being told how my mother would have behaved in my situation. Her situation was different, since she had a husband to take care of everything. Do you understand?"

"Certainly, Fräulein Annegret."

This had been the last time Frau Mertens had uttered a suggestion about how Annegret should behave, but it hadn't stopped her disapproval, which Margarete deliberately ignored.

Stefan closed the library doors and settled on the armchair opposite hers, spreading his papers onto the coffee table. As far as she discerned, they contained unimportant numbers about food supplies for the manor and she wondered what Stefan's real reason was to seek her out.

"I made some inquiries about that trip," he carefully said, looking over his shoulder. "A friend has recommended a trustworthy jeweler to use."

Margarete breathed a sigh of relief, even though the knot in her stomach tightened. With yet another piece of the puzzle put in place, she wouldn't have reason to delay the trip much longer.

"You looked worried," Stefan commented, just as the door opened and Dora came inside to serve coffee and bread rolls.

"Thank you, Dora. Could you please make sure nobody interrupts us? I need to carefully study these contracts," Margarete asked her maid.

"I'll let Frau Mertens know," Dora said with a conspiratorial wink. Dora knew that her mistress was sweet on the fisherman and covered for them however she could. Margarete had never told her the other reason why she needed to spend alone-time with Stefan, since knowing too much was dangerous in their line of work.

"For my part, I've arranged everything and can leave anytime for a few days." His blue eyes bore into her, leaving a tingling promise in her heart.

She mustered all her courage, took a sip of her coffee and then said, "This coming Monday it is then."

"Perfect. I'm looking forward to the trip with my wife."

His words made her blush furiously. That was another aspect of the journey she relished and dreaded in equal parts. Before she lost heart, she shoved a bread roll into her mouth. Despite the sugar rationing, Frau Mertens somehow managed to make them taste sweet and soothing. She drew reassurance from the bite and nodded. "Me, too."

Emboldened by her response, and the assurance that nobody would interrupt them, Stefan took her wrist and pulled her over. As soon as she settled on his lap, a wave of comfort washed over her. He had the talent to make her feel protected and loved. In his arms she always felt completely carefree. Wanting to savor these emotions, she snuggled up against his broad chest, inhaling the lingering scent of sun, wind and water, combined with traces of dried fish—and something acidic that tickled her nose.

"You came straight from the factory?" she asked as she rubbed her nose.

"Yes. How did you know?"

"I can smell the explosives on you."

"Do you want to taste them, too?" His bright blue eyes glinted with mischief. Without waiting for her answer, he tipped up her chin and lowered his head to give her a passionate kiss.

A delicious tingle spread from her lips all the way into her fingertips and even her toes, as she wrapped her arms around his neck, giving in to the need to be as close to him as humanly possible. Several heated minutes later she broke the kiss, her cheeks glowing, her entire body in emotional uproar.

"We shouldn't... I mean... What if someone..." she stammered.

"And here I thought Dora was keeping a lookout," he responded with a broad grin, even as he pressed a last soft kiss on her lips before letting her go.

The very instant Margarete got up from his lap, she acutely sensed the loss of his protective presence. All her worries seemed to have waited in the shadows and attacked her immediately, filling her with doubts about the upcoming trip.

Fraught with danger, so many things could go wrong...

Seemingly able to read her thoughts, Stefan assured her, "We'll be just fine. I'll be there to keep you safe."

"Thank you," she said, looking into his rugged, yet lovely face. "I love you so much."

"I love you too."

Then she straightened her skirt, brought him to the door and said loudly, "Thank you for going through these contracts with me. I'll return them to Oliver right away." She didn't expect prying ears, although one could never be too careful. With the inconsequential papers in her hand, she walked over to Oliver's office on the other side of the manor, but it was empty.

Instead of simply leaving the papers on his desk, she headed for the stables, hoping to find him there. Now that she had settled on a date for her trip to Berlin, she needed to inform him. She knew he'd hate the idea, since she might run into someone from her or Annegret's past. It was a risk she had to take because there was no other way to get the money they urgently needed.

She recognized Oliver's dark-blond, always tousled, hair from afar. He was talking to another man, small and thin, with cropped dark hair, wearing prison garb. She inwardly flinched, since she and Oliver had argued whether or not to give the prisoners who'd been transferred to the stables civilian clothes. Her point had been that it would give them some dignity, but he'd argued that it might raise suspicions. Also, that instead of buying civilian clothes, their money was better spent for food, which was the argument she'd ultimately accepted.

"Good afternoon," she greeted the two men.

"Good afternoon, Annegret," Oliver answered, while the prisoner cast his gaze downward, too afraid to look her into the eyes. "Do you remember Ladislaus? He's in charge of the new stable hands."

"I've heard only good things about you, Ladislaus," she complimented him.

His head jerked up, a mixture of pride and fear shining in his eyes, before he looked back to the ground again, murmuring something unintelligible.

It broke her heart, but she thought it better not to say another word, since she didn't want to be seen being too friendly to the prisoners. Therefore she turned toward Oliver again. "Do you have time to go for a ride? I have a few questions about the contracts you sent over for me to sign and would like to get out on horseback today." It was their standard excuse to spend time out of anyone's earshot.

Oliver nodded. "Ladislaus, will you please saddle Pegasus for Fräulein Annegret?"

The man hurried away, while Oliver said to her, "He's a

good worker and has a knack with horses. It was a good decision to give him the job at the stables after Piet left."

"He seems to be afraid of me, though."

Oliver laughed. "Hell, everyone is afraid of Annegret Huber!"

"Not you," she protested.

"Only because I've been here since childhood and my anger at... you then was much stronger than my fear."

Sometimes it was a burden that everyone kept their distance, but at the same time, it made her life so much easier, especially where the clandestine part was concerned. Although she often yearned for someone to lean on, someone who knew her true identity, and didn't depend on her, someone like Stefan. She caught herself in time before letting out a dreamy sigh.

While Oliver strode off to saddle a horse for himself, Ladislaus returned with Pegasus. He handed her the reins, his arm stretched out while the rest of his body seemed to want to dislocate itself from the arm to run away from her. "Here you go, Fräulein Annegret."

She took the reins and mounted the big horse. Once she looked down at the picture of misery at her feet, she couldn't keep herself from saying, "Don't be afraid of me. I really appreciate your work. We all do."

His head jerked up, showing an expression of disbelief. "No German has said a nice word to me in years."

A whirlwind of emotions filled her heart, and she bit back a tear, because she remembered all too well how being a harassed subhuman felt. "Here at Gut Plaun we acknowledge every human being, no matter where they come from."

Thankfully Oliver approached them with his own mount in tow. "Ready to go?"

"Yes. Where to?"

"I thought we might take the path down to the deer stand."

Oliver tapped the bag he'd tied to the pommel of his saddle. It was filled with food for the Jewish women hiding in a cave not far from said deer stand.

It was a thing they'd started last year, when the sword of Damocles of deportation to Auschwitz had hung over all their Jewish slave workers. They'd thought up an ingenious way to let workers "die" during the night and move them to the cave in the woods. The first groups had been issued with new identities using the Swedish protection passes that a friend of Stefan had given her. Unfortunately they had run out of these passes, with no way to procure new ones. Margarete really hoped the war would end before winter came.

They reached the deer stand, tied their horses and Oliver said, "You go ahead. I will climb up on the stand and keep watch."

The risk of someone wandering about this private part of the forest was minimal, but one could never be too careful. Margarete grabbed the bag with food and walked toward the cave, where she knocked the agreed sign to be let inside.

"Thank you for bringing us food," one of the women said.

"Can you tell us news from the outside?" another one asked.

"The Allies liberated Paris." Margarete enjoyed being able to give some good news. "Now it won't be long anymore. The Wehrmacht is losing ground each day."

"Who do you think will reach us first? The Americans or the Russians?"

"I really don't know. But you don't have to fear anything from the Red Army, they are coming to liberate you." Margarete was pretty sure that the same wouldn't apply to her, a free German woman, who supposedly was a Nazi. Panic rose in her chest every time she thought about all the unspeakable things the news reports said the Russian soldiers did to the women they found.

"Will they be here before winter?" Everyone knew that

living in a cave during summer, as inconvenient as it might be, was a piece of cake compared to doing so during winter.

"Very possibly." She wasn't half as confident as she made it sound, yet wanted to give them some hope. A few minutes later she left the women and returned to Oliver.

On the way back, she told him about her plan to travel to Berlin to sell some jewelry.

"I don't like it one bit. Berlin is a dangerous place for you."

"You said yourself that we urgently need cash."

"That doesn't mean I have to like the idea. Can't you send someone in your place?"

Margarete rolled her eyes. "Don't you think I have thought about this already? If there were someone I could trust with that errand, I wouldn't think twice."

"What about Dora?"

"Really?" Margarete suppressed a giggle. "My maid who looks and sounds like a Ukrainian from miles away? How long would it take for the jeweler to call the police?"

Oliver shrugged. "Frau Mertens, maybe?"

"Don't be ridiculous. We still don't know whether we can trust her. How would I explain the reason to her for selling the precious jewels of my oh-so-perfect mother?" She imitated Frau Mertens' strict tone of disapproval.

He looked up in surprise. "You're really good at imitating voices. You'd be a great actress."

I am indeed a superstar actress, playing a role day in day out, because my life depends on it, and my talent to imitate voices has more than once saved my behind. She decided it was best not to remind him of who she truly was. A fact they never mentioned, even when they were alone for fear of inadvertently blurting out a telltale detail in public. Instead she said, "There is no other way. I need to do it myself. The sooner the better."

Oliver shook his head. "I will worry about you every single second while you're gone."

"Leave the worrying to your wife, remember how she packed me about ten suitcases for a five-day trip to Stockholm last year? I was actually relieved when I left."

His features grew soft. "She considers it her prerogative to worry about the people she holds dear."

Even though she and Dora had formed a much stronger bond than was usual for a mistress and her maid, the admission warmed her heart. Despite being only a few years senior to Dora, she saw her much like a daughter, or perhaps a younger sister, for whom she cared and provided.

After several minutes of silence, Oliver offered, "I could accompany you."

"Where to?"

"To Berlin, of course."

She quickly looked the other way to hide the blush creeping into her cheeks, since she couldn't tell him that she already had male company who would take good care of her. "Thank you, but that won't be necessary. Besides, you are needed at Gut Plaun during my absence."

"How long are you planning to stay in Berlin?"

"Two days. Three at most. I don't want to take any unnecessary risks."

"Good." They had reached the manor. "Shall I leave you here and return Pegasus to the stables?"

"Yes, that would be nice. Thank you." She dismounted her horse, patted his neck and then climbed the impressive stairs leading up to the main entrance of the manor. She had plenty of preparations to make before traveling to Berlin.

15

Following Katze's visit, Ernst Rosenbaum had been transferred to a prison for political prisoners. Several months later, most of his wounds had healed well, although his body would show permanent signs of the torture he'd received at Thomas Kallfass' hands.

The physical pain, though, was negligible compared to the psychological burden of having betrayed his favorite niece. He knew he must forgive himself, but he just couldn't.

Lothar Katze hadn't mentioned her, so he feared for the worst. Margarete was probably dead by now, or worse, in some grinding labor camp. Ernst still pondered what he should wish for: that she'd been granted a quick death or that she was still alive. In the end he chose to consider her dead, if only because the certainty of death was easier to bear than the uncertainty of what other fate might have befallen her.

Most of the prisoners came here with a death sentence, and not everyone took it well. Obviously there were those making morbid jokes about their imminent demise. Like the convicted marriage impostor who had worked as a hairdresser before his arrest.

One day during leisure hour Ernst approached him. "Please forgive my curiosity, but how can you go around smiling at everyone, when you're living on death row?"

The man flashed him the most charming smile, that wasn't even impaired by a missing front tooth and a nasty scar on his check, courtesy of the Gestapo's treatment. "The way I see it, life here is close to paradise. I get two meals a day and never have to work. But the best of all, I'll be given six cigarettes to smoke on my last day. What's not to look forward to?" He broke out into boisterous laughter, before he walked on to pick a dandelion that grew in a corner of the yard. Shrugging he turned around and walked toward Ernst. "Here, for you. May it bring you some happiness. No need to waste the days we have left with bitterness."

The small exchange left Ernst reflecting for days. It was a strange irony that of all people a con man reminded him of the value of life. Since Ernst didn't believe in God, he couldn't pray for forgiveness for his horrible betrayal, couldn't undo it either or help Margarete, if she was still alive. But he could certainly help those who weren't blessed with the same exuberant zest for life as the con man was.

During the next leisure hour he approached the Catholic priest on duty, a man who received glowing references from all prisoners, independent of their own religious affiliation.

"*Pfarrer* Bernau, do you have a minute?" he asked the gaunt man in his late forties with benevolent brown eyes.

"Ernst Rosenbaum, is that right?"

Ernst nodded in awe. "You know me?"

"I make it a habit to look at all the prisoners' files. Yours was especially intriguing, since you are a Jew, but don't have to wear the yellow star." *Pfarrer* Bernau looked at him with open interest, devoid of the annoying gaze of curiosity.

Ernst felt as if it was entirely his own decision whether he wanted to tell the priest more about himself or not. "The Nazis consider me a Jew, purely because of my genealogy, because even though I was baptized as child, I have since come to the conclusion that no God exists and have converted to atheism. I hope that doesn't deter you from talking to me."

"Not at all." The priest's friendly gaze had never faltered. "I'm here to support all prisoners, whether they believe in my God, another one, or none at all. To be frank, I'm always looking forward to a good philosophical discussion with an educated man." The priest indeed lived up to the glowing praise the other prisoners bestowed upon him.

Ernst didn't quite know what to say, but he was relieved of an answer when the guard announced the end of the leisure hour.

"Why don't I visit you in your cell this afternoon?" *Pfarrer* Bernau suggested. "Except if our discussion is not meant for prying ears?"

"No, my cell is fine. I'll be waiting for you." Ernst watched the priest walk away toward the administrative part of the building, while he followed the other prisoners into the cell block. What he had to discuss wasn't secret, so he didn't mind his cell mates overhearing them, although the last remark had given rise to doubts that the priest wasn't as law-abiding as the Nazis believed he was.

Having watched his niece live under a false identity, pretending to be a staunch Hitler supporter while secretly helping the forced workers in her factory, he contemplated whether there was more to *Pfarrer* Bernau than met the eye.

Ernst shrugged. Whatever it was, it wasn't his concern—moreover he'd be better off not knowing anything. What a man didn't know couldn't be tortured out of him. The sudden pang of guilt knocked the air out of his lungs. He stumbled and the prisoner behind him grabbed his arms, heaving him up. "Steady, old man. There's no need to rush, the gallows are patiently waiting until it's your turn."

In the afternoon *Pfarrer* Bernau visited as promised and they had a long, pleasant conversation about everything under the sun, except Margarete and Ernst's immense guilt for betraying her. As a former professor of philosophy Ernst especially enjoyed meeting a conversationalist versatile in topics normal people usually rolled their eyes at.

"Thank you so much for what must have been the most pleasant hour I've spent in years," Ernst said.

"It was all my pleasure. While God has given me the task to support every human during this most difficult period in their lives, I must admit that I immensely enjoy the company of educated men. It challenges my own thought process to engage in arguments, especially with someone who holds different beliefs."

"There's one more thing."

"Please, speak up."

"You may have sensed that I suffer from horrible guilt. While I'm not willing to talk about my wretched deed, I want to atone for it. Not because of some God, or even the greater good, but very egoistically just for my own peace of mind."

The priest didn't seem surprised. "Go on."

"I heard there's a library in the prison."

"There is, and I rejoice at every prisoner who picks up a book. I'm sure there will be something for you as well, we have volumes of every great thinker, mostly German." *Pfarrer* Bernau's eyes twinkled with joy.

"Well, it's not for me, at least not ostensibly. I was wondering whether it could be organized that I will read perhaps a chapter of a book to a group of prisoners and then hold a discussion about the content with them."

"What a fantastic idea! I'm sure your fellow captives will appreciate the opportunity to break up the monotony of prison life."

Ernst felt a giddiness taking hold of him, he hadn't known in many years. It was almost as if he was returning to lectures at the university, a profession he'd loved with all his heart. "You think it would be allowed?"

"Don't worry. I'll talk to the prison director right away. He's a decent man." *Pfarrer* Bernau left the cell with the promise to arrange everything within the week.

Ernst returned to his cot, his mind whirling. Ironically, being a prisoner on death row had given him back a mission in life.

At Gut Plaun, Margarete was dealing with her own problems as she supervised Dora, who was packing her suitcase for the trip to Berlin.

"No, not that one, I want to go unnoticed. Look for the most understated dresses I own, since it won't do any good to attract attention." She had briefly considered asking Dora to lend her one of her dresses, but that would defeat the purpose with the jeweler. She had to tread a fine line between being too flashy and too drab, to both appear innocuous, but rich enough to possess her own valuables to sell.

A knock on the door interrupted them. "Go see who it is," said Margarete slightly annoyed, since she wanted to get done with the packing.

Dora opened the door and asked the visitor into the parlor adjacent to Margarete's bedroom, before she returned with a happy flush on her face. "Fräulein Annegret, Oliver wants to see you."

"Good afternoon, Oliver, what brings you here?" They had already organized everything for him to handle the estate affairs during her absence, and she wondered what else he needed.

"Nothing good, I'm afraid." His eyes were cast downward, as he turned an envelope with an official seal in his hands.

Dora, who'd followed behind her, let out a short squeak.

"Tell me." By his posture Margarete knew it was something awful.

"It just came in." He held the envelope out to her, and even before she recognized the seal of the *Wehrkreisersatzamt*, the authority responsible for conscription, her heart dropped to her shoes. "I'm drafted."

"But... but... you were exempted," she stuttered, while Dora slapped a hand across her mouth to suppress another squeak.

"It seems they are short on men." Oliver tried a crooked smile. "Franz Volkmer too."

"That is indeed bad news. Please have a seat." She turned toward her maid. "Dora, can you please bring us two glasses of schnapps. Or, better make it three," she added after looking at Dora's ghostly pale face.

Margarete downed the schnapps in one big gulp, the fierce burn warming her stomach. She had feared this day would come, since the causalities on the Eastern Front were horrific and the Wehrmacht had begun to summon up every able-bodied German male. It had been a long time coming, that those exempted for non-medical reasons would be drafted. Oliver though, had a medical discharge from the Wehrmacht, because one of his legs was shorter than the other after a devastating encounter with some shrapnel during the first year of the war.

"I'm so sorry," Margarete said, looking between Oliver who was putting on a brave face and Dora who seemed to be hanging on by a very thin thread.

Oliver shook his head. "As far as I know, everyone with two legs and two arms within the age range has received the same letter."

That meant, after her stud manager Piet, she was about to

lose her estate manager and her factory manager as well... and... her heart plummeted and she rasped, "Stefan!"

"I believe he's safe, since he's been deemed unworthy to serve," Oliver said grimly.

She didn't want to flaunt her delight in front of her two friends who were grappling with the news, so she lowered her head, trying to come up with something appropriate to say. Finally she offered, "I'll pay Katze a visit tonight and see what can be done."

"Thank you."

"You and Dora, take the afternoon off and spend some time together," she said, before she stood up to use the telephone. "Frau Mertens, can you please tell Nils to hitch up the horses, I need to go to Parchim right away."

"I'll see to it, Fräulein Annegret. Do you wish to eat before your departure?"

"That would be a good idea, one never knows how long the trip will take."

After Dora and Oliver left her rooms through the back stairs leading directly down to the patio, Margarete entered the bathroom to give herself a quick smartening up, tidying her hair and smoothing out her dress. For lack of time, she didn't change into more sophisticated attire. Greedy Oberscharführer Katze would have to put up with her like this.

About an hour later she arrived at Parchim and entered the headquarters, shivering at the memory of Thomas Kallfass, the man who'd pursued her relentlessly, voicing his undying love for her just days before turning around and wanting to send her to Auschwitz. She'd never trusted his smooth, charming façade, but she had still been surprised at the lengths he was willing to go to in the name of racial purity.

The ensuing events still caused her fingers to clench and the blood to freeze in her veins, even now in the scorching late summer heat. Grabbing her handbag tighter, she shrugged off the unpleasant thoughts.

She tapped on Katze's door and took a deep breath, pushing it open when he called out, "Enter."

"Fräulein Annegret, what a lovely surprise," Katze greeted her with a greasy overconfident smile. "To what do I owe this unexpected pleasure?"

"Herr Oberscharführer, I'm here because my business and factory managers were both drafted today, along with all of the German foremen at the factory," Margarete said without further ado.

"I heard everyone in the district received their papers today."

She raised an eyebrow. "Well, that is most unexpected. You know that I'm the first person to support our Führer, but how will I be able to meet the production quota and make money without employees?" She hoped he'd get the hint that his monthly bribe was in danger if he didn't get her the exemptions she desired. "If you could arrange for an exemption, if not for everyone, at least for my estate manager?"

"As much as I'd like to do that, my hands are tied. Orders are orders." He seemed genuinely contrite.

"Even your superiors must realize that a woman alone cannot run the nitropenta factory, let alone the stud and the farm. There must be some kind of solution." She cast him a gaze that she hoped conveyed damsel-in-distress.

"Indeed, that is a problem. We wouldn't want the source of your income to fizzle out, now would we?" Katze eyed her. "I might be able to spare a few SS men to help you out."

Margarete almost choked on his words. The last thing she needed was SS men snooping around her property. "Surely your men have much more important things to do than super-vise stables and a handful of well-behaved prisoners. Won't you reconsider?"

"I'm afraid the decision has been made by higher authorities. This issue is out of my hands. Do let me know if you want to take me up on my offer for help," Katze said.

Margarete inclined her head and made to leave when another idea came to her. She cleared her throat. "My trusted handyman Nils is too old to be a soldier. I can utilize him to oversee the farm and parts of the stable, but I desperately need someone with a scientific background to oversee the factory."

"As I said, I can help out with SS men." Katze stapled his hands on his desk.

"That is very kind of you, but apart from being needed elsewhere, I assume none of them has a degree in chemical engineering, which is essential to supervise the process of cooking the nitropenta."

Katze nodded, waiting for her to continue.

"I don't say this lightly, so please bear with me. Our production is vital for the war effort, therefore I'm willing to take desperate measures."

Curiosity flickered in Katze's eyes.

"It would be beyond reckless to leave this sensitive process in the hands of prisoners of war, or other dubious subjects, don't you agree?"

He nodded.

Margarete suppressed a contented smile. "We've recently asked a man to consult on the factory regarding quality control, under the strict supervision of Franz Volkmer, of course, and I'd like to ask for your permission to employ him full-time." Normally workers were assigned by the labor office, but since Stefan was banned from ever working in a war-relevant industry again, she needed an exception.

"Who is he?"

"His name is Stefan Stober, and he lives in Plau am See." Margarete hoped the dumb Oberscharführer wouldn't ask further questions.

"Isn't he the old fisherman?"

"No, he's his grandson and he has a degree in chemical engineering."

Unfortunately Katze was better informed than she had given him credit for. "Fräulein Annegret, I don't know what kind of lies this man has told you. He's a dangerous subject."

She gasped for effect.

"He's been classified unworthy to bear arms, because he's politically unreliable," Katze answered with a shake of his head. "You can't give someone like him full oversight over an ammunitions factory."

Margarete made a contrite face. "He swore that the unfortunate explosion at his previous work place was due to youthful negligence. He even showed me the results of the Gestapo's investigation completely exonerating him." She went out on a limb here, since the report only mentioned that there was no conclusive proof of malice. "He begged me for a second chance to prove his loyalty to our Führer."

Katze still didn't seem convinced.

"I wouldn't normally consider this, but we've fallen upon harsh times. Under the current circumstances it is more important to keep production up and running without hiccups than to continue punishing a good man for youthful error. Don't you think, Herr Oberscharführer?"

"What if he's secretly working against the Reich?"

Margarete shook her head, making a grimace of utter disbelief. "I can't imagine he'd be brazen enough to dare this. Not if he values his life. He knows that he's under surveillance already and if he truly regrets his prior mistake, which I wholeheartedly believe, he'll do everything to prove his support for the Reich."

Katze seemed indecisive, forcing her to pull out her biggest trump card. "If anything goes wrong, you can always blame me. Expose Herr Stober and myself, which will clear you of any fault. On the contrary, you'll be celebrated as a hero." If appealing to his ego didn't help, she didn't know what else she could try.

"That sounds sensible." He worried his lips, scrutinizing her. "But I wonder, why exactly are you doing this? Wouldn't a Jew like you rather work against our government?"

She had expected this question and looked him straight in the eye. "Because I want to survive. If the factory doesn't produce, I won't be able to pay."

"Hmm. Giving you a permit to employ this man is a great risk for me." He rubbed his fingers.

Fearing that he'd ask to increase his monthly allowance, she interrupted him. "Let's be honest, Herr Oberscharführer." Despite knowing the door was closed tight, she looked over her shoulder. "You and I both know that Germany won't win this war." Emboldened by his lack of reaction to her shocking claim, she continued. "And when all of this is over, it'll pay for you to have some persecuted people put in a good word for you." He didn't have to know that she had no intention to ever come to his defense.

"I have done nothing wrong. I only executed my orders," he said, but from the expression on his face it was clear that he knew it was a feeble excuse.

Margarete slowly shook her head. "It is not my place to decide whether that will be enough or not."

A visible jolt passed through his body, as he sat up straighter. "Enough of that defeatist talk! Germany will win this war! And to help her do so, I will ensure that this falsely accused man will get a second chance. He can show his support for the Fatherland by keeping production of ammunition at the desired level."

It was a stage-worthy performance and Margarete inwardly recanted her assessment of him. Katze wasn't half as dumb as she had believed. Perhaps she hadn't been the only one playing a role.

"Thank you so much, Herr Oberscharführer. We at Gut Plaun won't disappoint the trust you have placed in us."

She waited for him to sign the permission and then left the SS headquarters in a hurry. That building always creeped her out, especially since Katze knew who she really was. The conversation had gone well, as it could have ended with her being dragged away to some place of unspeakable horrors.

17

Stefan waited until it was completely dark before he left his fishing grounds and steered his boat toward the secluded beach he'd gone to with Annegret months ago.

He hadn't been completely honest with her, because the beach could be reached by land—if you knew your way around. It was a barely visible path through forest and thick underbrush that took you to the shore. From there it was a twenty-yard walk through shallow waters to reach the beach.

There, another one of Sandra's charges would wait for him. He only knew that it was a downed British airman who needed a safe place to stay for a few nights, before being sent onto the next leg of his dangerous journey toward freedom.

Stefan refused to know details, for once following his own advice. It was easy to guess though that the man's escape path would take him to one of the nearby ports and then across the Baltic Sea to Sweden.

The soft chugging of his motor seemed loud in the otherwise silent night. With the moon as his only source of light, he slowly approached the bay, switched the motor off and let the boat slide toward the beach.

Even before he reached it, two dark figures appeared from the bushes, walking knee-deep into the water to keep the boat from drifting ashore to avoid unnecessary noises like the screeching of wood on tiny pebble stones mixed with the sand. During the day this wasn't a problem, but at night every sound carried far across the lake, perhaps alerting someone that something was amiss.

It was the most critical moment of every pickup, because he could never be sure the two people were who he expected. He wouldn't be the first resister to walk straight into a trap. For this very reason he kept the engine in reverse gear, ready to start up and flee within the blink of an eye. It might not be successful, yet he preferred to be shot or drown than be dragged away for torture.

Seconds later the agreed owl-like howl whistled through the air and he relaxed. The two people came alongside the boat. He recognized Sandra's petite frame and reached out a hand to help the bigger figure come aboard.

She whispered, "Someone will pick him up in a few days. Ask them whether they have seen a great spotted woodpecker. They'll answer that there's a bunch of them on the Plauer Werder."

Stefan memorized the phrase, waved at her and started the engine, while he beckoned the airman to crouch on deck. As soon as he had reached deep water, he locked the steering in place and took the man below deck, where he'd prepared a hiding place behind plenty of fishing gear.

"I'm Stefan," he introduced himself.

"Thank you very much, I'm Anthony," the man answered with a heavy accent that would instantly give him away, despite his civilian clothes and innocuous looks.

"We'll be going ashore soon and from there I'll take you to a safe house. Don't talk, don't make a noise and trail me within a few yards' distance, understood?"

"Understood."

Not one to exchange unnecessary words, Stefan returned to steer the boat toward the boathouse near his grandfather's house, since disembarking with Anthony at the wharf in town was much too dangerous. If another fisherman asked his whereabouts in the morning—which was highly unlikely—he could pretend that he'd needed to fix something on the boat.

They reached the boathouse without incident, walking the short distance from there to his grandfather's house. Stefan hadn't had time to pre-warn Opa. But since this wasn't the first time a clandestine guest had arrived in the middle of the night, he would take it in his stride if he found Anthony there in the morning.

"Here we are," Stefan said as he locked the door behind them. "Are you hungry?"

Since Opa couldn't go fishing anymore, he spent his days at the house or in the garden, tending to a patch of vegetables and fast-growing salads.

"Like a wolf." Anthony grinned.

Stefan had made it a habit not to ask his guests about their stories, because the less he knew the better for everyone involved. After the first one, he'd decided not to allow himself to get attached, and treat them like the strangers they were. He didn't need the added complication of caring about them as people, since that would only lead to heartbreak when one of them got caught, which inevitably happened once in a while.

"I'll make you something. Have a seat."

He walked into the kitchen when he heard a voice from upstairs. "Is that you, Stefan?"

"Yes, Opa. I'm just preparing something to eat for a guest."

Instead of an answer he heard a loud snore and gave a sad smile. His grandfather deserved to spend his remaining years in peace and quiet, after working like a horse throughout his life.

After a mostly silent meal, he told Anthony, "Let me show you where you'll be sleeping. My grandfather lives upstairs with me and one of us will come and get you in the morning when it's safe. We rarely receive visitors since we live so far away from the village, but I'd advise you to stay in the basement as much as possible."

Anthony nodded and followed him down the stairs, where Stefan shoved aside several nets draped against the wall to expose a door barely big enough for a grown man to crawl through. "Don't worry, the room behind the door is much bigger. It used to be a storage cellar." He handed Anthony a flashlight. "Use it sparingly. There's a jug of fresh water and a waste bucket in the corner."

"Thank you," Anthony said, visibly exhausted.

"Sleep as much as you can." Stefan grinned. "There's nothing else to do anyway."

"I'll be fine," Anthony assured him and disappeared through the small opening.

Stefan closed the door behind him and carefully draped the fishing nets to conceal the entrance to the hidden room once more.

The next morning he came into the kitchen where his grandfather was preparing breakfast for three.

"You're up late," the old man commented.

"I worked last night."

"And brought us a guest."

Stefan knew he could trust his grandfather, yet he felt bad for loading the burden onto him. The timing of Anthony's arrival had been the worst possible, because he would leave later in the morning for Berlin with Annegret. "I wanted to refuse, but Sandra begged me, since two others had backed out already."

His grandfather looked at him with surprisingly astute eyes. "She's the boss of that operation, right? An amazing woman.

She'd be better suited for you than that heiress you seem to fancy."

"Opa."

"Don't Opa me. I may be old but not stupid. That Huber woman isn't good for you. Not only because she's way out of your league, but," the old man lowered his voice, "she's hiding something. She may fool everyone else in town, but this old fisherman knows how to observe. Let me tell you, she has a skeleton in the closet. A bad one. You'd better steer clear of her."

Stefan was tempted to tell his grandfather the truth about Annegret. If he knew her skeleton, he'd surely approve of Stefan's feelings for her. But it wouldn't be prudent, so he said instead, "I need to travel to Berlin to organize a few things."

"Things that have to do with Sandra's charges?"

It was probably best to let his grandfather believe this, as it wasn't too far from the truth. "Yes. I'll be only away for a few days. Three or four at most. Will you be alright while I'm gone?"

"Dear boy, I've managed on my own since your grandmother died forty years ago. I'm not going to change that now, even though you seem to think I'm an old fool who can't wipe his own nose. You seem to forget I was against Hitler and his NSDAP before you even went to school."

"It's just because of our guest. Someone might pick him up while I'm gone."

"Nothing I can't handle." Opa tapped his forehead. "Contrary to popular belief I'm still bright in the head. Tell me the code phrase and I'll send him onward."

Stefan sighed. He hated putting the old man at risk, but there was no way around it. Anthony's visit definitely couldn't have come at a worse time. "Ask them whether they have seen a great spotted woodpecker. They'll answer that there's a bunch of them on the Plauer Werder."

"How ingenious! I've never seen a woodpecker on that island." His grandfather mocked him.

"It wasn't my idea."

"Sure wasn't. You'd have chosen a phrase about a perch."

"You're right. I used to look forward to my perch-fishing summers up here with you at the end of the school year." Stefan grinned. "I still remember the first time I visited without Mom and Dad, when you taught me to bait my own hook."

"You couldn't tell the worm from the end of your finger." His grandfather chuckled.

"I only hooked myself once," Stefan recalled. "I was a fast learner."

"That you were. Those were the good days. Much better times." His grandfather sighed.

"Yes. I hope we can get back to that way of living one day soon. The war has to end sometime."

18

Dora couldn't seem to stop crying. Holding her five-month-old daughter on her hip, she watched Oliver get dressed in his old uniform, since he had to present himself for active duty later in the day.

"I can't believe this is happening," she sobbed.

"Don't be afraid, it might not be as bad as they say," he tried to calm her. Dora wasn't fooled though, since she could smell the fear emanating from him.

More tears spilled down her cheeks, since she loved him so much and couldn't stand the thought of losing him—especially not right now.

"What will happen to us?" she asked between sobs.

"You and Julia will be safe on Gut Plaun. Everything will continue as usual. During my absence Nils is in charge of the estate, together with Annegret. Ladislaus knows how to manage the stables—"

"The Pole?" Dora interrupted him.

"Yes. He'll do a fine job. I especially endorsed him to take care of the women should the Red Army arrive."

A shiver ran through Dora, since she didn't have any illusions about the treatment she'd receive at their hands. Oliver caressed her cheek with his thumb. "You have nothing to worry about."

But she did. Very much. Remembering her conversation with Olga a while ago, she said, "My friend Olga, she told me to pretend to be Ukrainian again, should it come to the worst."

Oliver bit his lip. "I really hate not being able to protect you myself. Hitler should do the only sensible thing and capitulate to salvage what is left of our country. But since he won't..." He didn't finish his sentence, because both of them knew the odds for him to stay alive weren't high. "Ladislaus will watch over you."

She nodded.

"You take good care of yourself and Julia."

"You know I will." She worried her lip, not wanting to cause him more grief, but on the other hand... he should know. She'd fretted for days about the secret she'd not told him and now it seemed she was running out of time.

Oliver used a finger to tip her chin up and asked, "Will you look after Annegret as well? She'll need someone to have her back."

He put on his tunic, slung the rifle he used for hunting across his shoulder and pulled her into a fierce hug. "I love you so much."

Dora dug her fingers into his tunic until they hurt. She couldn't be one hundred percent sure that her hunch was true, because she hadn't seen the midwife to confirm it yet. In any case, this was her last chance to tell him. "I should have told you earlier."

Oliver pulled away until he could look into her eyes. "Told me what, my darling?"

"I think I'm with child again." She twisted her head sideways, anxiously awaiting his reaction. Even before his being drafted it had been horrible timing for another child.

"That is fantastic news," he gushed, a huge smile spreading from one ear to another, a reaction she hadn't anticipated.

"No. It's not. You're leaving and—"

"—I'll be home long before this baby is born." Oliver kissed her passionately. "Thank you so much, my darling. You can't imagine how much this means to me. It may seem like a bad time to bring a child into this world, but the opposite is true. The war is about to end anytime now and our children will be part of a new generation, one that can hopefully grow up in peace. They can extend their hand to foreigners much like you and I have done to each other, instead of fighting them in battle." He winked. "And it will give me yet another reason to return."

"I'm afraid," she admitted. "Afraid of what might happen and how I will cope." She wouldn't speak out loud that she feared to become a widow at the tender age of twenty, with two small children to take care of all on her own.

"You're strong, you'll manage. And never forget that I fully intend to return to your side. To yours and Julia's and the baby's. When the war is over, we won't have to glance over our shoulder at every step and can live a life filled with joy and love."

"I'm looking forward to it. I love you." She leaned against his broad chest, wishing she could keep him with her, hide him somewhere so he didn't have to go to war.

"I love you too." After a minute, he carefully extracted himself from her. "I really have to leave. Don't want to be late on my first day at the new job." He gave her a crooked smile that couldn't conceal the fear she saw in his soul.

Then he stepped out into the bright sunshine, which was a stark contrast to Dora's gloomy feeling. She stood at the window, holding Julia and watched him walk away. Her heart grew weary, as a horrible sense of foreboding washed over her and she realized she might never see him again.

Thankfully Julia began to cry and distracted her. Fussing over the baby, she regained her composure. When Julia fell asleep, she proceeded to clean the small house, made the bed, put Oliver's pajamas under his pillow as if he'd return tonight to sleep in their marital bed.

Then she picked up her daughter and walked over to the manor to show up for work. Frau Mertens looked as unfazed as always, but Fräulein Annegret had the same forlorn expression on her face as Dora herself.

"How are you holding up?" her mistress asked once they were in private.

Dora gave a brave smile. "I'm fine. He isn't the first man who has gone to war. I still have Julia, you, and everyone left here at Gut Plaun."

"We'll get through this together. The war won't last much longer now."

"That is exactly what Oliver said." Dora busied herself cleaning Fräulein Annegret's room until the next shock revelation seemed to pull the rug out from under her feet.

"I'll be leaving for Berlin in the morning," her mistress said.

"Can't you stay here?" Dora pleaded, despite knowing the trip was a necessity. For some reason she feared that after being left without her beloved husband, the same might happen with the woman who'd become her friend and then she'd truly be left to fend for herself.

"Believe me, if I didn't have to travel, I'd stay here. It will only be for a few days, three or four at most."

"Yes, Fräulein Annegret." Dora didn't have the energy to say anything else, since part of her soul had left together with Oliver.

19

"The jewelry is wrapped in a velvet cloth inside one of your shoes," Dora explained as she handed Annegret the suitcase.

"Thank you." Margarete took up the piece of luggage that was much smaller than she would normally travel with. For her trip to Sweden last year, Dora had packed her several huge wardrobe trunks.

"Remember I'll be pretending to be Stefan's wife," she said to Dora.

"I'm so glad he'll be with you, taking care of you." Dora was the only person privy to the plan of selling the jewelry to bribe Oberscharführer Katze.

"I am too." Traveling alone for the entire journey would have been so much more frightening.

"Are you sure you have enough clothes?" Dora asked for the umpteenth time.

"I'll be gone only a few days, and, yes, I'm sure. Now, can you let Nils know I'm ready for him to take me to the train station."

"Of course, Fräulein Annegret," Dora said.

As soon as the maid was gone, Margarete removed the pearl

studs she usually wore and replaced them with tiny silver earrings the wife of a fisherman might wear. She and Stefan had discussed this. For all intents and purposes, Margarete would travel to Potsdam, the town adjacent to Berlin, as Annegret to visit a friend of the family. He would travel in a different compartment and *accidentally* meet her en route. Once they arrived in Berlin, they would travel together as Herr and Frau Stober, or, if someone demanded their papers, as unmarried lovers on a getaway. The thought filled her with exhilaration.

At the hotel, though, they would pretend to be a married couple, relying on the custom that the receptionist would only ask for the husband's papers. For this role she needed to travel light, looking like any other German woman and not the rich heiress.

All these precautions had been Stefan's doing, since they didn't want to risk the town gossips finding out about their liaison. Stefan's participation in the trip had turned out to be the most difficult part to pull off.

The capricious heiress Fräulein Annegret enjoyed the freedom to do as she pleased without having to fear any consequences or inquisitive questions. Stefan though, belonged to the working population with not one, but two jobs. In the end he had explained at the factory that he needed to meet up with several suppliers, while never actually mentioning Berlin, and instead insinuating he might travel up to one of the harbors on the Baltic coast.

In any case, since he was the new factory manager, nobody but Fräulein Annegret dared question his motives. As for his second job—the fish would be mute while they gladly waited another day to be caught.

"Frau Mertens, you'll take good care of the household while I'm gone," Margarete told her housekeeper.

"Of course, Fräulein Annegret. I hope you'll find your friend in good health."

"She seemed to be rather distressed, but I'm sure all she needs is a few days of company," she answered her, wishing she trusted Frau Mertens enough to tell her the truth. Apart from Stefan, only Dora knew the real reason for her trip to Berlin— and about the jewelry hidden in her suitcase.

In Oliver's absence, Dora had become her only confidante, giving her moral support. A pang of guilt stabbed Margarete for putting so many burdens upon her pregnant maid, and she vowed to lean more on Stefan from now on, despite the risk of gossip.

"Godspeed," the housekeeper said, and then added in a rare moment of emotion, "Take care! There's so much horrible news in the paper about the Allied bombings."

"I will. Goodbye." Margarete was in a hurry to leave. She knew all about the Allied bombings having survived a direct hit, during which the Hubers' villa had crumbled on top of her. It had been serendipity, since it had given her a new chance at life: shedding her identity as the Jew Margarete Rosenbaum, and becoming the spoilt daughter of a high-ranking Nazi. Despite the lucky outcome, she would rather not relive the moments trapped below the staircase in a destroyed house.

Nils was in the yard waiting for her with the coach. As they drove past the stables, the unofficial stud manager Ladislaus was working with a horse.

"Can you stop for a moment?" she asked Nils and got down from the coach box to talk with the Polish prisoner.

"Fräulein Annegret," Ladislaus said with his heavy accent.

"I'm going to be gone for a few days and I trust you to take good care of the horses."

He nodded, still subdued in her presence.

"Nils will be in charge of the estate, so anything you need, ask him."

"Everything will be done according to your wishes, Fräulein," Ladislaus assured her.

"Please know that I appreciate your work. You have a way with horses."

He beamed with delight. "Thank you."

Margarete thought for a moment, before she threw caution aside. "I don't condone mistreating people and I wish I could do much more."

His head jerked up in surprise. "We all know this and thank you from the bottom of our hearts."

"Perhaps one day we can meet under different circumstances." She smiled and turned on her heel to climb onto the coach box, where Nils was waiting for her. "Ladislaus is a good man, look after him, will you?"

Nils drew on his cigarette before he answered. "He doesn't need looking after. We are lucky to have him keeping the lads in check."

When he left her at the station she boarded the train, happy to find a seat in the crowded compartment. In Potsdam, she spotted Stefan's flaxen hair even before stepping off the train. A huge burden fell from her shoulders, because truth be told, she was afraid to be alone in Berlin. She didn't so much fear someone from her own past than an acquaintance of Annegret's. Her own friends were mostly in the same situation as she was and wouldn't denounce her to the Gestapo. There was a solidarity among the persecuted to help each other, while Annegret's ilk were the ones determined to extirpate the Jews.

"There you are, darling," Stefan greeted her, wrapping an arm around her waist as any young couple in love would do. He led her to a bench at the far end of the platform to wait for the connecting train.

"A friend recommended the Pension Birnbaum to me. It's conveniently located, clean, and attracts mostly young couples in need of a place to be alone."

She felt herself blush furiously, suddenly not as confident that her plan to share a bed with Stefan was a good one.

"Don't worry," he said, obviously aware of her self-consciousness. He dug in his pocket and produced two golden wedding bands. "My grandfather and grandmother's rings, just in case the hotel reception is not as lenient as my friends told me they would be."

"You thought of everything." Margarete hugged him, her doubts dissipating instantly. He was the man she loved with all her heart, and there was nothing to be afraid of being with him.

He slipped the smaller of the two rings upon her finger. It was a bit loose, yet tight enough not to accidentally lose it.

"May I?" she asked. Upon his nod, she took the larger band and slipped it on his finger, where it fit perfectly. The tiny movement sent an unexpected warmth into her body, along with a strong feeling of belonging. As if they were truly married, which they unfortunately couldn't do in real life, as long as that maniac Hitler was in charge of Germany.

Stefan seemed to experience the same emotions, because he took up her hand in a gentle gesture, gazing at the shining ring on her finger. His head moved upward to meet her eyes, and she saw so much love in them, it almost hurt.

"I love you so much, Gretchen." He pronounced her nickname with a soft promise in his voice that made her entire skin tingle. "It may not be the most appropriate or romantic situation, but I can't wait one second longer."

Her heart was beating a staccato rhythm, as the world around her faded away and the only thing that mattered was him. Looking into his clear blue eyes, she sensed the earth rumbling.

"Will you become my wife for real?"

She wanted to protest, say that it wasn't possible, that she couldn't start their marriage with a lie as big as being someone else entirely. But he seemed to know what she was about to say, because he put a finger on her lips. "Not now. Once the war is over and you can be your true self again. But I want to carry your answer in my soul, knowing that you are truly mine, even though circumstances forbid us to officially wed."

Her eyes filled with tears as she answered. "Yes. I want to be your wife, now and forever."

His hand squeezed hers and he gave her a peck on her lips, long enough to convey all the love he held for her, but not so indecent as to arouse unwanted attention. Then he jumped up, dragging her behind him. "We need to hurry, our next train has arrived."

With laughter in her heart, she ran across the platform toward the train door, where Stefan jumped onto the stairs and then swooped her up in his arms to carry her across the threshold into the carriage.

20

"It's not so bad," Stefan said as he set their luggage down by the side of the bed.

As his friend had promised, the hotel reception was more interested in a paying guest than holding up morale and hadn't asked for Margarete's papers after he'd introduced her as his wife.

Along with the rest of the hotel, their room was shabby, but clean. The velvet curtains must date back to the last century, thick enough to serve as black-out curtains. Against one wall stood a large matrimonial bed, on the opposite side a rickety table with one chair and a chest of drawers. In the corner was a washbasin with a jug of fresh water, while the toilet was outside on the hallway.

He held his breath to wait for Margarete's judgement, since she was definitely used to more luxury. She took a full turn, taking in the room, before she let herself fall backwards onto the bed with a happy grin on her face. "It's perfect." Seconds later an anxious frown crept onto her lovely face. "Are we going to the jeweler right now?"

"No. Tomorrow in the morning." He'd thought long about

how to best do this in a way that aroused the least amount of attention, and he'd come to the conclusion that they should reconnoiter the area first. Just in case something was amiss, he wanted to know how they could escape.

"I thought..." Margarete's face instantly tensed and he settled on the edge of the bed to caress her cheek.

"Trust me, it's better like this. Tonight we'll go out and have fun, and tomorrow we handle the business."

"If you say so..."

He could see she wasn't convinced. "I do. It's already afternoon and we don't want to get caught in an air raid with the jewelry on us."

Her eyes became wide. "You believe there'll be a bombing tonight?"

Since the Allies had been bombing Berlin incessantly, he was quite sure. Although knowing about her experience with the Huber villa collapsing on top of her, he didn't want to cause her more anguish. "It's a possibility. Though judging by the smoldering ruins we walked past, they'll concentrate on another borough tonight—if they even come."

Margarete exhaled deeply. "Let's hope so, by goodness."

"Are you hungry?" His own stomach was growling viciously.

"Very."

"Then let's go find us a place to eat." He extended his hand to help her up. With the jewelry securely hidden away, they walked down to the reception to ask for restaurant recommendations.

It had been a few years since he last visited Berlin and he barely recognized the city, as most of the iconic buildings had been reduced to rubble. A sudden anxiety took hold of him, that the jeweler didn't exist any longer and they would have to search for another one.

In the current climate, talking to the wrong person could

result in the police being called and then... he pushed the thought aside. *Nothing will happen.* He gave Margarete a reassuring smile. "Do you know your way around here?"

She nodded. "In fact, I do. We used to live here, before..."

He knew the story. Like many middle-class Jews, her family had lived in a nice neighborhood, side by side with their Christian neighbors, oftentimes not even knowing they were any different. Until the Jews had been forced to move out of their homes and had been relocated to Berlin's *Judenviertel*, boroughs that originally hosted mostly poor, working-class, so-called Eastern Jews, refugees from Eastern European countries mostly after the First World War.

Much to their disdain, the established German Jews who had assimilated the German culture for generations, were suddenly lumped together with Orthodox Jews, whom many of them saw as reactionary, poor people who barely spoke the German language. In the early years of persecution through Hitler's regime this had perhaps been the biggest humiliation of the successful middle-class people. Many families had used it as a breaking point to flee the country.

Unfortunately not all of them successfully: those who'd settled in France, Belgium, or the Netherlands had found themselves in the same predicament a second time when Hitler's Wehrmacht had overrun their new home countries.

Especially the French, who fully cooperated with the German government and handed over all *foreign Jews* not born in France, without batting an eyelid.

"Do you want to go left or right?"

As Stefan looked up, he faintly recognized the crossing. He had wanted to stroll along the beautiful boulevard Unter den Linden, which he vividly remembered from before the war, but realizing how destroyed the city was, he preferred not to blight the fond memories he had. "Let's turn to the left."

"It'll take us a bit longer," she said.

"Do you mind walking?"

"Not at all." Margarete snuck her hand into his, making his heart overflow with emotions. Here, in the anonymity of the capital, it was just the two of them. No need to worry about someone seeing them holding hands and laughing together. For the first time since falling in love with her, he could act upon his heart's desire. Emboldened by this revelation, he slid his arm around her waist.

When she leaned into him, warmth emanating from her body, he had to stop and peck her cheek, and felt his heart might burst with joy. It was an emotion he wished to preserve for all eternity. For a time after the war, when she had agreed to legally become his wife.

"Here's the restaurant the receptionist recommended." Margarete tugged at his hand, returning him to the present.

"We have to be back at the hotel before curfew," he said, after eating the only meal available on the menu.

On their way back, there were much fewer people out on the streets. Stefan involuntarily grabbed Margarete tighter, when he saw a pair of policemen approach them.

"Ten minutes to curfew," one of them said.

"Yes, officer, we are aware of it, just need to walk down this street," he answered, sensing how Margarete stiffened in his arms, which surprised him, since she usually wasn't shy in the face of government officials.

"Good night," the policeman said and left.

"Thank God," she hissed. "I really don't want them to have a look at my papers and get any ideas."

"Like why you're making out with a fisherman?" He grinned.

"That's not funny! And, yes, that is exactly what I'm worried about. Anything out of the ordinary will only lead to more questions and ultimately problems."

"I'm sorry, perhaps we should have taken off the wedding

bands before going out?" Guilt crept into his heart. While he'd been enjoying a carefree afternoon, she must have battled with tension, since it was her head on the line if someone recognized her.

"No, it's fine. It's just that this new role is confusing. I don't seem to know who I am right now and how to react, if you know what I mean?"

He realized how stressed she must be constantly living under a disguise. "I had no idea."

"Being Annegret has become my second nature, I barely even notice it anymore. I know how she talks, walks, and reacts. But this? I'm supposed to not be her, but also not be the real me, so who am I now?"

"My wife." His attempt to reassure her was met with a dry laugh.

"First of all that's a role I have no experience with and don't have the slightest idea how a real wife acts. Second, your wife doesn't even have a name, because we agreed that Annegret would never give the time of day to someone of your social class."

Stefan tightened his lips, because her comment hurt, despite knowing that it wasn't what she believed, just what her alter ego and the fine society did. For them he'd ceased to exist the moment he'd been forced to give up his job as a chemical engineer and became a lowly fisherman. Tumbled into oblivion. A working-class man, tolerated because he fed the population, not because those in power valued people like him or his grandfather.

He gave a deep sigh. "I so wish this war was over, because then we could finally be our true selves."

Her smile compensated his grief. "That's my wish, too." They had arrived in front of the hotel and she added, "For tonight, let's just be you and me."

"I would do anything to make you happy." He pressed a soft kiss on her lips, before he held the door open for her.

Upstairs in their room, Stefan closed and bolted the door, shutting out the world beyond. Due to the frequent electricity outages, they had been given two candles earlier. He lit them and switched off the lurid ceiling light. Instantly the room was cast in a cozy atmosphere.

He felt all his worries dissipate and walked toward her, putting his hands on her shoulders, "I want to make love to you, Gretchen."

"I want to as well, but... I'm nervous," she said with a feeble voice.

"No reason to be nervous. We'll take it slow." His hands moved down to unbutton her blouse while he first gently, and then ever more passionately, kissed her mouth. When the urge to throw her onto the bed became overwhelming, he took a step back, reminding himself that their coming together would be so much more fulfilling if he was patient.

"What's wrong?" she asked in reaction to his retreating.

"Nothing, my love. I just know the benefits of patience—I'm a fisherman after all."

Her eyes rounded with shock, before she laughed. "And I'm the prey you're going to catch?"

"Not at all." He closed the distance between them, removing the pins from her hair and watching it fall down to her shoulders. "I'm the one who has fallen for you hook, line and sinker."

She leaned against him, allowing him to brush his hands through her soft hair. They stood like this for several minutes, until she turned her face upward and said, "I'm not nervous anymore. I know you would never hurt me."

"That's quite the low bar. You're about to find out that I can do a lot better." He lifted a hand, cupping the back of her neck, placing gentle kisses across her forehead, down her cheeks and finally stopping to feast at her lips.

When they finally fell spent against the sheets and he pulled the quilt over their bodies, they both agreed it had been a marvelous experience.

She snuggled closer to him, her hand creeping across his chest, her head settling into the crook of his shoulder. Within seconds, sleep claimed them.

21

In the morning, Margarete woke with a huge smile on her face, and took a deep breath. She'd never been happier in her entire life.

After a frugal breakfast, they walked to the jeweler. They stopped across the street from the shop, which had lost all its luster, plaster crumbling from the walls, the windows boarded-up. It was a picture of decay and Margarete would have turned on her heel, if Stefan's hand in hers hadn't kept her in place.

In a city worn to the bone by the hardships of war, who had the money and the leisure to go shopping for gold and jewels?

"Ready?" Stefan asked, tugging at her hand.

"Yes. Let's go." Nothing was farther from the truth, but what alternative did she have apart from going inside and facing whatever awaited them there?

"Margarete? Is that really you?" A voice she'd not heard in years called to her, getting louder as it grew closer.

She turned her head in shocked surprise, recognizing one of her old classmates at the Jewish school, Thea Blume.

"It is you! Oh, imagine running into you here. It's been such a long time," Thea gushed, her gaze resting for a second on Margarete's chest, where the yellow star should be.

Margarete sent a warning smile toward Stefan. She needn't have worried, because he squeezed her hand, indicating her secret was safe with him. "Thea. This is indeed a surprise. How have you been?" Now she in turn scrutinized Thea and also found no trace of the detested sign the Jews were forced to wear.

"As well as can be expected these days." Thea gestured around her.

Margarete felt instantly sorry for the girl who must endure such hardships. These days, living as a Jew in Berlin was only possible if one went underground—constantly in flight, changing accommodations every few days, always looking over one's shoulder in fear of being discovered by the authorities. She could only imagine how this felt, it must be so much harder than her own situation. By comparison, Margarete lived a luxurious and comfortable life, protected by Annegret's papers and her social status.

Thea looked curiously at Stefan, taking in how he clasped his hand around Margarete's. "And you are?"

"A friend." When Stefan didn't give his name, Thea squinted her eyes for a moment, before she bestowed him with that precious smile of hers that had used to cast a spell over any boy within reach during their schooldays.

To Margarete's huge relief, though, Stefan didn't seem to be impressed. At school, all girls had envied, and sometimes loathed, Thea for the power she held over the other sex.

"He can be trusted," Margarete assured her former classmate.

"You can't imagine how delighted I am to meet you, Margarete," Thea said sweetly. "It's so uplifting to encounter someone from the past, instead of losing friends all the time. There are fewer of us remaining each day."

Margarete took all her courage together to ask the question that burned on the tip of her tongue. "Who... are there any of our other classmates?"

"Well, of those that haven't emigrated when it was still possible, there's just a handful left. One of them is Agnes."

"Agnes Goldmann?" Margarete remembered well the vibrant, lanky girl with pigtails, who had the most beautiful chestnut colored hair.

"Yes her. She was arrested a while ago. In the Rosenstrasse, you know? They had to let her go after a week or so because she's only a half-Jew." Thea kept her attention trained on Margarete's face, seemingly puzzled that her friend didn't know about the arrest and subsequent release.

Margarete ignored the subtle disapproval and pressed right on. "And her brother? David is his name, right?"

"Ach, him..." Thea made a dismissive gesture. "He's a veritable rabble-rouser."

"Are you sure we're speaking about the same person? He was always such a shy and kind boy." Back in their youth David had been a fervent, yet distant admirer of Thea's beauty, too shy to actually utter a word in her presence.

"He's nothing of that sort now. Anyhow, it seems the Gestapo arrested him on the grounds of some illegal activities, despite his protected status as half-Jew. It's such a shame really!" Thea looked contrite. "After his arrest, Agnes helped several of his friends to go underground. I haven't seen any of them since and can just hope they're alright."

"How awful," Margarete uttered.

"We need to get going," Stefan interrupted.

"Oh sure. Can we catch up later, please? I'm dying to know more about you," Thea begged.

"I don't know. We aren't planning to be in the city for long," Margarete hedged.

"Oh, come on. It'll be fun, just like the good old times. How often can we have fun these days?" Thea glanced around to make sure nobody was listening. "I'm so incredibly happy to have found a kindred soul. We must meet tonight, please?"

Margarete couldn't deny her old classmate the request and nodded. "But I can't stay long."

"That's wonderful, thank you so much. It's so lonely at times..." Thea furtively blinked away a tear, before she wrapped her arms around Margarete. "You can't imagine how happy I am to see you."

"Me, too."

"We need to help each other to get through this, don't we?" Thea said and gave Margarete the directions of where to meet her later that night. Looking over her shoulder, Thea suddenly seemed to be in a hurry. "I need to go. Not wise to spend too much time in one place. See you tonight. Bring your friend as well."

Margarete watched Thea hurry down the sidewalk, musing how little the other girl had changed since their schooldays. She still was ebullient, a human dynamo, who hadn't succumbed to the dejection most every person, and most of all the Jews, wore these days.

"I have a bad feeling about her, something isn't quite right," Stefan said as Margarete turned toward him again.

She squinted her eyes. "Thea was always like that, she hasn't changed one bit."

"But don't you think it odd for her to be so... happy?"

"Oh, come on. You of all people are judging her? Doesn't a Jew have a right to be happy, too?" Margarete couldn't believe her own ears.

He put up his hands in defense. "That's not what I'm saying, of course everyone has a right to be happy. It's just that her behavior doesn't match her situation, presumably living in hiding and all that."

"Not all people react the same way to a threat. Some over-compensate the situation by behaving the exact opposite than what is considered normal."

He chuckled. "Since when have you become a psychologist?"

"Since I've been reading a few books in the manor's library."

"A scholar of Sigmund Freud? There's a lot more to you than I ever suspected."

"Not Freud obviously, since his work has been forbidden." She took his hand in hers. "Let's focus on our task at hand."

He brushed her cheek with his lips, waking memories of the delightful happenings last night. "I've never met a woman who's so keen to get rid of her jewelry."

She broke out in laughter and the underlying tension that the encounter with Thea had left between them dissipated.

The jeweler was an old man who seemed to have lost his ability to smile or find joy in anything. "What can I help you with?" he asked drolly.

"We need to sell some jewelry and I was told you were the best in the city," Stefan said. They had agreed beforehand that he would do the negotiation, since it would look odd when a married woman spoke above her husband.

"Let's see what you have to offer." The man unfolded a black velvet cloth and placed it on the counter next to a lamp, indicating they put the goods there.

Stefan opened the pouch, where Dora had carefully wrapped several beautiful, but not too flashy, pieces. It might be illogical but Margarete was deathly afraid someone might recognize one of Frau Huber's more iconic pieces and trace them back to her, prompting all kinds of unwanted questions.

The jeweler widened his eyes as a pearl necklace, two gold bracelets, and earrings with a drop-shaped diamond came to lie on the velvet cloth. He put on white gloves and placed a magnifier in front of his eye.

Margarete watched in awe at how he held the magnifier in place purely by squeezing his eyes. Then he proceeded to scrutinize the pieces one by one, murmuring unintelligible words. With every passing second the urge to bolt from the shop grew bigger. She barely breathed, watching the jeweler turn the necklace to and fro, hoping he didn't find some hidden inscription that might allow him to trace it back to Frau Huber.

Stefan's hand pressed against the small of her back, as if he'd caught up on her nerves. Despite the turmoil inside her, she did her best to breathe evenly. Even if the jeweler somehow recognized the provenance, there was nothing illegal or even shady about it. Annegret was Frau Huber's daughter and legitimate heir. Even rich people sold jewelry for one reason or another, perhaps just because they didn't like the particular piece and wanted the money to buy another one.

The golden wedding band on her finger seemed to burn up and scorch her hand, causing her to question whether it would have been better to come alone. But she needn't have worried, since the jeweler was exclusively interested in the precious goods, caressing them with his wrinkled fingers as if with a lover.

Finally, he removed the magnifier from his eye and looked at Stefan. "Very nice things you have. I am able to buy them." Then he mentioned a price, but Stefan shook his head.

"I'm afraid they are worth a lot more than that."

The jeweler grimaced. "Young man, these are hard times. Nobody buys jewelry anymore and it's a great risk I'm taking on."

Margarete bit her lip in an effort to keep herself from telling Stefan to take the money and leave.

"You are right, the times are tough, otherwise we wouldn't even sell these fine pieces. You came highly recommended as an honest businessman." The implication in Stefan's words had an immediate effect.

"I certainly am," the old man protested.

"Then you should offer a fair price." Stefan crossed his arms in front of his chest.

Margarete looked from one man to the other, wondering what the jeweler would do. Apparently he was savvy enough not to ruin a good business deal, because he said, "Well, I can certainly give you more, if you agree to leave the goods on consignment."

Margarete all but gasped. She needed the money now and definitely didn't want to travel to Berlin again in the near future.

"I'm so very sorry, but we're wasting our time here." Stefan reached for the precious pieces, but the man stopped him.

"No need to rush this." The jeweler frowned miserably. "What you are demanding is going to ruin me."

"That isn't my intent. If you can't make a fair deal, I think we should take our business elsewhere."

The jeweler put his hands up in defeat and doubled the sum he'd initially offered. Margarete was sure it was still a low-ball offer, since the man knew very well that the people who sold their precious items were usually in need of fast cash.

Stefan glanced at Margarete and she nodded slightly. "You have a deal."

The jeweler wrapped the precious pieces into the velvet cloth and put them into a tray. "I assume you'll want your payment right now?"

Stefan nodded.

"Wait here for a minute, will you?" With these words he stepped through a curtain into what Margarete assumed was his office. She barely dared to breathe, praying nothing would go wrong at the last second.

Within a few minutes he returned with a stack of bills, dutifully counting them out over his counter. Stefan grabbed the bundle, gave half of it to Margarete, whispering into her ear, "Turn around and put them in your bra."

"What?" She stared at him, unbelieving.

He gazed at her, and when she didn't move, he put his free hand on her shoulder and turned her toward the wall. "Just do it."

Then she heard how he shuffled the bills, supposedly distributing them among several of his pockets. Margarete pushed away her embarrassment before she acquiesced to his demand, opened the uppermost button on her blouse and stuffed the bills evenly into both cups of her bra. When she was done, she buttoned up again and closed her light coat over what had become a bulging bustline.

"Ready to go?" Stefan asked. After her nod, he bid goodbye to the jeweler. "Thanks for doing business with us."

"Anytime you have more goods to sell, you're welcome to stop by."

Once they were out on the street, Margarete finally breathed again. The jeweler hadn't given them quite as much as she had been hoping for, however it was more than enough to ensure she would be able to pay Katze for at least six months, while keeping the people under her protection fed and alive as well as the factory running. After that, well—hopefully the war would be over by then.

"We should return to Gut Plaun immediately," Stefan said as they reached their room.

"Why the hurry? I thought we were going to leave tomorrow?" Margarete asked as she retrieved the money from her bra and handed it over to him.

Stefan withdrew the false bottom from his suitcase and stuffed the bulk of the money into the space, before carefully sealing the bottom again. "I have a bad feeling and would rather leave the city behind."

"You're being paranoid. Everything went absolutely perfectly. Besides, I'm meeting Thea this evening." Margarete took the remainder of the money and padded the extra lining Dora had sewn into her travel costume with it.

Stefan gave her an incredulous look. "Surely you're not actually planning to go?"

"Of course I am." Margarete became slightly annoyed with him. "It's the first time I've met someone from my past, apart from Uncle Ernst. Plus Thea might need my help. You of all people should know how difficult it is to live as an illegal."

"That's exactly what I'm worried about. She was much too confident walking the street than anyone in her situation should be."

Margarete swept his objection aside with a gesture of her hand. "You wouldn't say that if you knew her. Thea has always been more self-assured than the rest of us put together. She has this natural ability to command attention and have everyone eat out of the palm of her hand."

Stefan shook his head. "I still think it's not safe to go. Who else will be there? Can you trust all of them? What if someone recognizes you? What if they start asking questions?"

"Please." Margarete was getting increasingly cross with him. "Can't you understand how important this is for me? I haven't spoken to a classmate or friend in years. Nobody even knows that I still exist!" As she was speaking she realized that this reunion with Thea wasn't so much because she liked the girl, or even wanted to help her. No, the true reason was to reassure herself of her identity. Thea, a person who didn't know anything about Annegret Huber, would be able to see Margarete as the person she had been before all of this. By talking to her former classmate, Margarete could prove that her former personality had actually existed and wasn't some kind of wicked dream.

Over the years of living in someone else's skin, she had

begun doubting her own memories, ruminating if she'd been making up her past life, and perhaps had indeed been born as Annegret. Thea's testimony would serve as an anchor to ground Margarete to the reality.

"Look. I know how hard this must be for you—"

"No you don't," she interrupted him. "You don't have to hide your personality day in day out. You don't have to be on guard every single minute of every single day, anxious to avoid a mistake that could give you away. You don't know how it is to be someone else. All I want is to be myself for just a few hours. Tomorrow morning I'll return to Gut Plaun, and resume my role as lady of the manor, but tonight I need a break!"

He looked at her with so much love in his eyes, it almost hurt. "I do understand your need for a break. But you can't afford to indulge in it. It's not safe. We must leave tonight."

"I'm not leaving," she insisted.

"Then, at least, don't go to that reunion. Please, I beg you." He reached out to take her hand, but she shoved it away.

"No. I'll go and that is my last word." She used the tone she did with her employees, letting Stefan know who was calling the shots here. After navigating the perils of a false identity for close to three years, she wouldn't give anyone, not even him, control over her decisions.

"Well then, if I can't make you see reason, be my guest and go. However, I'm not going to risk my life for such a sentimental folly." His usually calm voice clearly indicated how upset he was.

Margarete, though, had no time for hurt feelings. Should he want to sulk that she wasn't going to do his bidding, he could. She had to get ready to leave the hotel if she wanted to arrive on time. "Suit yourself." She removed the wedding band from her ring finger and put it on the nightstand, before she went to the bathroom a few doors down the hallway to refresh herself.

Looking into the mirror, she decided to go for a very subdued look, imagining this was what she would look like if she were still her former self. Deep inside she hoped that despite being adamant about leaving immediately Stefan would wait for her in the hotel when she returned in a few hours.

22

Mentally cringing, Oliver looked around at the comrades he'd been assigned to fight alongside. It had been four years since the Wehrmacht had discharged him with one leg shorter than the other one. Yet, he probably was the most capable of this ragged bunch of hastily drafted boys and old men who'd never seen an enemy up close.

Even the old handyman Nils, a veteran from the last war who was way beyond sixty years, would make a better soldier than his new comrades. At least some of the young lads, boys only, made up in enthusiasm what they lacked in experience, whereas the older men had the fatalistic expression of people who knew their last days had come.

Three days of training and off to the front it was, never mind they didn't have proper uniforms or even a weapon for every soldier. Mostly, the older men had brought their rusty equipment from the last war, while the boys made do with no weapons, and second-hand great-coats with Nazi armbands hastily attached. This truly was Hitler's last-ditch attempt to miraculously turn the tide on a war that was already lost.

The door opened and in walked their new leader, a man

barely twenty years of age, whose uniform indicated he was a Feldwebel, an air force sergeant with the lightning bolt of a radio operator to be precise. "Alright, lads, get your gear packed. We leave in two hours."

No explanation where to, nothing. Oliver thought about Dora and how much he loved her. He'd do everything in his power to stay alive, because he yearned to return to her and Julia's side—and to their unborn baby. Looking at his comrades, he tried a timid smile. "That's it then, I guess. Off to war we go again."

"What do you mean again?" a young lad called Kalle asked.

Oliver indulged him. "I fought in Poland and later in the Operation Barbarossa before a Russian bullet shattered my leg and I was discharged from active service on medical grounds."

"So why are you here, when you've been discharged?" Kalle was too young to grasp the absurdity of the current situation.

Since Oliver couldn't tell the truth that Hitler was desperate enough to send anyone in possession of a penis into his lost war, he answered instead, "It seems the Wehrmacht is short of soldiers, so they gave me the honor to defend my fatherland a second time."

"You don't seem happy about it," another young comrade called Lutz chimed in, his brows knitted together in a dark stare.

"He's a cripple, for God's sake," an old man, whom Oliver had seen a few times around Plau am See, but didn't know the name of, tried to defend him.

"His leg seems fine to me. It might be a ruse to evade service." Lutz spat at Oliver's feet.

Oliver took a deep breath. As much as he wanted to knock that insolent boy out, it would only get him into trouble. Instead he returned wordlessly to his bunk, where he stuffed his belongings into his knapsack.

Kalle sidled up to him. "Sorry about that."

"No need to apologize." Oliver had no intention of dwelling on the nasty incident.

"For what it's worth, Lutz is an asshole." Kalle paused for a moment. "Do you think we'll see real action?"

Oliver took a step backward to scrutinize Kalle's baby face, which didn't show the slightest growth of beard. "How old are you?"

"Sixteen."

A wave of sympathy hit Oliver. That boy should be at home with his mom instead of being used as cannon fodder. "My track record isn't exactly clean," he said, nodding toward his leg. "Nevertheless, I managed to at least stay alive during my stint at the front. Stay close by my side and do whatever I do."

Kalle nodded eagerly.

"Now go and pack your stuff, we don't want to get on the bad side of the boss."

When Oliver shouldered his knapsack, the older man who'd defended him earlier, sidled up to him. "Lutz is quite the asshole, don't let him vex you. Always trying to stir up trouble and then running to the boss laying the blame on whoever engaged him."

"Good to know."

"I'm Gerald, by the way." Gerald held out his hand.

"Oliver."

Just as Gerald turned around to leave, Oliver asked, "What about you? You seen action before?"

Gerald snorted. "Not in this war. Fought in the First World War. I still have nightmares about the comrades I buried in the trenches in France. Horrible times. Never thought I'd have to go through this again." He grabbed his rifle tighter. "Between us, these guns will do us no good in combat. The Russians have tanks and artillery, think we can defeat them with the few Panzerfaust anti-tank weapons we have? If you ask me, we're all doomed."

Lowering his voice, because what they were discussing was treason, Oliver answered, "We just have to hold out long enough."

"You do that and take care of that kid." Gerald nodded toward Kalle on the other side of the barracks. "I'm old and my wife died during a bombing several months ago. I'm ready to go and reunite with her."

Lutz approached them with a suspicious gaze. "You two cowards conspiring about how best to defect?"

"Get lost!" Gerald said, turning his back to the rabble-rouser.

"I'm watching you!" Lutz said, before he exited the barracks.

The rest of the men followed suit and soon everyone climbed into the back of an open truck to take them to whatever place they were needed.

23

A twinge of guilt for leaving Stefan behind at the hotel tugged at Margarete. It was their first fight and she so wanted to turn around to make up with him. But then, she wouldn't be able to meet with Thea.

Torn between Stefan and Thea, she realized this was her only chance to see her former classmate. If she didn't show up today, she'd most probably never see her again. Thea might need help. She had even said so. Her words still echoed in Margarete's ears. *We need to help each other to get through this, don't we?* Even if she couldn't help her classmate, maybe the opposite was true? Living in the underground for any length of time, Thea must have useful contacts she could share with Margarete. Document forgers. Corrupt bureaucrats who issued documents for a bribe. Anyone who resisted the government. Even if nothing came out of the reunion, nothing would be lost either.

She'd talk to Stefan once she returned to the hotel. Then he'd see how foolishly he had behaved. It was a good thing to be cautious, yet his anxiety was bordering on paranoia. Still, she had misgivings when walking down the street and felt for the papers that identified her as Annegret Huber, an Aryan. If she was stopped by police on her way, she had nothing to fear. She wasn't an illegal Jew in hiding like poor Thea.

Squaring her shoulders she walked to the address her classmate had given her, located in a well-known area downtown. The structural damage to the city was beyond her wildest imagination. When she'd left for Paris three years ago, there had been only a few destroyed buildings. Now it was the reverse: barely a building stood unscathed.

Miraculously, there hadn't been an air raid last night, despite the receptionist's warnings that this occurred almost every single night.

A few people hurried to their homes in the settling darkness of this winter evening, giving Margarete a sense of urgency to reach her destination. Used to the comparative peacefulness of Plau am See, the palpable tension in Berlin kept her on edge, despite repeating to herself that she was safe and had nothing to fear.

Finally, she located the correct building, and knocked on the door as Thea had told her to do. Nothing happened. She knocked a second time with the same result. Disappointed, she readied herself to return to the hotel.

With hunched shoulders she walked onto the sidewalk, when she suddenly gasped in shock. Thea, accompanied by two men in SS uniforms, stood a few steps away from her. Frozen with anguish, she didn't really comprehend what was happening. Thea didn't seem to be particularly dismayed, on the contrary, she smiled. How could she smile when she'd just been caught by the Gestapo? She must know what fate awaited her as soon as they verified she was indeed a Jew, even more so because she illegally walked outside without the yellow star.

Before Margarete had time to process the situation and

draw her conclusions, Thea took a few steps toward her, saying in her sweetest voice, "Margarete, there you are! You better come with me. And don't make a scene."

"What?" Margarete's mouth hung agape as the realization trickled into her mind.

"You heard me right. Fugitive Jews like you are taken to the Jewish Hospital."

Thea made it sound like a good thing, despite the fact that everyone knew the hospital was actually a prison and transit camp from where transports to the extermination camps in the east departed on a weekly basis.

"I'm not..." Margarete didn't finish her sentence. It was crystal clear that Thea had changed sides and worked for the Gestapo as a *catcher*, a Jew ratting out fellow Jews.

"This is Margarete Rosenbaum. She used to go to school with me," Thea said to one of the Gestapo men with a gracious smile. "Haven't seen her in years, I didn't even know she was still alive. But here she is, for you to pick up."

Perhaps Margarete could still talk her way out of this. "I'm not who you think I am. I have papers. I don't even know who this woman is—"

One of the men rammed his rifle butt into her back. "Shut up and get into the truck."

Biting back a groan, Margarete followed the soldiers and climbed into the back of their truck. If only she had listened to Stefan... Hot and cold shivers ran down her spine as she thought how deeply worried he would be when she didn't show up at Gut Plaun the next day, or any day for that matter.

Sitting in the back of the truck together with some other obviously Jewish prisoners, she still couldn't grasp the concept that Thea had turned on her own people and was working for the Gestapo.

Guilt crept up on her as she thought about not only her own fate—deportation to certain death—but also that of so many others who depended on her for protection. She had risked their lives for the egotistical pleasure of reconnecting with an old acquaintance. She bit on her lip, swallowing down the horrible lump in her throat as she became aware that she urgently needed to control the damage that was already done.

24

After Margarete left their hotel room, Stefan sunk to the bed. He had a very bad feeling about her visit to Thea and was stung with remorse for arguing with her. It was their first fight, and he hated to leave without telling her how sorry he was.

Sure, she'd been unreasonable, reckless even, but that didn't justify him letting her wander alone through the streets of Berlin. With a sigh, he grabbed his coat, intent on going after her. If he couldn't make her see the danger, he could at least ensure she was alright. Unfolding the city map, he searched for the address Thea had given them and then left the hotel in pursuit of Margarete.

Throughout the walk he grew more and more nervous. He didn't understand what exactly was worrying him so much, but working undercover for so long had taught him to trust his instincts, therefore he sped up his steps, hastening along the street as fast as he could risk without attracting unwanted attention to himself, since he had no time to waste for a check of papers.

As he turned the corner onto the given street, he stopped cold in his tracks at the scene unfolding in front of him. Two men in SS uniforms were forcing a woman at gunpoint to climb into the back of a truck. Curbing his instinctive reaction to rush to her aid, he disappeared into the shadows, knowing full well that he was no match for two armed soldiers.

He was about to walk away, when something caused him to look back in the very moment the captured woman turned around to look out of the back of the truck. A split-second later his eyes met hers, sending a searing pain through his body, as he recognized Margarete.

It was a momentary gaze, yet it conveyed such abominable desperation it pressed all the air from his lungs. His fists instinctively clenched in anger, watching helplessly as the SS men hopped onto the truck, their weapons at the ready.

"I love you." He mouthed the words, just as she was pushed further inside the vehicle and it took off with screeching tires, taking the love of his life away.

Stefan fell back against the wall behind him, dry sobs erupting from his throat, when a couple walked by a short distance away. The blonde mane belonged to Annegret's former classmate and he took after them, trying to get to the bottom of the events. Just as he caught up with them, Thea gave a ripple of laughter and said, "Another Jew caught off the streets. Where do we go next?"

Thinking quickly, Stefan slowed down his pace and turned at the next corner. He didn't feel any joy at finding the evidence that his foreboding had been justified: Thea was a catcher. A Jew who worked for the Gestapo hunting other Jews. If he could have done so, he'd have strangled this vile woman with his own hands for her abominable betrayal of human decency.

After taking several deep breaths, he pondered his next steps. The authorities had taken away the woman he loved. Unfortunately, there was nothing he could do for her, but pray. He shook his head, trying to clear his thoughts. Now was not the time to succumb to emotions. He needed a sharp mind to mitigate the damage. His foremost duty was to get himself to safety—and see that the money reached Gut Plaun. The least he could do was continue Margarete's work and save the Jews in her factory by finding a way to keep bribing Lothar Katze without giving away the fact that he was in on Margarete's deceit.

Sometime later, Stefan found himself standing outside the hotel. He didn't remember how he got there, just that he'd started walking mindlessly, his soul weeping for the loss of his beloved Margarete—knowing what he knew, he had little hope to ever see her again.

"*Guten Tag*," he greeted the receptionist hurriedly so as not to risk her asking questions about his wife's whereabouts. Upstairs in the shabby room, Margarete's things sitting on the dresser caught him unawares, so he sank down onto the mattress, burying his head in his hands. Anger at her recklessness mixed with guilt for being too late to save her knocked the air out of his lungs. Grief, horror, sadness, angst... a multitude of emotions whirled in his soul, making it difficult to breathe and almost impossible to think clearly.

After a while he got up to drink from the jug of water, stretching his arms over his head and forcefully shoving away any feelings except for a healthy dose of fear. Because fear kept a man alive. It heightened the senses, alerted to dangers and pushed reckless notions away... at least for those men who'd learned to welcome fear into their hearts and listen to what she had to say.

Looking around the room, his gaze fell on Margarete's travel outfit. Should he take her things with him? On the one hand it might raise suspicions if he left it in the hotel, and the Gestapo might somehow connect the supposed Frau Stober with either Margarete Rosenbaum or Annegret Huber—and neither of those outcomes boded well for him. On the other hand, if he was asked to open his suitcase and the police found women's clothing in there, they might ask more questions than Stefan cared to answer. There was really no good solution to his conundrum, except... He undid the seam of her dress to recover the money, then he stuffed the bills beneath the false bottom of his suitcase. Making sure there was nothing to betray either of Margarete's identities, he packed and left the hotel with one suitcase in each hand.

Since he'd already paid in advance, there was no need to check out. He cast the receptionist a quick smile and said, "My wife has met a friend and we're leaving earlier than planned."

Before the woman could answer, he hurried outside. It wasn't long until he saw a young woman clambering across a ruined building, picking up household wares that had survived the explosion.

"Fräulein, was that your house?" he called out to her.

Her empty eyes in the dirt-streaked face spoke before her lips formed the words. "Yes. Direct hit two nights ago. The police wouldn't let me in before, because it was still smoldering."

"I'm so sorry," he said as he approached her and put the suitcase at her feet. "These things belonged to my wife. May they serve you now." Without waiting for an answer from the stupefied woman, he quickly vanished.

At the train station, he bought a ticket to Plau am See, his heart weary, but his mind working feverishly on a plan of how to continue Margarete's legacy. Now he was grateful that she'd made him the acting factory manager, because that position enabled him to keep its forced workers fed and clothed—and prevent the deportation of the Jews.

For now he'd have to feign ignorance about Annegret's whereabouts, claiming he hadn't seen her since before her trip to Berlin. He just needed to find a way to let Oberscharführer Katze know that nothing had changed, except for the fact that Stefan would from now on deliver the bribe.

Sitting on the train home he couldn't help but feel the burden of being responsible for so many lives pressing down on him. With Oliver drafted and Margarete arrested, it was only him and Dora holding up the clandestine operation to help the prisoners. In any case he had to seek Dora out first thing in the morning, to let her know about her mistress' arrest and devise a plan to keep it a secret, since they couldn't tell anyone that the Gestapo had caught her for being a Jew.

He promised himself to continue the resistance work to the best of his abilities. Margarete's sacrifice should not be in vain.

25

Margarete reeled with the shock. She scolded herself for being so gullible, stupid, even outright reckless. After hiding beneath a different personality for three years she should have known better. She should have listened to Stefan, should have... it was futile to dwell on the things she could have done better.

The harsh reality was that the Gestapo had arrested her, shoved her into the back of a truck, no doubt headed to the infamous transit camp at the Jewish Hospital in Schulstrasse. A million thoughts ran through her brain, trying to come up with a way out. But there was none. The two armed SS men guarding the prisoners wouldn't hesitate for a second to shoot her. No, she imperceptibly shook her head. If she wanted to have a—however slim—chance to survive, she had to oblige.

Unadulterated hatred spread through her cells as she relived the seconds of her arrest. The way Thea had smiled. Stuffing her hands deep down into the pocket of her coat, she felt the fabric of her wallet. The sensation caused goosebumps to erupt all over her skin. Inside that wallet were Annegret's papers.

It was a lifeline. Perhaps now that Thea wasn't present to

denounce her, she could bluff her way out of this situation? Tell the SS guards it was a huge misunderstanding, and she wasn't really who they thought she was.

Those men must have heard this excuse a million times, her inner voice said. That might be true, yet she had the advantage of owning original papers, not fake ones of dubious quality. She also had dozens of people who could vouch for her, testify she really was Annegret Huber, the rich Aryan heiress.

Thomas found out about your real identity, what makes you think these people won't?

Well, that was a point to consider. The Gestapo weren't exactly known for being clueless fools. They'd find out the truth easily enough, especially because it was Thea's word against hers. Even if they believed her, they'd surely check up on Thea's claim. Lying to them and then being found out would make things much worse, because apart from herself it would also implicate everyone at Gut Plaun.

Under any circumstances, she had to keep Annegret out of this, because that was the only way to protect Stefan, Dora, Frau Mertens, Nils and all the prisoners working for her. The realization hit her hard, making her shiver. She was on her own. Absolutely, totally, utterly and completely alone. Nobody would come to her aid.

Closing her eyes in dismay, her mind drifted back to Stefan. She so regretted their argument and wished she'd listened to him. Now she might never get the opportunity to apologize and say how much she loved him. The pain in his eyes when he'd seen her on the truck, it broke her heart all over again.

The vehicle stopped and one SS man jumped off, leaving only his comrade to guard the prisoners. Two people in plain clothes signaled to a café, presumably to arrest more Jews inside. Margarete wondered whether these two were catchers like Thea. How many Jews had betrayed their own race to work with the enemy? And why? To save their own skin? For financial gain?

Disgusted, she shrugged the thought off and moved toward the back of the truck. Not to escape, because she knew that she stood no chance, but because she realized this might be her only chance to get rid of Annegret's papers. She slipped them from her pocket and just before two people were shoved inside, terror etched on their faces, she used the commotion to toss the *Kennkarte* to the ground.

Nobody noticed. The second soldier jumped inside once more, and seconds later the vehicle set into motion. Margarete laid her head back against the metal frame and closed her eyes. Without the papers that had kept her safe for such a long time, she had returned to the same precarious situation she'd been in three years ago, when Herr Huber had announced that he was sending her away to a labor camp in the east.

It seemed fate had caught up with her, and the Jew Margarete Rosenbaum was finally on her way to extermination.

26

Dora had left her little girl with Frau Mertens so that she could walk into town to run some errands. She also needed to stop at Olga's place to deliver foodstuffs for the Jewish girl she and her employer were hiding. Secretly she hoped to receive some news from home, since Olga seemed to have ways to get word from the Ukraine.

She was paying Frau Bracke, the owner of the haberdashery, when she heard a kerfuffle outside. Vile gossip that she was, Frau Bracke had a long neck, but couldn't see anything through the window of her shop.

"I better check what this is about," Frau Bracke said, handing Dora her change and shuffling her out of the shop. Locking the door behind them, Frau Bracke set off in the direction of the noise, which unfortunately was the exact direction Dora had to take on her way back to Gut Plaun. She'd rather keep her distance from the horrible woman who'd insulted her many times for being a subhuman Slav out to steal a good German man. Gratefully, after Fräulein Annegret's show of support, the open hostilities had ceased, although Frau Bracke continued to give her nasty looks.

So Dora dawdled, to bring as much space between her and the nosy woman, as she headed for the main square. Her plan was to pass the square at the far end, steering clear of the commotion happening there.

Even though she had nothing to hide—having already delivered the foodstuffs to Olga—she preferred not to get involved with the authorities, since one could never know what they were up to. But as she looked up, she immediately covered her mouth with her hand to hide the gasp of shock.

SS men were dragging someone across the cobblestoned main street. As she took a second glance, she recognized two victims: an old white-haired man and a younger one with reddish hair. Both were badly injured, most likely from being tortured. Horrified, she told herself to get away from the depressing scene, but her wobbly legs wouldn't obey. Bile rose in her throat, causing her to sway until she had to lean against the wall of a nearby building.

Recently she'd been getting nauseous easily, which she took as proof that she indeed was with child again. Despite the awful situation, she smiled to herself, thinking of Oliver and how much she loved him.

As she regained her composure, she made to leave, having no intention of witnessing the cruel spectacle, but it was too late. SS men had cordoned off the main square, blocking all streets leading into it, and herding villagers into the open space.

"Fräulein, move over there." One of them indicated toward the majestic town hall, a beautiful red-brick building that was almost entirely covered with ivy. Suddenly the noise ebbed to nothing, as the mayor stepped through the dark green door onto the outside staircase of the town hall.

He halted on the uppermost step, looking down at the gathered folks for several long seconds, before he raised his voice. "Our great SS has just caught these two traitors, conspiring to harm Führer and Fatherland."

A murmur went through the crowd.

"We're here to witness how they receive their just punishment."

The crowd cheered enthusiastically. Some shouted, "*Sieg Heil*", others cursed the traitors.

Dora didn't dare to take her eyes off the mayor, afraid someone might denounce her for not supporting law and order if she showed how disturbed she was by this public spectacle.

"These two men have caused unspeakable suffering for the German population. Anthony Walker"—the mayor pointed at the red-haired man, who was promptly dragged toward the streetlamp to the right of the town hall's entrance—"is a child murderer. One of the vilest men in history. He's one of the English bomber pilots who kill our loved ones. He ran away after being shot down..." The frenetic shouting of the masses forced the mayor to interrupt his speech. He spread out his arms to calm the noise, before he began once more. "This criminal has been hiding out with the help of one of our own citizens."

The mayor pointed to the old man, who was now being dragged to the other side of the staircase. "Old fisherman Stober. A vicious traitor if there ever was one."

Dora suppressed a gasp. This was the grandfather of Stefan Stober, the man her mistress was sweet on. She would be devastated on Stefan's behalf.

"Hang them. Hang them," chanted the crowd. Dora's legs threatened to give out under her and she frantically searched for an exit, but all corners were manned by SS men.

"If this is the wish of the people," the mayor responded, causing the crowd to chant ever louder, demanding to hang the two men.

Dora watched in horror as the SS men produced two ropes and made nooses into them. Another wave of nausea hit her, much stronger than before. Retching, she fled to the corner of the market square, vomiting the contents of her stomach next to the brightly polished boots of an SS man.

"I'm sorry," she hastened to say. "Forgive me, I wouldn't normally. But being with child, I can't seem to keep it in."

The man gave her a benevolent smile. "Perhaps these happenings are a bit much for a woman in the family way. Would you rather leave?"

Her relief was immeasurable. "Please don't think me a bad person. I want the traitors punished as much as anyone else, I just can't..." Another retching emphasized her words.

"Good woman, go and take care of your child. The Führer needs healthy soldiers to be born."

"Thank you," Dora muttered and fled the scene, reeling equally at the cruel spectacle and the thought that her unborn baby was earmarked to kill other people even before its birth if Hitler had his way.

On the walk back she pondered how best to tell Fräulein Annegret what had happened to her lover's grandfather. Stefan Stober was a kind man, who adored his grandfather with whom he'd been living the past few years. He'd be so heartbroken when he returned from Berlin.

Oliver would know how to break the news in a gentle way... Thoughts of her husband saddened Dora, since she'd had no news of him for quite a while. *No news is good news*, Fräulein Annegret always said to comfort her.

Dora so much wanted this to be true. As long as she didn't receive the dreaded telegram, she would pretend everything was fine. Oliver just had to return to her side.

27

After hours of marching, they had finally arrived their destination. Oliver lay exhausted on the ground, Kalle and Gerald sitting next to him. He massaged his injured leg to disperse the cramping, after the strenuous hike.

"Alright, men, we're to support a rifle company that's been trapped by a tank breakthrough. They're bunkered down and waiting for us to retrieve them, since most of them are injured. They're not expecting us until it gets dark, but I'd rather fight an enemy I can see," their leader announced.

Oliver listened as the Feldwebel outlined his foolhardy plan to advance in plain sight, thus risking the injured men who presumedly could run away if needed. Some of the veterans in the unit argued with the Feldwebel, who was adamant that he knew better and wouldn't take their advice.

Going in at dark would be a much safer option, as well as giving them the element of surprise. At least that's how Oliver's old officer back during the Polish Campaign would have done it.

"Split into two teams and get going," their leader commanded them. Oliver looked around to make eye contact with his newfound friends. Gerald, the old man, immediately understood and dawdled until nasty Lutz had chosen his group, before they casually walked to the other side, taking young Kalle with them.

"Can't trust that lad," Gerald said.

Oliver nodded. They'd have their hands full with the enemy, there was no need to risk getting stabbed in the back by a supposed friend. Kalle's face was white as a bedsheet, looking as if was about to shit himself at the prospect of encountering real action.

"You stay by my side, alright?" Oliver told the shivering boy. It wasn't that he was free of fear himself, just that he'd learned to control his emotions and focus on the task at hand. In this instance he remembered the men he fought alongside in Poland. Back then they'd all been real soldiers, not babies like Kalle, who'd learned to shoot a gun during his Hitler Youth, but never had any proper military training.

"Oliver and I go first," Gerald ordered. "You stick with us and keep your head down. No need to get yourself killed right away."

Kalle nodded wordlessly.

Then they crept in the direction their leader had ordered. As soon as he moved forward, Oliver felt his old training taking over. Instantly his only focus was survival, while everything else faded to the back of his mind.

They finally worked their way around the line of enemy fire only to discover the remaining men of the rifle company were being pinned down by at least dozen Russians with guns and plenty of ammunition. Oliver and the others in his group had just squatted down to assess the situation, when the other half, led by the inexperienced officer, walked boldly into the line of fire.

"Stupid idiots," Oliver groused as he witnessed the ensuing massacre. They had no choice but to rush the enemy from behind, drawing some of the fire away from their comrades boldly walking toward their deaths.

When the skirmish ended, they had lost five men, including Lutz, and many more were injured. Oliver seethed at the unnecessary casualties, since most of them could have been avoided had their officer not disregarded the advice of the veterans.

Kalle was a shivering mess, but by sheer miracle hadn't sustained any injuries. The youngster would have to grow up real quick if he wanted a chance to survive.

"That was a debacle," Gerald said.

"Shush, or you'll get into trouble," someone else hissed.

"More trouble than we're already in?" Gerald smirked. "The way this goes, none of us will make it out alive."

Oliver feared the same, but he had a wife and soon two children to return to.

28

As soon as the truck stopped in front of the Jewish Hospital, the prisoners were shoved into cells in the dank and dark basement. One by one, they were taken away, until only Margarete and a young man called Zim crouched on the empty ground.

"Never seen you before, where have you been hiding?" he asked.

Unsure whether she could trust him or whether he was another catcher working for the Gestapo, she shook her head. "I'm not from Berlin."

"That would explain why Thea got you. All the illegals around here know to run fast when spotting her blonde mane."

"Is she kind of famous?" Margarete asked.

He snorted. "That woman? We call her 'the blonde poison'. I'd wager she's helped catch more than a hundred Jews. Maybe two hundred."

"That many?" Margarete didn't know whether she should be shocked upon that number or relieved that she hadn't been the only gullible soul falling into Thea's trap.

Zim cocked his head. "You really have no idea how all of this works now, do you?"

"No." She shook her head. "Like I said, I'm not from here."

"However did you manage to survive this long? Or..." he walked around her, taking in her well-kept appearance "... are you working for the Gestapo, too?"

"Me? Of course not!" she said disgusted.

"Hey, just asking." Zim held up his hands. "It's just... you're clean, well-fed, have a nice haircut and even nicer clothes. Illegals don't look the way you do."

Margarete didn't want him to suspect her of working for the Gestapo, so she explained. "I had good papers and lived a well-protected lie until I met Thea."

"How does she know you if you're not from Berlin?" The lad was clever.

"We went to school together."

"Aha." Zim walked around her once more, as if he could get answers by just inspecting her from all sides. "Why did you come to Berlin? You must have known it wasn't safe."

"I had to." She held his gaze for quite a while, getting the feeling he could be trusted. Although she wouldn't make the same mistake twice, there was probably no harm done if she told him in vague terms about her reasons to travel to Berlin. "Others depend on me."

"Other Jews?"

She shrugged.

"Aren't you afraid I'll tell the Gestapo what you said and they'll beat the names out of you?"

She shrugged again. "I don't even know their names. And aren't you afraid I might turn on you and work for the Gestapo like Thea does?"

Zim gave a hearty laugh. "I like you."

Their conversation was cut short, because the cell door opened and a guard came in, pointing at Margarete. "You! Come with me!"

He took her upstairs to the office of the transit camp leader

SS-Hauptscharführer Walter Dobberke. "Well, well, Fräulein Rosenbaum," he said jovially. "I had to dig quite deep to find your papers, since it seems you died years ago in a bombing. Perhaps you could explain how a dead person looks so very much alive to me."

Margarete thought quickly. If he'd found evidence of her real identity, and had Thea's testimony, it made no sense to deny who she was. The one thing she had to do was to keep everyone else, especially Stefan and Dora, out of this. "You are right, I didn't die during the bombing. I left my papers next to a random body to make sure they would be found and went underground."

"Aha," Dobberke said. "You expect me to believe that?"

"It's the truth."

"We'll see." He walked over to an elegant cabinet, opened the door and took out a bullwhip. Margarete's mouth went instantly dry as he whirled it in his hand, striding toward her. "I'd like to know the names of those who helped you."

"Please, nobody knew, I kept hidden—"

The whip came down hard on her shoulder, leaving an excruciating sting. "The names." Several more whip lashes rained down on her, making her crouch on the floor, before the sadistic man finally paused to relax his wrist.

Her entire body burned like fire, leaving her gasping for air, hoping against hope he was finished with his interrogation. Apparently her prayers had been heard, because he looked down at her sobbing misery with an indulgent gaze.

Yet, his next words shattered her soul. "You're such a pretty woman. I'm afraid this will get rather unpleasant if you don't tell me what I want to know."

Margarete had tasted enough pain to know she wouldn't hold out for long before she started betraying everyone dear to her—including Stefan. Despite the dire situation, the thought of him sent a ray of sunshine into her heart.

She loved everything about Stefan, and she genuinely admired his incredible courage, combined with an unwavering loyalty and the astuteness to pull off dangerous actions. What would he do in her situation? Suddenly she felt his comforting presence in the room and his spirit whispered into her ear. "If you can't fight them, you must join them—let him believe you're on his side."

His advice was, of course, spot on. Her only way to protect those she loved was to think ahead. Gathering what little wits she had left about her, she returned Dobberke's gaze, conjuring up a confidence she didn't possess.

"Please stop beating me. I will tell you everything you want to know," she whimpered through swollen lips.

"I'm all ears."

Margarete glanced down at the nasty rupture on the skin of her lower arm, a coiling red stripe that would form an ugly scar. "I... you were right, I had help." It wasn't difficult to make her voice shiver with fear. "But... you... you... have to protect me from them."

Apart from raising an eyebrow, Dobberke didn't show his surprise. "Where you're going, nobody will be able to find you."

That probably wasn't the reassurance he wanted to evoke, since she knew exactly where those transports were headed. Yet, she forced herself to show relief.

"Stand up," he ordered and then called out, "Get her some water."

Moments later a chubby woman in a nurse's uniform with a yellow star on her chest showed up, holding a glass in her hand. She led Margarete to a chair in front of Dobberke's desk, and helped her to sit down, before she handed Margarete the glass, while whispering, "Tell him everything you know, and he'll let you be."

Briefly, Margarete wondered whether that woman was a random nurse, or if she had some kind of relationship with

Dobberke. Perhaps she worked for him in a similar way Thea did. She inwardly shrugged, since it didn't make any difference.

"Thank you," Margarete said, struggling to sit upright despite the agonizing pain.

Dobberke had taken a seat behind his desk, grabbing a blank piece of paper and a pen. "The names, if you'd be so kind."

"I worked for SS-Standartenführer Huber and when he died in 1941 in the same bombing I supposedly perished in, his son Reiner took me under his wing to protect me."

"You're lying," Dobberke spat out.

"No, it's all true. He hid me in his villa in Wannsee, where I stayed until I was sent word that he'd died in Paris."

"Whyever would he do this? He's SS and you're a filthy Jew."

Once again, thinking of Stefan emboldened her to go all in. She would not only protect the man she loved more than her own life, but drawing from his strength, she had a fantastic idea. Perhaps her testimony could cause a few high-ranking SS-officers to be arrested for the gravest crime of all: *Rassenschande*, sexual intercourse with a Jew. She needed to reach deep into her soul to unearth the memories of the vile things Reiner had done to her.

Thus equipped, her voice quivered miserably as she began to speak. "He wanted... intimate favors. He... he threatened to have me deported if I didn't obey."

Dobberke furrowed his brows, apparently unsure what to think of her confession. The way he'd looked at the perky nurse clearly showed that he wasn't above getting paid in sexual favors, either. "I believe Reiner Huber was killed by the French Résistance quite some time ago."

Margarete nodded painfully. "Yes. I hoped that would mean an end to my suffering, but..." she sobbed for effect "... even while he was still alive he had frequently offered me to his friends. They then took over 'caring for me' as they called it, until I was finally able to escape being a sex slave to a dozen or more of these men. Until I was caught by Thea."

"She's a great agent, isn't she? My best one." Dobberke grinned. "Although in the beginning she was recalcitrant, just like you."

Margarete feared he'd offer her the same deal he'd offered Thea. Under no circumstances would she work for that scumbag and send her fellow Jews to their doom. To prevent him from getting any ideas, she emphasized once more. "Throughout my ordeal they passed me from one to the other on a regular basis. But I never met any other Jew. It was always just me and my current rapist."

"Now that's a grave accusation. If what you say is true, I might even spare you from going on the transport."

"Really?" She barely dared to get her hopes up.

Dobberke gave a serene nod. "You'll understand that I can't let you go, but I can take your name off the list and keep you here indefinitely. But I need proof for your accusations. Names and places. Any detail you remember. Anything at all. Every single bit may be useful to catch these people."

Margarete could see that he was already delighting in the thought of a possible promotion and she began to talk. She had no qualms about accusing every single Nazi she had ever met, and she strained her brain to remember the names of Reiner Huber's friends, whether her accusations were believable or not. She was as good as dead anyway and if she could do nothing else, she would at least take as many of the vile Nazis with her as possible.

When she was finished, Dobberke had written down two pages of names and locations, shaking his head in disbelief. "This is huge. If this is true..." He looked directly into her eyes and asked, "Are you sure they didn't hide any other Jews?"

"I feel sure they probably did. But none that I was actually aware of. They always blindfolded me, except when someone wanted to use me for their pleasure." Her ears started burning with shame, since this part of her story wasn't entirely made up. Embarrassed, she looked down at her feet.

"Put her into a holding cell," Dobberke hollered. Moments later two guards arrived and dragged her into a room that was crowded with miserable men and women awaiting their fate.

Margarete, though, clung to the promise that Dobberke would keep her off the transport list, as a treat for collaborating so well.

29

Ernst was in the prison library discussing a classic book when a guard came in to announce, "Rosenbaum, you have a visitor."

Wondering who that might be, Ernst closed the book and said to his audience, "I'll see you tomorrow." Then he followed the guard to the visiting room at the end of the hallway. "Who is the visitor, if I may ask?"

The guard was one of the friendlier ones. "Some official, that's all I know."

"What does he want?" Ernst said more to himself.

"You'll find out soon enough." The guard stopped in front of the door to the visitor room. "You have thirty minutes, if you're done earlier, knock on the door and I'll come and get you."

"Thank you for your kindness." Ernst smiled at the man who'd never harassed or beaten him, although he proudly wore his Nazi party badge at all times.

As Ernst stepped into the visitor room, he recoiled at seeing Lothar Katze waiting for him. "Herr Oberscharführer."

"Let's make this short," Katze said. "Your good days are over. You'll go on the next transport to Auschwitz."

Ernst swallowed hard. "May I ask why?"

"I don't need you anymore. The entire reason to keep you in here living like a king was because of your precious niece. She was paying me handsomely to keep her filthy Jewish identity a secret and so I kindly agreed to keep you alive to make sure she wouldn't hoodwink me. She's a deceitful Jew after all, isn't she?" Katze guffawed as if he'd made a hilarious joke.

Ernst wasn't so much distressed for himself, but apparently Margarete was in dire straits. Perhaps there was something he could do to help her. "What happened to her?"

"The stupid chit got herself arrested. She's in a transit camp as we speak, no doubt going on the next transport to Auschwitz. You might even reunite on the train." Another heartless guffaw erupted from Katze's throat.

Ernst felt an excruciating pain in his soul. If she'd been caught that meant all the workers in the factory were without protection, too. What he didn't understand was how and why it had happened, and why Katze had come especially to tell him? He needn't wait long, because the Oberscharführer glowed with importance and started talking again.

"That woman thinks she's so intelligent, but she has under-estimated me. I know everything about her and her pathetic attempts to help the prisoners in her factory, but like I said, she has underestimated me."

"How sacrilegious of her," Ernst murmured, despite being of the opinion that Katze was equally dumb as he was cruel and corrupt.

"It is. She's the stupid subhuman here, not me! Anyhow, I have a friend in Schulstrasse and when he mentioned a bitch who claimed Reiner Huber and several of his friends had hidden her in exchange for sexual favors, I immediately smelled a rat. That hag was none other than your precious niece Margarete Rosenbaum, also known as Annegret Huber. Can you imagine? Accusing the very family whose name and heritage she stole to safeguard her squalid existence?"

"Very heinous, indeed." Secretly, Ernst admired Margarete for such a bold action of resistance. Instead of giving up without a fight after having been caught, she'd decided to take as many Nazis down with her as she could. It probably wasn't the wisest decision, although it might not matter, since once inside the gas chambers everyone was alike.

Ernst still grappled to believe the notion of industrial scale murder in the camps, even at the hands of the Nazis. Yet, the evidence had become overwhelming and anyone who was able to add up two numbers had to accept even the wildest rumors as truth. Or how else could it be explained that hundreds of thousands of Jews were shipped to Auschwitz and other camps, without those camps overflowing with prisoners? Where did everyone go? Through the chimney, as people had written in carefully coded letters from better places in the east—no doubt forced to write under the watchful eyes of the SS-guards. Yes, murder was the only explanation that made sense.

One of his new friends in prison, an Aryan, had received a postcard from a Jewish friend, saying that all of his relatives were living happily with an esteemed uncle. The only problem was, said uncle had died years ago. After more of his friends had received similar postcards with references to dead people, he'd come to the conclusion that it was a hidden way to warn those still roaming freely of what awaited them at the other end of the train ride.

"You don't seem upset," Katze stated.

Ernst felt the implicit need to respond in some way. "Herr Oberscharführer, I am certainly disturbed that my niece should have been captured, although I'm not surprised that it happened."

"Well, her luck ran out, and with it yours." Katze grinned with genuine pleasure. "It's your time to join the rest of the scum. Say goodbye to your cozy prison cell, your next stop will be much worse." With that said, Katze got up and knocked on the door. "I'm done here."

"Enjoy your freedom, because it won't last long," Ernst said to the man leaving.

The next day Ernst was taken to a transit camp for Jews.

30

Afraid someone had seen him with Margarete in Berlin and might follow him back home, Stefan disembarked the train about halfway to Plau am See and spent a night in a cheap hotel. When he was sure nobody had made the connection between the arrested Jewish woman and him, he finally boarded another train.

As soon as he arrived at the Plau am See train station, he walked to his grandfather's house, without going into town. First he needed to hide the money in a safe place and check up on his grandfather. The British airman would hopefully have been moved on to another place by the time he arrived.

Despite the cold weather, there was no smoke rising from the chimney. A sense of foreboding made his skin crawl and he hastened his pace, while giving himself a hundred logical reasons for his observation. His grandfather might have fallen asleep and let the fireplace go cold, or he hadn't been able to carry wood inside, or he'd fallen down and was lying there help-lessly... Stefan fell into a jog, imagining his grandfather with twisted legs at the bottom of the stairs.

"Opa?" he called out as soon as he reached the door. There was no answer. He raced upstairs into his bedroom, which was empty. The kitchen, the living room, the outhouse, everything seemed deserted.

Stefan's heart constricted, because the old man rarely ventured from the house, except to sit on the porch or walk down to the shore. It was entirely too cold and cloudy to sit outside, yet he checked the porch. He'd already expected it to be empty, so then he raced down to the shore, concerned that his grandfather might have slipped on the icy ground and drifted into the shallow water.

Even though he wouldn't drown, he'd freeze to death within an hour if he couldn't stand up and get out of the icy water. Horrible memories of Margarete's near-death experience in the lake almost a year ago attacked him, pressing the air from his lungs. He bit his lip, casting the troubling emotions aside, since he needed a clear head. There might be a logical reason for Opa's absence. He might have taken the airman to the meeting point with whoever would take over next. Although it wasn't the agreed procedure, changes of plan happened all the time.

As he returned to the house, he decided to check his theory and walked into the basement where they'd hidden the airman. The hidden door was slightly ajar and nobody was there, although the room looked as if someone had just left, which was worrisome to say the least.

Opa would have removed any trace of the illegal guest the moment he'd been moved, unless... something had happened. The tingling sensation at the back of his neck intensified.

Foregoing caution, he stashed the money in a hiding hole, put on his coat and walked into town. His first stop was the wharf, hoping his grandfather might have gone for a chat with old friends.

His boat was there. Empty. Next to him, another fisherman

sat on his boat, smoking a pipe. Stefan approached him and called out, "Hein, have you by chance seen my grandfather?"

The man's face fell. Ever so slowly, he removed the pipe from his mouth. Stefan was about to scream aloud, such was the bad feeling rolling off of the old man. "Haven't been around, have you?"

"No. Just returned from out-of-town business. Where's my grandfather?"

"I'd rather not be the one to tell you. There's no way to sugarcoat it. The Gestapo got him, for hiding a foreign soldier."

Stefan clenched his fists in anger. Despite knowing it was probably pointless, he asked, "Where is he now?"

"Dangling from a lamppost in the town square. The mayor forbade anyone to take him down, wanted to make a warning example."

Stefan swayed on his feet like a leaf in the wind, feeling as if someone had just punched a hole through his torso. He couldn't breathe, and neither could he comprehend that his grandfather wasn't here anymore.

"Sorry, lad."

Stefan shook his head furiously and stormed down the dock, ignoring the other man's warning. "Don't do anything to get yourself arrested too. Best to just let things be."

Stefan's steps slowed as he reached the town square, some acquaintances giving him sympathetic gazes, while others quickly looked the other way. Two bodies hung from lampposts, flanking the entrance to the town hall like flags flying in the wind. Stefan balled his hands into tight fists as he first recognized the British airman and then his grandfather.

Casting all caution aside, he ran toward his grandfather's stiff corpse and made to untie the rope around his neck, when an SS man exited the building and yelled, "Hey, what do you think you're doing here?"

Stefan knew the man and said, "Look. I'm going to give my grandfather a proper burial."

"You'll do no such thing. He was a traitor and will stay here to remind everyone what happens if you betray the Reich."

"Come on, he was an old man who's never hurt anyone."

When Stefan didn't budge, the SS man closed the distance between them and hissed, "Everyone knows he was a rabble-rouser. Hiding the enemy was just the worst of his crimes."

"I wasn't in town for the past few days, perhaps he was confused and thought the Englishman was one of ours? My grandfather's mind has been in sharp decline the past few years," Stefan tried to argue, because he couldn't stomach the notion of his beloved Opa dangling like a heinous criminal, for everyone to spit at and mock his memory.

"For the sake of old times, let me give you this advice: back off and never mention your grandfather again. Unless you want to take his place at the end of the rope, that is."

Knowing when a battle was lost, Stefan held up his hands in defense. "Sorry for the inconvenience. It won't happen again." Then he took a last glance at the dead body of the man he'd loved so much, turned on his heel and walked back to their empty house.

Once there, he made himself a cup of *Ersatzkaffee*, feeling Opa's presence in every corner, despite knowing he was dead. He settled in his grandfather's favorite armchair, staring out of the window toward the lake that had been the old man's biggest love. Having lost the two people he loved most in this world within a few days, Stefan didn't have the energy to get up, so he simply sat there, staring at the beautiful landscape, not comprehending how he could ever feel anything but grief again.

He must have fallen asleep, because he woke from the mug in his hands shattering on the floor. It was still dark outside, yet a glance at the clock told him it was time to get ready for work.

Stretching his hurting back, he picked up a dustpan and brush, cleaned the mess and made himself another coffee.

Still weary with grief, he somehow gathered his resolve to keep going. He would avenge what had happened and make sure Opa hadn't died in vain. Taking a deep breath he determined to seek out Dora before going to the factory, since she had a right to know what had happened to her mistress.

31

Dora was worried sick about Fräulein Annegret. She should have been back from Berlin by now, but hadn't returned and hadn't sent word about a delay either. When she'd carefully voiced her worries to Frau Mertens, the housekeeper had simply answered, "Fräulein Annegret has always been capricious, she might have met an old friend, or she might simply have gotten bored of the quiet life at Gut Plaun."

Dora, of course, knew this wasn't the case, but she couldn't tell Frau Mertens the truth. Still shaken about the fisherman's grandfather's death, she wondered whether she should seek him out. Then she realized that since he and Fräulein Annegret had gone to Berlin together, he most certainly wouldn't have returned either. Perhaps the trains weren't running, or they'd been held up by bombing, or something else. These days one never knew and anything could happen.

Since Oliver had left for service, she and Julia had moved back into the manor, mostly for practical reasons, but also because she didn't feel safe alone in the gardener's house next to the entrance gate. She was just returning from delivering food to the prisoners working in the stables, who weren't allowed to eat at the manor, when she noticed a figure trudging through the gate.

It took her a second glance to recognize the person with the slumped shoulders and the skulking gait as the energetic fisherman.

"Herr Stober!" She waved at him, recoiling in shock when she saw the dreadful expression on his face that indicated he knew about his grandfather already. She sped forward to meet him and her heart broke for the sorrow she saw etched on his face.

"Hello, Dora," he greeted her.

"You've been to town?" she asked. When he nodded, she bit on her lip to keep herself from crying. "I'm so sorry. I only met your grandfather a few times, he seemed to be a wonderful and courageous man." Even with nobody else in sight she didn't dare say how much she'd admired the old man for working underground against the Nazi regime.

"Thank you." He gazed around, before he said, "Is there anywhere we can speak in private?"

Dora's stomach forcefully clenched together. "Yes. We can go to my house."

He nodded, seemingly exhausted.

"Do you bring news from Fräulein Annegret?" she asked as they walked side by side toward her house.

"I'll tell you inside."

His words hit her like a punch to her chest, and she barely suppressed a gasp. "Has something happened?"

He ignored her question, waiting for her to open the door to the small house. Once inside he locked the door behind them, before he turned around and said, "I'm sorry to be the bearer of bad news. Your mistress was arrested by the Gestapo."

"What?" Dora's hand flew to her mouth, covering up the screeching sound that came out of it.

"I couldn't do anything. I just stood there and watched

them drive her away. I... I don't know how I even made it back here..." He fell onto the sofa, burying his head in his hands. "We might never see her again."

"How horrible!" Dora genuinely cared for her mistress, who'd become not only a good friend, but a mentor and example for her.

After a struggle to regain his composure, Stefan locked eyes with her and said, "I will continue her work supporting the forced workers at the factory, but I need your help."

"Anything." Despite knowing the danger involved with the clandestine activities, Dora agreed. Someone had to help the poor souls. If her idol Fräulein Annegret had risked and possibly lost her life, she could do the same.

"First of all we need to explain Annegret's absence," Stefan said.

Dora shook her head. "We can't tell anyone the truth. That would only create more problems. But if we don't say anything, Frau Mertens will soon alert the authorities, and we'll all be in trouble. We need an excuse for Fräulein Annegret's extended absence."

"Yes, that was what I was thinking. Perhaps we could make up a story that she met friends in Berlin and decided to stay with them for a while. That she's had enough of the boring countryside," Stefan suggested.

"That might work, since Frau Mertens has said the same thing, about her being capricious and getting bored with the quiet country life. Just, who's going to tell her? She'll get suspicious if you or I break the news, because at the very least she'd expect a phone call from Fräulein Annegret herself."

"Right." Stefan seemed shaken. "She'll need to hear directly from her... a phone call isn't possible, though... How about a letter?"

"We could certainly write a letter in her name. But Frau

Mertens knows her handwriting and will realize it has been written by someone else." Dora shook her head.

"That's too dangerous. Perhaps... How about a typewritten letter?"

She thought for a moment. "That might work. I don't know how to type though."

"Let that be my worry, I have a friend in town who's a typist. She'll do it for us. We just need Annegret's signature. Would Oliver have anything with her signature on it?" Stefan asked.

"I'm sure I can find something in his office," Dora offered.

"Good. Can you replicate her signature using a signed slip of paper to trace the contours? I would do it myself, but probably a woman's hand would be better suited."

Dora felt the grief emanating from him. Despite the short time he and her mistress had been secretly together, Dora had always known that Herr Stober truly loved Fräulein Annegret, even before knowing about her true identity. Unlike Oberscharführer Kallfass, who'd set his eyes on her for what her social status could do for him. Thinking about him, she pressed her lips into a thin line.

"Let's make a draft of the letter to type up," Stefan said, looking around. "Do you have pen and paper?"

"One moment." Dora walked into the kitchen and returned with the requested things. Together they drafted a letter from Fräulein Annegret, letting the housekeeper know she wouldn't return for the time being, since she was staying with a friend.

"Shouldn't we add instructions for Frau Mertens and Nils, what to do during her absence?" Stefan asked.

Dora nodded. "And you should include instructions for yourself, or it will look strange."

"Good point." After they were finished, Stefan tucked the paper into his pocket. "Once my friend has typed it up, I'll let you know. Meanwhile, try to find her signature on some paper in Oliver's office, will you?"

"I'll go there later this afternoon. Currently Ladislaus is the only one who uses the office when he needs to arrange for deliveries, but that's always in the mornings."

"Good. Take care." Stefan smiled at her. "For the time being it's just the two of us."

Emotions threatened to choke her, but somehow she managed to say, "I'm really sorry about your grandfather and Fräulein Annegret."

"I know you are, but there's nothing that can be done to bring them back. All we can do now is honor the legacies they began and help as many people as possible. Chin up and act normal. I know it's hard, but we must keep Annegret's secret at all costs. Can you do that?"

"I will. I'm glad at least you're here," Dora said and turned to leave the house. "Better wait a few minutes before leaving, we don't want anyone to suspect unsavory things happening here." She put a hand on her stomach, where she could feel a small bump from her growing child.

32

The nighttime bombings had intensified, so that even deep down in the basement of the Jewish Hospital, Margarete flinched with each explosion. In the morning, in spite of the all-clear sounding, there was no sense of relief.

On the contrary, a strange tension took hold of the transit camp and all its inmates. Margarete couldn't make sense out of it, until she finally asked Zim for an explanation.

His answer was a derisive sneer. "I really have no idea how you managed to survive this long. Today's the weekly transport."

"The one to Auschwitz?" she whispered, afraid to speak the name out loud.

"Sure, where else?" He shrugged. "As we speak, the final revisions of the list are made and anyone who wants their names crossed off better have enough money to pay."

"Money?" In her fake identity as Annegret she'd had enough of it, but in here? The Gestapo had meticulously searched her clothes and even her body, so it eluded her as to how anyone might smuggle money inside.

"Yes, money. You'll need to learn a lot of things very fast, if you want to stay alive," Zim said.

Since Dobberke had promised to keep her in the Jewish Hospital as a reward for her collaboration, she wasn't overly nervous. Although a nagging doubt remained, since she had learned never to trust a Nazi to do the humane thing where a Jew was concerned. Therefore she asked, "How does one know who's on the list?"

"You ask the Jewish orderly, Ralf. If he's in the mood and you have the money, he can usually get you off the list. For another week."

"Just for a week?" she almost shrieked.

"Yes, the Gestapo has quotas. Every week a transport leaves. So as not to waste precious coal, it has to be full, too." Zim turned away to indicate the conversation was over.

Several hours later, SS men entered the crowded room, yelling out names. Margarete assumed these were the unfortunate ones who were on the transport. Reassured by her status as earmarked to stay at the camp, she didn't pay too much attention to the names, focusing instead on observing the shock, horror and grief whenever someone recognized their name.

Despite having seen so much human suffering, it was one of the most awful situations she'd been through in the past year— the veil of evacuation to the east had long been lifted by means of secret messages, hearsay and boisterous bragging, so that the selected people knew exactly what awaited them.

Those who had given up hope long ago walked toward the door with stoic fatalism, while others cried tormented tears on the way, leaving a few hotheaded youngsters to rail against those sending them to their deaths with a violent, yet futile attack, leaving their bloodied bodies crumbled on the floor.

Margarete was musing about the evil emanating from one man, spreading through an entire nation like gangrene spread across limbs, apparently with no means to stop it, when she heard her name. Not actually believing her ears, she stayed quiet, observing the other inmates. When nobody moved, the SS man called out a second time, "Margarete Rosenbaum."

Just now realizing they truly meant her, her blood froze in her veins, even as her feet set themselves into motion toward the door. Time seemed to slow down as she waded through waist-deep molasses wanting to keep her in place. Yet, somehow she reached the Jewish orderly, standing next to the SS men. As soon as she had reached him, the molasses vanished, and somehow her brain started to work once more.

"That must be a mistake. Hauptscharführer Dobberke promised to keep me off the list."

Ralf gave her a vile grin, exposing a missing tooth. "Did he now? I guess he lied." Then he winked at two SS men to shove her outside into the yard, where a furniture van was waiting.

"No, you can't do that!" Margarete cried, panic-stricken.

"I can do anything I want to, but you, you're just another destitute Jew."

"You're a Jew yourself."

He shook his head. "No, honey. As soon as the war is over, Dobberke promised to make me an honorary Aryan."

Her heart filled with disdain, shame, and pity for the deluded man. It was one thing to be an anti-Semite if you were a Christian, but a Jew hating those of his own kind? How utterly disgusting was that? She didn't have time to ponder on Ralf's behavior, because the SS mercilessly propelled them forward, generously doling out kicks and punches at those who stumbled or didn't run fast enough.

The van was only half full, when it was closed and set into motion. Margarete huddled in a corner, her arms around her legs and her head resting on her knees in the almost complete darkness, oblivious to the direction they were taking. Truth be told, she knew deep in her heart that this might well be her last journey and she had a very good idea where it would end.

Suddenly, the van stopped, the doors opened and more prisoners were shoved inside. Opposed to those from the Jewish Hospital wearing civilian clothing, the new ones were clad in prison garb. Not the threadbare striped clothes from the camps, with colored triangles to distinguish the different prisoner categories, but a slightly sturdier monochrome cloth without markers. A commotion ensued, as more and more people were shoved inside, literally landing atop the ones crouching on the floor. Long after the doors had been clanked shut, the inmates were still sorting limbs and trying to find a space. It had become so crowded, there was no way to sit down, so Margarete stood up, swaying vicariously as the van careened around the corners of Berlin.

Someone struck up a conversation and she learned the new people had come from a prison for political prisoners, which gave her hope, since Zim had told her that usually politicals weren't sent to extermination camps.

Her good spirits didn't last long, because at the the next stop, everyone was propelled onto a train ramp under the constant shouts of *"Schnell! Schnell!"*, urging the prisoners to hurry up. An elderly man behind her stumbled and she turned around to help him climb down from the van.

Not believing the illusion in front of her eyes, she took his hand, leading him toward the other side of the ramp. He was just a random old man, a prisoner like everyone else.

"Is that really you, Gretchen?" he said with a cracked voice.

She shook her head, still not believing what her ears and eyes told her. The man in front of her looked so much worse than she remembered him. It was absolutely impossible that this broken creature was her beloved Uncle Ernst.

"How?" she whispered.

"Katze kept me nearby to ensure your collaboration. Until... he didn't have further use for me when you got caught. I'm so happy to see you alive."

Margarete hugged her uncle, moving to the farthest end of the ramp, since it was always best not to be trapped in the middle of a mass of bodies. New energy surged through her veins, because whatever happened next, she wasn't alone anymore.

Two SS men strode toward the ramp, talking to the man guarding the exit. Margarete perked up her ears and caught snatches of their conversation. "Bomb damage... prisoners... clearing work."

Given the choice between going on a transport to Auschwitz or clearing rubble, she much preferred the latter one. She grabbed hold of Ernst's arm and whispered, "Stand up as straight as you can and look strong. We're going to get out of here." Then she drew near the SS officer, albeit keeping a safe distance, until one of them yelled, "We need twenty volunteers."

As usual, they didn't say what the volunteers were needed for, and even if they did, it probably was a lie, that much she'd learned from Zim. Therefore the crowd hesitated, yet Margarete didn't. She was willing to take the gamble based on what she'd overheard. Quickly closing the distance, she stepped in front of one of the SS men, adopting the submissive posture of a harassed Jew, as opposed to how she would have approached him if she were still Annegret, and said, "Herr Scharführer, we volunteer."

The man seemed pleased that she called him properly by his rank, at least until he noticed Uncle Ernst. "He's too old."

"Sir, that man is incredibly strong. You'll see."

Since not many people were taking up his offer for volunteers, and most of them didn't exactly look strong and healthy either, he shrugged. "What do I care. Assemble over there." He pointed to a space away from the ramp, away from the danger of a train taking them toward Auschwitz.

It seemed she had cheated death once again, at least for a

few more days, which was all she desperately yearned for right now.

Once twenty people had gathered, the SS man opened a gate and led them out of the pen. "Get in the van. *Schnell!*" he barked at them.

As soon as they had settled inside the dark furniture van, she squeezed Uncle Ernst's hand tightly, afraid she might have made the wrong choice.

"We'll be fine," he said as if reading her thoughts.

"How are you?" Margarete asked, pressing herself tight against him. It was such a relief to finally have an ally again, a person who she could trust implicitly.

"I'm so sorry for betraying you." His confession left her speechless, so that several seconds later he continued apparently needing to explain himself. "We all like to think we're stronger than we are. But I'm not made of sterner stuff, I'm just an old man who studied philosophy. In the end it became clear that I'm no hero and I told them anything they wanted to know, just to make the pain stop."

Margarete's heart flowed over with sympathy, remembering her own encounter with torture. If it hadn't been for Stefan's inexplicable appearance in her brain showing her a way out, she would have betrayed anyone and everyone herself.

Thomas had bragged about torturing her uncle to get the truth out of him, but until experiencing the same, the intractability when finding oneself in this situation hadn't really registered in her brain. "It wasn't your fault. Nobody can withstand the Gestapo's torture."

"Some do." Ernst smiled, apparently deep in thought. "I had the honor to meet some of the bravest souls, heroes who defied their captors to their last breath, hurling defiant words at their torturers, even under the most agonizing pain. I wasn't one of them. I succumbed. And I beg your forgiveness for that."

Margarete had never held it against her uncle that he'd told

Thomas her true identity. Indeed, the interrogation at Schulstrasse camp had proven the point that she wasn't cut from hero material either, and only her clever idea of accusing high-ranking Nazis of sexual crimes had saved her from betraying those she loved.

"There's nothing to forgive," she said, patting his hand. "Especially since Thomas' plot didn't work out the way he planned it. It may please you to hear that Horst Richter didn't believe him and sent Thomas to Mauthausen labor camp." She decided to omit the part of the story where Horst Richter had forced her to jump into the icy lake and she'd almost drowned, had it not been for Stefan... *Stefan,* her heart continued to ache with regret over arguing with him. If only she could tell him one more time how much she loved him. Unfortunately, that would most probably never happen. At least she sensed deep in her heart that he had returned to Gut Plaun unscathed, and for that she was immensely grateful.

"I find no pleasure in the misfortune of others, but I'm incredibly delighted to see you well and alive."

That she was well was an exaggeration, but she was alive, which was everything that counted these days.

"And now tell me how you ended up here?" Uncle Ernst asked.

She didn't want to dwell on her mistakes and merely said, "It boils down to trusting the wrong person. I thought she was a friend, but she was a Jewish woman who'd chosen to work for the Gestapo."

"Oh my dear." Uncle Ernst was genuinely shaken.

A short while later, the van stopped and they were herded outside, equipped with brooms and shovels, and ordered to clear the debris from the streets. It was tedious work, despite being in the lucky position of not having to carry fallen pieces of concrete like other groups of prisoners they saw.

Margarete made sure her uncle always had the lightest

work. In the evening, when she tried to give him some of her soup, he sternly shook his head.

"I appreciate that you want to take care of me, but you need to eat too."

"I ate well for the past years on Gut Plaun, so I can afford to fast a while."

"No you can't. We don't know how long this will last, so do me a favor and eat your portion."

Margarete took back the offered bowl, happy and sad at once. Hunger like she had never known before was nagging at her intestines, and despite her reassuring Ernst that she had enough reserves, she felt her strength dwindling every day. The sweeping that had seemed light work on the first day, had gradually evolved to being tiresome, grueling and all but impossible over the past weeks.

Working day after day from dawn to dusk, and huddling in bare shelters at night that didn't do anything against the biting cold, had worn her down and dampened her energy.

On their first day, every prisoner had been issued with a blanket, which was barely thicker than a bedsheet and certainly not adequate to keep them warm. Only huddling together with Ernst and another woman they'd made friends with, kept the worst of the cold at bay.

The days passed like an immemorable gray mass, time always passing too slowly, since every waking moment was an ordeal. Only at night, the hours rushed past with incredible speed. She always felt as if the guards came to wake them up again for another day of agony the very moment she fell asleep.

Without even noticing it, the old year ended and 1945 arrived, and with it whispers of an imminent Allied victory, bolstered by the absolute air supremacy of their bombers coming every night and every day to unload their deadly cargo on Hitler's capital of evil.

Then, one day in early January, the van usually taking them to yet another street in ruins, disgorged them onto a train ramp.

"What's going on? Where are we? Where are you taking us? Why?" Many voices spoke over each other, but as usual no answer was given.

The ramp filled with desperate people, all of them wearing the yellow star. Just when Margarete believed there was no room left for a single additional person, a locomotive puffed into the station, pulling a dozen or more cattle cars.

The blood draining from her face, she grabbed Uncle Ernst's hand and said, "That's it. This will be our final trip."

He had physically weakened over the past weeks up to a point that he seemed to be a mere shadow floating in the air, yet he had retained his wits. "It's not over until it's over."

"Then we'd better hang on." Margarete sighed.

"Where are we going?" one younger girl asked as they were herded into the cars.

"Auschwitz. Make your peace with God. You'll be seeing him shortly," a man replied from the midst of the car.

Margarete saw the resignation and defeat on the girl's face and closed her eyes, knowing the sentiment was probably reflected in her own eyes. This was it. She only hoped she could face death with the same courage that had helped her pretend to be Annegret for so long, since she didn't want to die a coward.

33

Stefan often felt like the last man standing. The only man fit for military service still at Gut Plaun, and the only person still actively working for the resistance. After his grandfather's death he'd made cautious inquiries and had found out that Sandra, the organizer of this part of the escape line, had been sent to a camp.

Now it was just Dora and himself. He knew she had some contacts in town, although he never asked who and what exactly she did, the same way that she never asked about his true activities in the factory, where he was sabotaging the ammunition production.

With Franz Volkmer and most of the German foremen drafted, it had become so much easier, because he could do as he wished. Still, he needed to be careful, not for fear of being discovered, but because he didn't want to risk any innocent lives. The chemicals were dangerous, and he had to take great care not to end up injuring or even killing the workers because of his sabotage work. He wanted to shorten the war, not become the prisoners' worst nightmare.

He'd thrown himself into work like a madman, for the sole

reason to dull the heartache he felt. Missing Margarete like he would miss a limb, he mostly avoided having idle time on his hands that would allow his thoughts to linger on her. Deep in his heart, he still felt that intense connection between them, giving him hope that she might still be alive, although he preferred not to go there.

After a long day of work, he walked up to the manor to use Oliver's office to order new raw materials, when a loud clopping sound caught his attention. He turned in the direction of the stables and as he rounded a corner, he witnessed several horses being coaxed into waiting trailers.

"What's going on here?" he asked one of the Wehrmacht soldiers.

"We're taking the horses with us," the soldier answered.

Meanwhile a completely overwhelmed Ladislaus sidled up to Stefan. "Thank God you arrived. These men won't listen to me. Perhaps you can tell them that these horses aren't broken in yet. They won't be of any use for the Wehrmacht."

Stefan had no experience with horses. Nevertheless he nodded. "I can try." Though secretly he doubted the soldiers would listen to him any more than they had to Ladislaus.

"Sir, may I have a word?" He approached the highest-ranking officer.

"Who are you?"

"I'm the manager of Gut Plaun." He purposefully omitted that he was only responsible for the nitropenta factory. With a nod to Ladislaus he added, "My stable hand just told me that your men are taking all the horses. They haven't been properly trained and according to our contracts—"

"Those contracts are null and void. My orders come from the very top. We need every able-bodied horse, and we need it now."

"Sir, with all due respect, half of the mares have been bred,"

Ladislaus said in his thick Polish accent, his gaze directed downward.

"Who's that foreigner? And why does he think he can speak to me?" the officer asked.

"I'm so very sorry," Stefan chimed in. "Since our stable manager was drafted we have been using foreign workers to keep the stud working. He's their foreman, because he also speaks German."

"He's still a bloody Slav and has no right to talk to me."

"I beg your pardon. It won't happen again." Stefan gave Ladislaus a sign to move out of sight, since it was best to avoid a further altercation with the Wehrmacht officer. "Can you at least leave the brood mares with us?"

"I'm afraid my orders don't give me the liberty to say otherwise. You should be proud of every horse that serves in the total war for the ultimate victory."

"We certainly are. We at Gut Plaun always strive to serve the Fatherland the best we can." Those were the words Annegret always said on the occasions she had to deal with Nazi officials. Once again, he sensed an immediate connection with her, just by using her words. It was both comforting and disturbing. He still regretted not having tried harder to convince her not to go to meet Thea. At least he should have accompanied her, or intervened when she was arrested... *Please forgive me, my darling. I should have protected you,* he thought, riddled with guilt.

"*Sieg Heil,*" the soldier saluted, and Stefan had no other choice but to return the salute.

It didn't take long until all the horses, except for a few foals were loaded and the last trailer rolled down the driveway, leaving nothing but a waft of dust behind. As soon as the vehicles were out of sight, Ladislaus returned to the yard, shaking his head.

"I'm sorry, there was nothing I could do," Stefan said.

"Now what?" Ladislaus indicated the dozen prisoners who had been assigned to the stud. "What will happen to them?"

Stefan knew they feared being transferred to some camp supervised by the SS. "They'll stay, of course. Ask Nils if he needs help around the house and garden. If not they can work in the factory until spring arrives, when we will need the hands for the farm and orchard."

"Can we still sleep here?" one of the other prisoners asked.

Stefan wondered when and by whom he'd been nominated the lord of the manor. Perhaps it had been inevitable, since Ladislaus was a foreigner and Nils, while good with his hands, lacked the intellect to oversee the business side of things. "I don't see why not. Just make sure to always appear busy in case someone comes to check up on us."

Ladislaus grinned. "Even with the horses gone, there's more than enough work for us to do. For starters, the stables need plenty of repairs."

"You're a good man. We're lucky to have you."

"Herr Stober, may I ask a question?"

"Sure."

"What happened truly to Fräulein Annegret?"

Everyone at Gut Plaun had been fed the same lie: that Annegret had met old friends in Berlin, and, bored with the country life, had decided to stay with them for a while.

"She's with friends," Stefan hedged. He had no reason to doubt Ladislaus' loyalty, but the fewer people knew about her real identity, the better. Even now.

"Is she...? I mean, is she alright? She's such a nice person and we all want her to be safe."

Stefan shook his head. "I can't say for sure, but I doubt she'll ever return."

"That's a shame." Ladislaus turned to leave, then looked back and said, "For what it's worth, when all of this is over, if she or anyone on Gut Plaun needs my help..."

"Thank you. I really appreciate that. Let's hope the war ends sooner rather than later." With these words, Stefan left the stables and headed for the manor to make some much needed phone calls to suppliers of raw material for the factory.

There, another unwelcome visitor waited for him.

"Oberscharführer Katze, what brings you here?" Stefan asked, despite having expected his visit since the day Margarete had disappeared. Not wanting to risk an altercation with the SS man, for the past two months Stefan had sent Nils to Parchim, delivering the bribe under the guise of sending papers to be signed and authenticated. This month he'd on purpose not sent the bribe to find out what would happen. Perhaps he could convince Katze to agree to a lesser amount.

"At the factory I was told you'd be up here. Are you the new estate manager now?" Katze asked.

"No. I was kindly allowed to use the office for dealing with suppliers, since all the documentation is up here. It was easier than moving the papers down to the factory." Stefan itched to knock out Katze's teeth, since his greed was ultimately the reason for Margarete's arrest. Without his callous blackmail, they wouldn't have needed to go to Berlin to sell the jewelry and then she wouldn't have met Thea... But it was futile to think about what could have been.

"Let's go in this office anyway and have a chat in private," Katze said.

"As you wish, Oberscharführer Katze." Stefan led him along the hallway, past the kitchen, where Dora and Frau Mertens were preparing dinner. As they entered Oliver's office he offered, "Please have a seat. Shall I get you something to drink?"

"That won't be necessary." Katze closed the door, before he gazed around the office. "Nice place."

"You haven't been here before?" Stefan was genuinely surprised.

"No, unfortunately I haven't had the opportunity yet.

Fräulein Annegret preferred to come to my office in Parchim, which is so much bigger than this one here."

If the situation weren't so sinister, Stefan would have laughed out loud at Katze's ridiculous need to have the biggest, greatest, and most beautiful of everything. He purposefully didn't say a word and rather enjoyed the discomfort in Katze's face.

Finally, the other man cleared his throat. "Your employer and I had an agreement and I have come to collect my dues."

"I'm sorry, Fräulein Annegret didn't leave any instructions for me. Does it concern the factory?" Stefan decided to play stupid and see if Katze would give him any leverage.

"It certainly does. She was very keen on exemptions for certain indispensable workers. I'm a man with a soft heart." Katze uttered the lie without batting an eyelid. "Therefore I helped her, but these things are very costly, if you understand."

Stefan opened his eyes wide to pretend he was shocked. "I can't believe Fräulein Annegret condoned bribing someone. I certainly don't."

Katze seemed confused, though he quickly regained his composure and said, "I'll be frank with you. No monthly payment, no more exemptions for your Jewish workers."

Something in Katze's eyes emboldened Stefan to take the gamble a bit further. "I'm afraid I don't have access to money that's not in the books, if you understand? Perhaps you should ask Fräulein Annegret personally? She's staying with friends in Berlin."

"That's what they made you believe?" Katze made a comical grimace.

Stefan nodded, speculating whether Katze knew she'd been arrested.

"Ha. Nothing could be further from the truth. That stupid Jew was arrested by the Gestapo."

Cold shivers ran down Stefan's spine, yet he managed to

school his features, playing the innocent. "What Jew are you talking about? The only ones I know of are prisoners in the factory."

"Fräulein Annegret. Your precious lady of the manor was in fact a Jew."

Widening his eyes Stefan groused, "Fräulein Annegret a Jew? How dare you accuse her of such a horrible thing? She's from one of the most esteemed families in the area. Aryan more than six generations down. She has the most stellar genealogical tree you have ever seen. There's a drawing somewhere in the library, I can show you—"

Katze interrupted him with a wave of his hand. "You're a dumb bloke. The woman that came here after the oh-so-tragic death of her family never was Annegret Huber, but a vile impostor. A Jewish bitch posing as her."

Obviously Stefan had known this all along, yet, he called out, scandalized, "Are you sure?"

"Sure as hell I am!"

"Such a heinous deed! I barely met her a year ago. But I simply can't imagine how she got away with such a deceit, pulling the wool over the eyes of the townspeople and the employees who knew her as a child," Stefan deliberately said.

"And yet she did. Which just proves that Jews are cunning and lying scum. Though she couldn't fool me." Katze gloated. "I immediately smelled a rat."

As far as Stefan knew Thomas had been the one to expose her, while his subaltern Katze took advantage of the situation to blackmail Annegret once his former boss was out of the way. That knowledge gave him an idea. "How did you even find out, when she fooled everyone else?"

"Well," Katze put on an important face, obviously proud of his achievement. "For someone with my skills and my connections it wasn't all that hard. I suspected her from the moment she stepped onto Gut Plaun. But since that Gestapo officer

Richter was protecting her, I couldn't investigate too obviously. Suffice to say that her uncle finally gave her away. Her own uncle! A squalid Jew who had no qualms betraying his family to save his own miserable life."

Stefan balled his hands into fists, since he had a pretty good idea of the torture inflicted on Margarete's uncle, before he'd succumbed and spilled the beans. "I am speechless and distressed. How could I not have noticed?"

"It's not your fault to be so naïve, that's what the SS is for, to expose the criminals in our midst. But enough of that, your employer is no more—the Gestapo surely has sent her to Auschwitz by now." Katze lowered his voice to a conspiratorial whisper. "It seems you're the boss of the estate now, with no one to oversee your actions. What do you say we team up? I give you all the papers and documentation you need to keep running the factory, and in exchange we divide the profit fifty-fifty?"

Stefan said nothing for several seconds, quickly assessing the situation and how he could use it to his advantage. Lothar Katze was as dumb as he was greedy, and a coward on top. If Stefan played his cards carefully, he could get rid of the black-mail once and for all. "So you knew all along that this woman was a Jew pretending to be the heiress Annegret Huber?"

Katze preened and nodded. "Yes. She tried to fool me but I figured it out."

"How long ago?" Stefan inquired softly.

"Does it matter?"

"Just humor me. I'm curious because I never had a clue that she was anyone other than she appeared to be."

"I have known for almost a year, actually," Katze confirmed.

"Uh huh. And you never told anyone else about your knowledge? Never reported her to your superiors?" Stefan asked, his voice getting softer even as his expression hardened. When Katze opened his mouth to defend himself, Stefan shook his head and held up a finger, silencing him. "Let me clarify this for you and you can nod if you understand. You, an SS Ober-scharführer, hid the knowledge of a Jew impersonating a very notable young lady. A lady who was also in charge of a muni-tions factory tasked with making weapons to help in the war effort?

"Instead of turning her in and preventing her from causing unimaginable damage to our Fatherland, you decided to black-mail her for your own personal gain." Stefan shook his head and mocked, "Not very sporting of you, keeping that knowledge all to yourself." He paused, observing the light of understanding creeping into Katze's eyes. "So, this is how we will proceed, you and I. You will leave Gut Plaun right now and never return. You will not collect any more bribes from the Gut or the factory. You will not mess with the exemptions in place, nor will you attempt to deport even one of the prisoners currently assigned to my factory."

Katze once again tried to interrupt, but Stefan simply kept talking over him. "If you ever try to extort money from us again, I will personally go to the Gestapo headquarters in Berlin and report you. I will tell them how you had knowledge and kept it to yourself and how you were blackmailing the estate." He met Katze's eyes, recognizing the fear lingering there. "How long do you think you'd last during a Gestapo interrogation?"

Katze swallowed heavily and shook his head. "I don't think we'll need to find out."

Stefan smiled sardonically. "It's in your hands whether you will. Good day."

Katze scrambled from his chair and almost ran out of the office. Stefan watched from the window as the man raced to his car and left the premises with screeching tires.

"I guess we won't have to worry about the money to pay him after all," he muttered to himself. "I only wish Margarete had been here to see her nemesis taken down so easily." Although if she'd still been at Gut Plaun, he wouldn't have been able to pull it off. This way her arrest had at least amounted to one good thing. Because now he could use the remaining money from the jewelry sale for the subversive activities of hiding people and smuggling them out of Germany, rather than bribing a vile Nazi.

Feeling morose, Stefan left the office and decided to head out to the lake on his boat, since he needed to calm his mind. Fishing always had that effect on him, whatever the time of the year.

34

Oliver was so tired of fighting. Of seeing bodies littering the streets and hearing the wounded cry piteously. Years ago he'd stopped believing in Hitler's vision of a unified Europe under the leadership of Germany. Margarete had opened his eyes to the plight of the Jews and Hitler's abhorrent idea to extirpate an entire race from the face of the earth.

Nothing in this war was worth fighting for, even worse, the Wehrmacht didn't stand a chance. All the talk about ultimate victory was just that: talk. The Wehrmacht was getting crushed: men, material, even the animals spent, depleted, with no way for them to be replaced, whereas the Russians seemed to have an unlimited supply of, if not soldiers, then at least tanks and artillery.

Oliver's unit fought with guns and the odd *Panzerfaust*, an anti-tank rocket launcher, against tanks or the Katyusha rocket launcher, nicknamed "Stalin's organ". A defeat was inevitable and every day of fighting simply served to produce more dead and maimed. More young men deprived of their future, more widows, more orphans, more suffering.

Ultimately it seemed Germany turned the war on their

own, because instead of fighting against the enemy, they had been moving across the land from town to town, searching homes and basements for stragglers, hanging them from the next lamppost for "cowardice in front of the enemy".

Families were herded outside, all "able-bodied men", including twelve-year-old boys and half-blind grandfathers, were conscripted on the spot. Forced to join their unit, without a uniform or bullets for their guns—if they were even issued one.

It was worse than a nightmare come true. Yet, Oliver stayed the course, because like almost every human being, he was self-ish. His goal was to return to his beloved Dora, little Julia and the unborn baby. So he followed his orders, no matter how stupid or senseless they were.

"Sweep the town," barked the leader of their ragtag bunch, that hadn't received replacements for the killed and injured men.

Oliver sighed as he and his comrades began walking through the town. Out of necessity, they'd taken to doing house searches on their own when usually they were supposed to go in pairs. An elderly woman opened the door, fear in her eyes. Her frail frame spoke of the deprivation she was enduring.

"Are there any stragglers, Jews, or other subjects hiding in your house or on your premises?"

"No," she answered, grabbing the door with both hands to steady herself.

"I need to look and verify that for myself," Oliver told her as nicely as possible. Unlike some of his comrades, he didn't see any benefit in destroying or stealing material possessions while searching for hidden rooms or doorways. Because he much preferred not finding anyone in hiding, he undertook only a superfluous search each time.

"Thank you, that will be all," he said to the old woman as he left her house. Then he continued on, searching house by house, until he came to a large farm property at the edge of town. There he met with several comrades who'd been assigned different streets in town.

"Anyone?" their leader asked.

"No. Nothing. This village is clean," one man said.

"Only old women left, it looks like everyone else fled weeks ago."

"Evacuation of civilians is forbidden. There are orders that everyone has to shelter in place until we have halted the Russian advance and thrown the Red Army back behind the border."

Oliver thought this statement was bordering on delusional, since nobody in their right mind could actually believe the depleted Wehrmacht might recapture even a single town in these useless final battles.

He sympathized with every woman living in one of the East Prussian villages threatened to be overrun by the Red Army in the near future who sought her luck in the escape. A horrid thought occurred to him. What if the Russians captured Plau am See? What would happen to Dora and little Julia?

He squinted his eyes for a second, willing Dora to stay safe. Then he relaxed. She was Ukrainian and spoke some Russian. If she told the Red Army soldiers that she had been abducted by the Germans, they might just let her be.

That thought calmed him. Dora might never have enjoyed a formal education, but she possessed a shrewdness that would serve her well in her fight for survival. And she had Annegret by her side, who arguably was the most cunning person he knew —though in a good way. If anyone was going to get out of the war unscathed, it was her.

"I can't believe you didn't find a single hidden person. What bunch of useless idiots you are! Search again, and this time more thoroughly!" their leader barked, visibly agitated.

Oliver wondered why he was so keen on wasting their time

to search for civilians, when their actual duty was to fight the enemy.

"Search every square inch of this sorry place," the officer commanded as he organized them into pairs.

Oliver and his partner headed for the cowshed. "This is a total waste of time," he complained.

"It's not. Finding the deserters teaches a lesson to others and helps keep morale high," his comrade answered.

In spite of having a different opinion, Oliver nodded. He opened the door to the cowshed, peeking inside. There was a woman in wellington boots, who jerked around when she saw them.

"What are you doing here?" his comrade asked.

"Checking on the cows."

"At this time of day?"

"Let her be," Oliver said, trying to drag him outside.

"Nah. She's hiding something, I know it."

"What could she possibly hide here?"

"That is our duty to find out." His comrade went on to search through the shed, without finding anything. In a foul mood, he left the barn. Outside they came across other comrades who shouted at them, "In the hay barn. The boss says there's someone up there hiding beneath the straw. We found a prisoner's discarded clothing behind the bushes."

"Really? These people should know better than to hide escapees from the camps."

Oliver didn't join the conversation. He silently took the hay fork that was handed to him and went upstairs to stick it into the bales, under which supposedly someone was hiding, although he took great care not to dig too deep in case there really was someone there.

He certainly had no intention of finding and killing an escaped prisoner. As he moved toward the back, he thought he heard a noise and immediately thereafter his fork struck something. Instead of probing deeper, he removed the fork from the hay and took a big step to cross whatever, or whoever was there. If indeed people were hiding beneath the hay, they would be shot on sight, along with the young woman offering them shelter and everyone else who lived in the house.

The prospect of such a senseless bloodbath was more than Oliver could stand. So, he quickly finished his row and called out, "There's nothing here. Let's go, we're only wasting our time."

Since nobody was too keen on chasing elusive prisoners, they retreated and reported to their officer. "All checked. The barn is clean."

"There must be someone!" the officer screamed. "I can smell a Jew from a mile away. And this place stinks!"

"We could leave to make them believe they are safe, but post a guard and catch them as soon as they try to slink away under the cover of the night," someone suggested.

"What if we're wasting our time?" Oliver asked in an effort to lead his unit away.

"What's your urgency to get away? Are you in cahoots with the Jews?" his officer asked.

"Certainly not, sir," Oliver protested.

"Then, I guess you won't object to searching the barn again. We won't leave this place before we have found them."

With that said, the entire unit was tasked to leave no stone— or hay bale—unturned, and as their leader had predicted, about half an hour later, two escaped Jewish prisoners, both female, were dragged out.

A vile gleam entered the officer's eyes as he turned toward Oliver. "You'll shoot them."

"But... why me?" Oliver recoiled at the idea of having to shoot two civilians whose only crime was to be Jewish.

"This way you can prove your loyalty."

"They... they are civilians."

"They are Jews. Escaped Jews. They are a danger for the public health and safety. Or are you a friend of the Jews?"

"Certainly not, sir." Oliver was shivering. He could not—he would not—kill these two young women in cold blood.

"Then, what are you waiting for? Shoot them!"

Oliver wracked his brain to find a way out, but all his possible solutions were flawed. Finally he gave a resigned nod, while training his gun at the escapees. "Get over there." He beckoned them toward a copse of trees. When they passed him by, he hissed at them, "When I shoot, fall down and pretend to be dead."

Then he aimed and fired two shots. Both women dropped to the ground like felled trees. He turned around and walked over to his unit leader, declaring, "Mission accomplished."

"Well done," his officer said, and then called out to the two youngest men in the unit. "You two go and get the corpses, we'll nail them to the door for everyone to witness what happens to those who escape from the camps."

Oliver felt the blood draining from his head, because he knew his two comrades wouldn't find the corpses. At least the two youngsters didn't have weapons, so he hoped the two women would have had a chance to escape.

Minutes later the two returned, "Sir, we couldn't find anyone. No trace of a person, living or dead."

"What?" the unit leader screamed, before he turned toward Oliver, his furious grimace proof that he knew what Oliver had done. "You... you are a traitor. And you'll get what you deserve."

He raised his weapon and before Oliver even knew what happened, the world around him went black. His last thought was with his beloved Dora and their little girl.

35

The train arrived at what Margarete presumed to be the infamous Auschwitz, yet everything was so different from what she had expected. Usually the Germans were exceptionally orderly, having everything under control. From all her experiences with the Nazis, she'd imagined that the business of killing hundreds of thousands would be no different, an efficient, streamlined process running like a well-oiled machine without the slightest hiccup.

Not so here at the ramp, since it seemed as if the entire camp was in a state of utter chaos. SS, guards and prisoners, presumably Kapos, were barking orders, assembling groups of inmates that marched along the train ramp to whatever destination.

Margarete had never been to an actual camp before, except for the one attached to her own munitions factory, but she knew that this was completely out-of-the-ordinary. Something huge was happening. Fear coursed through her veins, making her knees tremble. She grabbed Uncle Ernst's hand tighter, as much for his benefit as for hers. Whatever was happening here, she feared having to face it alone.

Though it seemed nobody attended to the recent arrivals, not even the SS usually so apt in herding the Jews to their final destiny. Frantically searching with her eyes for someone, anyone, to ask what was happening, she froze in place, when a shot rang through the air.

"Assemble in rows of five!" an SS guard shouted.

After a moment of shock, the mass of people recently disgorged from the train, scrambled about like a frightened flock of rabbits. Margarete dragged Uncle Ernst behind her, instinctively seeking protection in the middle of the row of five.

Ernst though, who'd been weak before boarding that cursed train, barely managed to stay upright on his legs. A crazed expression, caused by maddening thirst had taken hold of his face and he tugged at her hand like an unruly toddler, wanting to get away from his mother.

"Please, Uncle Ernst, we have to stay together," Margarete whispered with a hoarse voice. Throughout their journey of several days, the only water they'd drunk had been the condensation they'd licked from the wall of the cattle car.

Now the snow at the other side of the ramp looked alluring, but from the twisted corpses lying there, she understood that any attempt to reach the tempting liquid would result in being shot.

As soon as the crowd had assembled in a sufficient order, one of the guards commanded them to march through the main gate into the camp. As soon as she passed beneath the wrought iron with the inscription *"Arbeit macht frei"*, work brings freedom, a dreadful chill ran down her spine, a harbinger of unspeakable things to come.

"Form rows of three!" The next order came, causing a ruckus as the mass of depleted walking dead somehow reorganized itself. They seemed to undergo some kind of inspection, because left and right stood SS guards, picking prisoners from the crowd, ordering them someplace else.

As she and Ernst approached the guards, heavy goose-bumps erupted on her arms. She fought with herself to stand straight, keep her shoulders back and not let anyone know how horrified she was.

"You! Out!" the guard shouted as her line had reached him.

Barely able to keep her legs from giving out under her, she forced them to change into the direction he was indicating.

"Not you, stupid bitch! Him!" This time there was no doubt he meant Uncle Ernst.

Fearing for the worst, she begged, "Please, he's my uncle. We need to stay together."

For a split-second something like empathy seemed to cross the guard's eyes, before the stone-cold gaze returned. "He's much too frail, he has to stay."

Uncle Ernst was too delirious to utter a word, merely following the orders. Margarete watched him walk a few steps before he slumped on the frozen ground to join a group of equally spent prisoners, all of them more dead than alive. Only then, did he raise his face to send a smile in Margarete's direction and voicelessly mouthed the words, "I love you. Stay strong."

Desperation hit her deep in her guts. In this very moment, the last thing she wanted was to be strong. In fact she wished to drop down next to him and face whatever awaited her alongside a beloved family member.

Soon the forward motion of the crowd came to a stop, as more decrepit creatures emerged from the barracks on the far side of the huge square. Whenever a sufficiently big group was assembled they turned to march out of the exit gate to an unknown destination.

"We need to hurry up, or they'll catch us red-handed," she overheard an SS guard say to his colleague. Still speculating what he meant by his words, her group of new arrivals was ordered to join a group of old hands in slightly better condition than the rest.

Still crazed with thirst, Margarete used the opportunity to catch a handful of snow in an unguarded moment and shoved it into her mouth. The cold substance melted, moistening her tongue, gums and cheeks until a few drops ran down her parched throat.

It wasn't enough to satiate her thirst, yet it revived her determination to stay alive, despite the recent blow of being separated from Uncle Ernst. As they marched on toward an unknown destiny, she realized that to survive she needed to focus all her energy entirely on each next step and push everything else out of her mind. Whatever was going to happen to her, would happen whether she fretted about it or not. So it was wise to conserve the little energy she possessed.

The roadside was littered with emaciated corpses of those who hadn't been able to withstand the hardships. Their legs and arms twisted unnaturally, most of them with a red hole at the back of their heads.

She took her eyes off the macabre scene, vowing not to become another Jewish corpse that no one would ever mourn.

36

"Dora," Frau Mertens pronounced her name so hesitantly that Dora knew instantly something was terribly wrong. "There's a telegram for you."

A dreadful sense of foreboding attacked Dora as she stared at the envelope in Frau Mertens' hand, unable to move, or even to breathe.

During the past months the middle-aged housekeeper and the young maid had become more like mother and daughter, while they were jointly running the household at Gut Plaun, feeding dozens of forced workers employed at the stud, along with women from town helping out with whatever work was needed in exchange for something to eat.

Frau Mertens doted on little Julia as if she was her grand-child and mothered Dora who was now heavily pregnant with her second child, although she still had about six more weeks before the baby was due.

Seeing that Dora was frozen in shock, Frau Mertens asked, with a sympathetic voice, "Shall I open it for you?"

It could be anything, Dora told herself, though deep in her heart she knew that telegrams were only sent for two reasons: killed in action or missing in action. "No, I'll open it."

She took the envelope and opened it, her mind not truly comprehending what was written on the paper, until her eyes got caught on the word "killed".

"No!" Dora cried out, even as she was overcome by faintness and fell to the floor. Coming to, she sneezed heavily, because Frau Mertens was holding a flask of smelling salts beneath her nose.

"Are you feeling better?" the housekeeper asked, visibly worried.

"I don't know if I'll ever feel better again in my entire life," Dora murmured, deprived of the energy to fight against the huge, black hole threatening to swallow her whole. It felt like a maelstrom tugging at her soul, wanting to rip it from her body. A sweet promise to sink into the darkness and follow her beloved husband into eternity.

"You must get up." Frau Mertens' words didn't make an impression on her. She wouldn't know how to use her legs to follow the order, even if she wanted to. The hard kitchen floor was strangely cozy, tempting her to stay curled up like a toddler, never having to face the debilitating grief.

She was about to give in to the temptation, when a sharp pain in her abdomen caused her to scream.

"What happened Dora? Are you hurt?"

"No. Just..." She took Frau Mertens outstretched hand, letting the older woman help her up. Just as soon as she stood on her wobbly legs, she gasped and crumpled over. A vicious contraction stole her breath and moments later she felt liquid running down her legs. Unable to utter a word, she bent forward, bracing herself against the kitchen table, welcoming the physical pain because of its promise to drown out her overwhelming grief.

"Oh dear! Your waters have broken. It's much too early for

the baby to come." Frau Mertens, who usually ruled the household with a calm hand, showed hectic red spots on her cheeks. "I'll take you to your room and send Nils for the midwife."

Dora didn't care. Whatever happened next didn't concern her, since her soul had retreated into itself, refusing to acknowledge that Oliver was dead. That her beloved husband would never return home to see her and Julia again, or to meet his soon-to-be born child.

She didn't even worry about the baby that was much too early to see the light of day on this dreary, cold day of January 1945. All she wanted was to blissfully forget the world around her, and the excruciating pain of each contraction was strangely exactly what she needed. As far as she was concerned, the labor could last forever.

The next few hours passed in a blur. Dora barely registered the arrival of the midwife, more or less automatically obeying her orders, while her soul sobbed for the loss of the love of her life. Only when the midwife cut the umbilical cord and pressed a tiny baby into her arms with the words, "It's a boy. Small but healthy," did she return to this world, looking at the little man in awe.

"He's so beautiful," Dora whispered.

"Yes, he is."

Delighted with her son's striking blue eyes and the small shock of blond hair, tears stung her eyes, and she vowed to protect her children with all her might.

Silently she conversed with Oliver. *My dearest husband. This is your son. I hope, wherever you are you can watch over him. Please know that I loved you with all my heart and will never stop doing so.*

One by one Frau Mertens, Nils, Gloria, and the regular employees of Gut Plaun entered the room to admire the newborn. It seemed that during these days filled with gloom, everyone delighted in the arrival of an innocent soul on this earth.

"Have you thought of a name yet?" Frau Mertens asked.

Dora had pondered many names throughout the last months, but in this instant she tossed them all aside and said, "His name shall be Oliver, because he looks so much like his father."

"I think that's a wonderful tribute," Frau Mertens agreed, visibly moved. "You get some rest. Meanwhile I'll cook a hearty chicken broth for you."

Dora smiled, since the housekeeper's medicine for all ailments, ranging from broken limbs, a severe cold or emotional distress, was always chicken broth. "I'd love to have some, the birth was quite exhausting."

Two days after little Oliver's birth, Dora ventured into the kitchen and insisted on resuming her duties.

"Nonsense," Frau Mertens said. "With Fräulein Annegret staying with friends, and most of the men drafted, there's not much to do anyway. You stay in your room and recover your strength."

"Thank you." Dora wasn't going to argue, since she was still grappling with her grief.

"I'm afraid we'll need our strength sooner than we all would like," Frau Mertens muttered as she shooed Dora out of the kitchen, thus reinforcing Dora's own fears of the Red Army. At this point it wasn't a matter of if, but only of when they arrived. By then she hoped to be sufficiently recovered to face whatever they had in store for her, although she prayed she wouldn't have to endure the atrocious rapes she'd heard about.

Perhaps it was high time to polish up her Russian language skills as her friend Olga had suggested. Then the soldiers might spare her.

37

Ernst was too feverish to care what happened to him. When Margarete had marched out of the gate, he'd stared after her for what might well have been hours. With her, the last shred of his zest for life had left him, and not even the thought of his beloved wife Heidi was able to rekindle the flame of life that was slowly dying within him.

One man, whom he'd met several times in the prison prior to his deportation, stumbled down beside him, just to crawl onerously onto all fours.

"Ernst Rosenbaum? That you?"

"Yes." Ernst didn't have the energy to waste words.

"We need to get up and go inside, or we'll freeze to death."

In spite of sitting on the frozen ground, Ernst was bathed in sweat. His entire body was burning up from within, yet he couldn't make himself care. If it was up to him he'd simply stay in this very place, patiently waiting until eternity claimed him.

Robert, though, had different plans. "I heard there's an abandoned SS warehouse up that way, with food inside."

"Really?" Ernst wavered between wanting to eat and

staying in the snow, since the food would only prolong his suffering.

"Yes. Come." Another prod got Ernst onto all fours, and for lack of strength to walk upright, the two men crawled side by side to the nearest hut, where they grabbed onto the wall to push themselves up.

"I can't anymore," Ernst said as soon as he stood on his feet. He peeked inside the mostly empty hut, where only a few moaning and groaning men remained, apparently too weak to leave their beds.

During the long ride in the cattle car, Ernst had become accustomed to the putrid smell of feces mixed with sweat and fear, yet the stench he encountered inside the barracks caused him to retch. It was such a disgusting scent, he feared he might never cleanse himself from it, even if he lived to one hundred years.

Aware of the ridiculousness of his thoughts when he was much closer to dying within the next one hundred minutes, he inwardly shrugged and stumbled to the nearest bed.

"You stay here while I go and seek out the abandoned warehouse. Perhaps there's food," Robert said.

Ernst immediately fell into a feverish sleep, not caring about the world outside his head. He did not even feel his body anymore, as his spirit seemed to hover above it, looking down on the twisted, scarred, tired, hungry body that had long ceased to be a comfortable home for him.

When Robert returned, Ernst fought him tooth and nail, yet the other man somehow managed to sit him upright in the bunk and feed him with morsels of bread dunked into some richly-flavored sauce. It exploded on his taste buds, returning not only some energy into his body, but also long forgotten sensations of savoring a meal. This definitely wasn't the stuff the Nazis had fed their prisoners.

Yet, he was too weak to ask what it was, or even to care,

since all he wanted was to sink back against his mattress and sleep, which was exactly what he did, after devouring the food with the hunger no free man would ever feel.

Robert must have been exhausted from foraging in the SS store, because he fell next to him onto the bunk, securing the sack with precious food between their bodies and crouching together against the biting cold. Ernst woke up several times with the need to relieve himself, but was too weak to get up.

When he woke again he noticed the space next to him in the bunk was empty. Shortly after, he felt a mug held to his lips. The next thing he knew, there was a blanket covering his body and Robert by his side once more, although he had no recollection of how or when this had happened.

Ernst spent the next ten days in a feverish delirium, only interrupted by short bursts of consciousness, which Robert used to feed him hot soup and morsels of bread. During one of his wake moments, the door suddenly burst open and soldiers stormed inside. His initial reaction was to hide beneath the blanket, until he recognized their uniforms. The Red Army had arrived to liberate them.

Finally, Ernst's war was over.

The soldiers looked shocked to the core and more than one stormed outside with a green hue on his face, followed by retching noises soon after. Again, Robert was by Ernst's side, grinning from ear to ear. "You were in a delirium for exactly the ten days it took for the Red Army to arrive and liberate us. How do you feel?"

Apparently, the fever had broken, at least that's what Ernst assumed since he could focus and think clearly again. "So how did I survive?"

Robert looked around the hut, pointing at two comparatively sturdy looking prisoners. "They helped me to construct an oven. Once we got it running, we could heat the hut and cook soup from raided foodstuffs and melted snow."

Ernst gave a faint nod and wanted to thank his companion, when several prisoners came inside the hut.

"What's up?" Robert asked.

"Soviets ordered us to get everyone out of the barracks."

"Into the snow?"

"Yes. Blankets have to stay, too. Everything will be cleaned and disinfected, before people can return inside."

Ernst looked anxiously at the distance from his bunk to the door, but he needn't have worried, because two of the prisoners grabbed him under the shoulders and carried him outside.

To the side of the street lining an endless row of huts, corpses were thrown on piles that grew faster than another work detail could throw them onto wheelbarrows and take them to hastily dug mass graves. For a fleeting moment, Ernst feared they'd throw him atop the tower reaching way up into the sky so he made an effort to croak out, "I'm alive."

Nobody acknowledged his words, though they soon settled him on a patch of frozen earth. He wasn't the only one more dead than alive, either. The huge yard was filled with people, since the Soviets had tasked every walking prisoner with carrying their comrades outside, so that local Polish women could thoroughly clean the huts to avoid the further spread of diseases, lice, and whatever other ailments.

By some miracle, not much later, Robert arrived with two women in tow. They carried a huge pot of steaming hot broth and began distributing it to the sick.

Ernst was too weak to hold the bowl, so Robert spoon-fed him, until he had eaten the entire soup.

"Thank you." Ernst closed his eyes for a moment, since the mere act of eating had exhausted him. It took a while until the energy provided by the food reached his system, spreading a warm and cozy feeling into his limbs. Then he lifted his face toward the sky, suddenly aware of the biting cold, despite the glorious sunshine on his face. "Thank you for saving my life."

Robert smiled sheepishly. "Actually it was you who saved mine first."

"How so?"

"Back in the prison, I had given up on myself. You and your reading circle revived my will to survive."

"I'm glad I could help." Ernst gave him a genuine smile.

"Now, let's get you out of the cold. The Red Army has sent dozens of medical orderlies, food and clothes. Some of the stronger men have left already, despite the Soviets' orders to stay in the camp. Although, in your condition, I guess you'll have to stay anyway. Let me see if I can convince someone to admit you to the field hospital. Wait here." With these words, Robert walked away, leaving Ernst to himself once again. Even if he'd wanted, he wouldn't have found the energy to get up and walk a single step.

Not much later, Robert returned with two medics, who then carried Ernst to a makeshift hospital set up in one of the barracks that looked clean and smelled of disinfectant.

"I can't stay," Robert said.

"Don't worry about me, I'm in good hands. You go and find your family. Maybe one day we'll meet again." There was nothing else to be said, so Ernst raised a hand for a last goodbye to the stranger who'd stepped up in a time of need. Without Robert's determination, he wouldn't be alive today.

Under the care of the doctors, Ernst slowly regained his strength and his health over the next months. For the rest of his days, he'd walk with a slight limp, because the torture he'd endured at Thomas' hands had left him forever disfigured. But he was alive.

"When can I go home?" he asked one of the nurses several weeks after being liberated.

"Soon. Soon."

"When?"

"Soon. Soon." That was the only answer he ever got, until

he assumed the nurses, and doctors, and perhaps even the military command in charge of the former camp simply had no idea what to do with all the liberated prisoners.

He yearned to return home and find Heidi, although that seemed like it would have to wait until later. One day he had the chance to talk to a nurse who spoke passable German and he asked her, "Is the war finally over?"

"Not yet. While most of Poland has been liberated, the war is still raging on in Germany, and there's no way for you to go back there yet."

"For how long?"

"It's a matter of days, perhaps weeks. Not more."

It wasn't what he had wanted to hear. With no other options, though, he intended to use the time while he was stuck in the former camp to heal and rest. And as soon as the war was over, he'd move heaven and earth to return to Leipzig and find Heidi.

After everything he'd heard about the so-called death march of prisoners leaving Auschwitz before the Russians arrived, he harbored little hope that Margarete had survived. Nevertheless, once he was settled in Leipzig, he'd go about searching for her.

38

Almost a week had passed since the prisoners had been herded out of the camp and forced to march through snow and ice. Margarete had watched countless emaciated men and women stumble and fall down, or fail to get up after a rest. If they weren't already dead, the guards shot them, and forced the dwindling rest to continue.

She estimated that more than half of those who'd left the camp had already succumbed to the harsh conditions of walking endless hours without food and with only snow to drink. Most prisoners were clad in rags and wooden shoes that weren't in the slightest fit to withstand the cold.

Margarete herself still wore the same clothes she'd worn when the Gestapo had arrested her and was grateful for her sturdy shoes. Nonetheless, she had oozing sores on her feet, which turned the march into a never-ending agony.

On the second day she observed a comparatively well-fed old-time prisoner ravage a corpse for useful things. Disgusted, she looked away, but the scene wouldn't leave her mind.

During the day while marching she was too tired to think, let alone speak, but in the evening as they sought shelter in an empty barn, she sidled up to one of the women who always seemed to be well informed.

"Where do you think they'll take us?"

The other woman answered, "To another camp."

"But why?" The war was as good as over, that much was clear. The prisoners whispered of the Red Army being near, shelling the area around Auschwitz for weeks already.

"Are you really that naïve? To kill us all, of course."

Margarete barely suppressed a shocked gasp. "But... why not leave us in Auschwitz then?"

"Because with three of the crematoria razed, they can't kill us fast enough to hide the evidence."

Margarete grabbed the blanket that every prisoner had been given at departure tighter around herself as she felt a chill sweeping her soul. It was one thing to hear about the atrocities from boasting Nazis and assume the rest, but sitting here, witnessing hundreds of people around her dying on a daily basis, and hearing this woman matter-of-factly state the master plan of killing an entire race was a different thing altogether.

"They force us to march day in day out, just so they can kill us when we reach another camp?" she asked with a feeble voice.

The remark earned her a hard stare. "How did you survive this long with that attitude? Here we fight for every minute, every hour, every day."

Margarete ashamedly looked downward. When had she become so fatalistic?

"Take this advice: in the camps there's no humanity, no kindness, no friendship, not even hope. Once you've been inside this death machine for long enough, the only thing still alive in you is your instinct for survival. You form alliances, not out of a sense of amicability, but because the other person can help you survive, and vice versa. So if I were you, I'd start this very moment to fight for the next minute and the next..." With these words, she turned her head away, indicating that the conversation was over.

Margarete, though, had a lot of food for thought to chew on. She huddled together with a group of women to share each other's warmth, and while the others one by one fell into an exhausted sleep, interrupted by nightmares, she stayed awake staring into the darkness. The air was filled with noise: coughing, wheezing, sneezing, screaming, and murmuring of hundreds of tortured souls.

Her mind wandered back to Plau am See and to Stefan. If only she could see him one more time, run her hand through his flaxen hair, see the irresistible smile on his lips, feel the warmth of his hand on her skin, tell him how sorry she was for their argument... and how much she loved him.

In that instant she felt a sudden connection with him, as if his soul had reached out to hers across hundreds of miles and she knew without the shadow of a doubt that he was still alive. He just couldn't be dead, his unwavering determination, his zest for life, his resilience, all the traits she loved so much, would enable him to withstand whatever fate threw at him.

The image of him opening his arms to embrace her caused a surge of new energy to course through her veins. Yes, she would fight every minute of this horrid march, fight to survive so she could return to his side. He was worth every pain, every horrid experience, everything.

The next morning a drastically shrunken group of prisoners reached a train station, where everyone was herded onto open cattle carts. Margarete welcomed the prospect of not having to march any longer until she realized that the train ride merely exchanged the agony of marching with the one of huddling unsheltered in wind and weather. All around her, people died of the biting cold, literally frozen to death.

At that point in her journey, Margarete was past showing piety for anyone but herself and followed the example of those barely alive to build a barrier of corpses against the biting airstream. Together with three others she snuggled inside that little cave, praying to God that this, too, would pass. If only she made it to wherever this train was destined.

During short intervals when she could think clearly, she realized that it had been a blessing in disguise for Ernst to have been left at Auschwitz. With the crematoria razed, and most—if not all—SS guards on the march, her uncle might actually have a better chance at survival there. At least she hoped so.

Three agonizing days later, she dropped her head on a bunk in a camp on top of a hill.

Three days later without being given food and only rain to drink, she heard artillery shelling in the distance, followed by hurried steps and shouting. Curious, she got up from her bunk to see for herself if this was the long-awaited liberation. Peeking out of the hut, she saw absolutely nothing. The huge courtyard was empty. As the minutes ticked away, more and more prisoners came outside, Margarete with them, until she finally noticed the difference: the guards were missing.

Apparently they had fled as soon as the Red Army reached the village down below the camp. Unsure what to expect, most of the inmates settled on the ground waiting for their destiny. It took only a few hours, before the first soldiers of the Red Army arrived.

The prisoners who spoke Russian engaged with them and soon enough word got round that the war for all inmates was finally over. Those who were healthy enough danced in the street, hugging each other and their liberators, who were closely followed by an army of medical orderlies.

Food was distributed, wounds were cleaned, sick people cared for and everyone was disinfected to get rid of the lice. Margarete smiled to herself. Against all odds she had survived.

Much to her dismay she learned from the medics the Russians brought into the camp that the battles in Germany continued to rage on, as Hitler foolishly mobilized all reserves, including the crippled, the half-blind, young boys, and veterans from the last war.

Again, she thought about Stefan, praying that he and his frail grandfather had been spared from the *Volkssturm*. Now that she was free, she yearned to return to Gut Plaun hoping the man she loved had survived. There was so much she wanted to tell him, foremost that she loved him with all her heart and never wanted to be separated again, not even for a single day.

39

APRIL 1945

Stefan had moved into one of the servants' rooms at the manor. He said it was more convenient, since it was closer to the factory, whereas the real reason was that he felt the need to protect Frau Mertens, Gloria, Dora and the two children.

Nils, the only other remaining male on Gut Plaun, except for the foreign workers, had received his drafting papers about a month ago. The *Volkssturm* was the last of Hitler's utter follies, dragging out the inevitable and causing thousands of needless casualties without making a dent in the war effort. The Führer though had determined on this last ditch resort of drafting men over sixty and boys from age twelve upwards into an army that was already breaking apart under the constant onslaught of the Allied forces.

The hastily thrown up *Volkssturm* units were equipped with little more than their fighting spirits to oppose the enemy. No uniforms, no weapons, no bullets. Nothing. Every half-witted imbecile knew the poor sods had no chance against an enemy that was superior not only in numbers, but also in arms, training and experience.

Stefan himself had escaped conscription, because apparently even in his last desperate attempt to alter the course of the war, Hitler wasn't willing to use those he deemed politically unreliable.

Sadly smiling to himself, Stefan half regretted this directive, since he would have been able to wreak so much havoc among the German lines, in spite of knowing full well that his sabotage would have most certainly resulted in being hanged.

Returning from the factory, he passed the stables, where some of the foreign workers still resided, despite the fact that they didn't have horses to care for.

"Herr Stober, can I have a word?" Ladislaus approached him.

Stefan liked the other man for his logical thinking and grasp on organization. "Sure. How can I help?"

"It's just... I've been thinking about what to do when the Russians arrive."

Stefan nodded pensively. There was no doubt whatsoever that the Red Army would conquer Plau am See, it was just a matter of when. Even according to the official news from Goebbels' propaganda ministry, the Wehrmacht was withdrawing on all frontlines. "I've been worried about this myself. We're definitely not going to sacrifice more people by resisting. I'll have a word with Frau Mertens to prepare white flags to hang on every building, especially the manor."

He didn't mention how much he worried that the Russians would act according to their reputation and go on a rampage of rape, murder and mutilation at Gut Plaun.

"That's a good idea," Ladislaus said, his face revealing he didn't think it was enough.

"Did you have anything else in mind?" Stefan asked, the responsibility for the well-being of dozens of workers, Germans and foreigners, as well as several hundred prisoners weighing heavily on his shoulders.

"Please don't think me preposterous," Ladislaus hedged. For

a Pole, having been treated as an inferior human by the Germans for so many years, it must not be easy to speak his mind, despite the cordial treatment he'd experienced from Stefan.

"Certainly not." Stefan leveled his eyes at him. He decided to humble himself to make the other man feel as an equal. "The burden to keep everyone under my care safe is a lot to carry and I certainly welcome any advice or help offered."

Ladislaus gave a tiny smile. "You're a good man. Everyone here from Fräulein Annegret herself, Herr Gundelmann and his wife Dora, even the rather scary housekeeper Frau Mertens has treated us well, and believe me, we've experienced otherwise. Therefore, perhaps as a form of repaying your kindness, I wanted to offer my services dealing with the Russians once they arrive. I can't promise any results, but I do speak their language, and might be able to negotiate lenience for the people living here."

The mention of Annegret caused a sharp sting to Stefan's heart. Ignoring the pain, he answered, "That is a very generous offer, and I'm immensely grateful. I trust you to have the best interest especially of the women in your mind. So, when the time comes, please do what you consider best and don't feel obliged to get my permission first. You might only have one chance to get the Russians to listen to you."

"I will. And thank you for your trust." Ladislaus beamed with pride beneath his serious expression.

"For now we should stock up on provisions, water, wood and coal, anything really to weather at least four weeks without access to outside supplies."

"I'm on it," Ladislaus said.

After bidding him goodbye, Stefan was in a very pensive mood. The prospect of the Red Army conquering the area was both hopeful and frightening at the same time. As bad as the Nazi regime was, life would probably be worse under the

Russians, at least for those who had been born into the German master race.

His heart grew even more weary when he thought of Margarete. From everything he knew about the treatment of Jews in the camps, logic told him that she must be dead by now, yet he refused to acknowledge it. Something in his soul sensed that she was still alive, because every time he thought of her, he felt that intimate connection as if she were right by his side. No, he would know if she had died. *My darling Gretchen, it'll be all over soon. Just hang on for a few more weeks.*

———

It was on a bright sunny day at the beginning of May 1945 when the Russians arrived at Plau am See. Stefan was in the factory when several tanks drove up to the gate, Red Army soldiers with machine guns rushing out.

They arrested him alongside two other German workers, while they set the prisoners free. Without anywhere to go though, most of them opted for staying on in the factory premises, with the only difference that everyone stopped working.

Stefan was dragged onto a truck following the tanks and driven into town, where the Russians had already set up some kind of temporary administration. After a short process of jotting down his personal data, he was unceremoniously thrown into prison. Unsurprisingly he found himself in the company of the town's few remaining SS men and the mayor.

Stefan had half expected such a treatment, despite him never having been on the Nazi's side, but he was more worried about the women at the manor than about himself. Thus he placed his trust in Ladislaus and his ability to protect them, especially Dora and her two little children.

The next afternoon the door to the prison cell opened and

none other than Ladislaus showed up together with a Russian soldier, pointing at Stefan. "That's him."

For a split-second Stefan feared for the worst, hot and cold shivers rushing down his spine. He took a calming breath telling himself that he couldn't have misjudged the Pole so starkly and put on a brave face.

Then, the soldier beckoned with his machine gun at Stefan, whose heart began to gallop wildly, and said, "You are free. Go."

Not quite believing his ears, Stefan somehow managed to nod, scrambled to his feet and walked out of the cell. Only Ladislaus' encouraging expression kept him in good spirits, following the soldier upstairs while at the same time fearing they'd lead him directly to the gallows.

A huge weight fell from his shoulders when he was led into the former police chief's office, where another soldier handed him his papers. "Here you go."

Out on the street in front of the police station, Stefan finally breathed again the sweet smell of freedom. He turned toward Ladislaus. "Thank you so much for getting me out. You probably saved my life."

"Sorry that it took so long, I had to make sure the women were safe first," Ladislaus said.

Stefan almost cried with relief, since he'd been worried about the women at the manor the entire time. "How can I ever pay you back for this?"

"Actually it's me paying you back, since you treated me and my compatriots so well."

During their hour-long march to Gut Plaun, Stefan finally asked the question that had been on the tip of his tongue ever since Ladislaus had shown up in his cell. "How did you pull this off?"

It was as if the tension of six years of war fell off Ladislaus in that very instant, since he broke out into a huge grin as he explained. "It wasn't that difficult actually. When the Russians noticed our prisoner garb and shorn heads, they immediately lowered their weapons."

Now Stefan was glad he'd insisted on them keeping up the pretenses, so as not to be mistaken for civilians, which would have led to problems, not only with the Nazis, but apparently also with the Russians.

"They were quite surprised about me speaking their language and immediately brought me to their commanding officer. After downing several glasses of vodka,"—Ladislaus gave a half grin—"which I was barely able to stomach after years of abstinence, the officer and I became best friends. Another vodka later, he tasked me with running Gut Plaun until he gets a better grasp on what needs to be done. He said he's busy setting up some kind of administration and desperately needs farmers to produce food."

"How serendipitous." Stefan had no problems to being relegated to working under Ladislaus, since he knew the man to be honest and fair.

"Yes. I've grown quite fond of the remaining foals and people here. Anyhow, after making my plea for the integrity of the women under my care—and I took the liberty to include not only the employees at the manor, but the former female prisoners as well—I then told Major Dobrolev that I absolutely needed your expertise to keep up food production on the farm and that you had always behaved correctly toward the prisoners."

"Once again, I thank you so much for probably saving my life."

The two of them silently walked side by side, until Stefan spoke up again. "I assume the munitions factory has ceased to produce, so we could ask the ex-prisoners if they would be willing to work for us on the farm? We'll need all the hands we can get to sow and plant."

"Yes, that's what Major Dobrolev was worried about too. It

seems that in huge parts of Eastern Europe the fields are lying fallow, as there are neither farmers nor enough grain to feed the population come winter."

Winter was still half a year away, so that seemed to be a rather pessimistic statement until Stefan remembered listening to his grandfather's tales of the big famine after the Great War. As they approached Gut Plaun he asked, "Did your new friend, the major, have an estimate how long the war will last?"

"He thinks it's a matter of days, a week at most. The Russian troops are already on the outskirts of Berlin, having overrun the rural area around here without encountering much resistance."

"Well, if that isn't good news, I don't know what is." Stefan only wished Margarete could be here together with him. The pain whenever he thought of her threatened to break his heart, until he deliberately chose to trust in her incredible courage and resilience that would return her to his side.

40

Margarete had been biding her time in the refugee camp. Once word of Germany's surrender came, she was anxious to return to Gut Plaun, where she hoped find Stefan, Oliver, Dora, and the rest. She even dared to hope that by some miracle Uncle Ernst had made it out of the hell that was Auschwitz.

By now she knew that around ten thousand of the sickest inmates had been liberated ten days after all the healthier prisoners had been evacuated. Though the numbers didn't allow much optimism, she clung to the idea that he'd somehow managed to survive.

About two days after the capitulation, she walked into the camp administration and asked, "When can I return home?"

"Where's your home?"

She paused for a moment, since her real home was in Berlin, yet her immediate concern were the people she'd known under her disguise as Annegret Huber. "In Plau am See, about one hour north of Berlin."

"You're lucky. Unlike many others whose home is now under foreign jurisdiction, you'll be allowed to return as soon as we have processed everyone."

Margarete nodded, though she had no intention of waiting for the slow Russian bureaucracy to catch up with the never-ending influx of displaced people. At the first opportunity she simply walked out of the refugee camp to embark on her journey to Plau am See. It took her several weeks, mostly on foot, sometimes on a train, until she entered the familiar town.

At the sight of the old St. Mary's Church tower reaching high into the sky, she almost cried with relief. She stopped at the nearby fountain to drink some water, speculating where she should go first to search for Stefan, when two women approached the fountain with pails.

Margarete didn't follow their idle gossip until one of them said, "Such a shame about the fisherman."

Instantly her ears perked up, as she listened in on their conversation.

"Yes. Who would have thought that he was hiding an enemy airman. He was such a nice man."

Margarete couldn't hold her curiosity any longer and asked, "Excuse me, ladies, who was the fisherman, you were talking about?"

"Stober," one of the women said.

The shock settled deep in Margarete's bones, threatening to drag her into a whirling, black abyss of misery.

The woman squinted her eyes at Margarete, "Are you alright?"

"Yes, I'm fine. It must be the exhaustion." Ever since her arrest, Margarete had slowly changed back into herself, speaking, walking and behaving like the Jewish girl once again.

"You remind me of someone, does your family live here?" the other woman asked.

Having worn the same dress for the past six months since leaving Gut Plaun, she apparently looked too disheveled for these women to recognize her as the elegant heiress she'd once pretended to be.

"No, I'm passing through here, after being liberated from the camps the Nazis sent me to." Margarete couldn't help but answer with bile in her voice.

At the mention of the camps and seeing Margarete's regretful condition, the two women quickly looked elsewhere and hurried to get away from the fountain.

Absolutely devastated by the news of Stefan's death, Margarete sat next to the fountain for a long, long time, at odds with the fact that she should have survived when he hadn't. Only the prospect of seeing her beloved again had kept her fighting all this time, and now that she'd finally made it home, he wasn't there anymore.

After what seemed like an eternity, she finally found the energy to get up. Going to the wharf or Grandfather Stober's house made no sense anymore, so she decided to walk the five miles to Gut Plaun. Perhaps she would at least find Dora and Oliver there. Along the way she didn't meet a single person and with every step her grief, her pain and her anxiety grew.

When she passed by the stud, she saw neither horses in the corrals nor people in the vicinity. Fear constricted her throat and she unconsciously increased her pace, bracing herself for more horrible news.

The manor itself stood unscathed. Like on the first day she'd come here almost three years ago, the majestic building impressed her and made her feel small. Hesitantly walking up the stairs, she knocked on the front door. Moments later it was opened and Dora stepped outside.

"How can I help?" Dora asked.

"It's me." Margarete slipped effortlessly into the high-pitched tone of Annegret's voice and seconds later observed how recognition washed over Dora.

"Fräulein Annegret! What a joy to see you again! We've been so worried—"

"It's Margarete Rosenbaum. Annegret Huber has been

dead for a long time." At the displaced persons camp she'd had plenty of time to think about the best course to restart her life. In spite of the conveniences being Annegret had afforded her, she much preferred being herself again. Dead poor, but with a clear conscience. Furthermore, it would probably make her life under the Soviet occupation easier, at least she hoped so. Although she had never thought further than returning to Gut Plaun, since all her focus had been on reuniting with Stefan and the others.

"Oh, Fräulein Margarete." Dora fell back into her annoying habit of curtsying, when she was nervous, doing it not once, but three times.

"Just Margarete, please."

"Yes, Fr— Margarete." It apparently would take a while until Dora came to grips with the reality that Margarete wasn't her mistress anymore. "It's so good to see you. We thought for sure you were dead."

"Who else is here?" Margarete worried her lip, anxiously awaiting the answer how many of the people dear to her had survived.

"Oh, Fr— I mean, Margarete, you'll be so pleased. Nils has returned from the front, and Frau Mertens is here, and my two children and," she said, smiling with delight, "Herr Stober."

"Stefan is not dead?" Margarete's knees gave out beneath her and it was only thanks to Dora's quick reaction, catching her around the middle, that she didn't tumble to the ground.

"No. They arrested him on the same day when the Russians came here, but Ladislaus got him out. He also protected all the women at the manor—"

"Wait. Not so fast." Margarete interrupted her, still not quite believing that her beloved Stefan might still be alive. "Please can I get a glass of water and maybe something to eat?"

"Of course, how rude of me. Follow me." A few steps before

they reached the kitchen, Dora turned around and asked, "What shall we tell Frau Mertens?"

"She doesn't know?"

Dora shook her head. "After you were arrested, Herr Stober and I thought it best not to tell anyone, so we invented the story that you, I mean Fräulein Annegret, had met some old friends and stayed with them."

"I guess we'll have to tell her the truth." Margarete didn't look forward to that conversation, but since she'd decided to start her new life with a clean slate, there was really no way around it.

"She currently is in town. Herr Stober, though, should be in Oliver's office."

Margarete seemed to notice a sudden severity as Dora mentioned her husband's name and asked, "What about Oliver? Where is he?"

Pressing her lips into a thin line, Dora shook her head before she answered. "He was killed in action."

"I'm so sorry for you." Margarete genuinely grieved not only for the man who'd become a good friend, but also for his widow and the children who'd have to grow up without a father. She barely dared to ask her next question. "What about your second child?"

"He's fine. He was born much too early, but has developed well. I named him Oliver in honor of his father."

"If I can help with anything..." Margarete offered, before she remembered that she was a destitute Jewish survivor, without a single penny to her name.

"Thank you. I'm fine." They had reached the kitchen, where Dora poured her a glass of water and cut a piece of bread, which Margarete devoured within an instant.

"Do you want to see Herr Stober now? He usually doesn't like to be disturbed when he's in the office, but I know he'll want to see you. He's been eaten up with guilt over having to leave you in Berlin."

Margarete suddenly felt acutely aware of her sorry condition. Even without looking into a mirror she knew that she must look like a scarecrow with her emaciated frame and the wrinkled face of an old hag. "Wait. I'm not sure I'm ready..."

Just in that moment, the door to the kitchen opened and a flaxen-haired head peeked inside. "Dora, can you please..." Stefan stopped mid-sentence, looking as if he'd seen a ghost. All of the color drained from his face and his eyes filled with disbelief. "Gretchen? My darling! Is that really you?"

She nodded, too overwhelmed to utter a single word. Until this very moment she hadn't really believed Dora's assurances that he was alive. Taking a tentative step forward, she suddenly was swept up in his arms, his lips pressing on hers as he feverishly pulled her against his body, as if he never wanted to let her go again. Out of the corner of her eye, she noticed how Dora backed out of the kitchen to give the two of them some privacy.

"I can't believe you're here," he said, rubbing her back. "So many times I despaired, thinking you were dead for sure."

"I thought the same thing many times, but by some miracle I survived."

"My love. My sweet, sweet love. Now that I have you back, nothing else is important anymore. Let me hold you." He pressed her even closer against him. "I still can't believe you're really here in my arms."

"Dora, I thought I heard someone crying. Is everything—" Frau Mertens stopped speaking as she entered the kitchen and saw Margarete wrapped in Stefan's arms.

"You're home," Frau Mertens stated unnecessarily.

"Yes. There were times I didn't believe anymore that I would ever return," Margarete answered.

"What happened after you were arrested?" Stefan asked.

"Why on earth would anyone arrest you? And why didn't

you send us a note to let us know?" Frau Mertens seemed outraged that such an injustice could happen.

In that moment Margarete remembered Frau Mertens still thought she was Annegret. She had wanted to break the news in a gentler manner, but now she was backed into a corner without the time or leisure for explanations. "I wish I could have told you differently, Frau Mertens." She gave the housekeeper a vague smile. "I'm not Annegret Huber. I was the Hubers' maid in Berlin. When Annegret was killed during a bombing raid alongside her parents, I adopted her identity to save myself."

"You are... what?"

"My real name is Margarete Rosenbaum and I'm a Jew."

Frau Mertens' eyes became as big as saucers, before she gave a frustrated scream and stomped from the room, slamming the door behind her.

Margarete started to go after her, but Stefan held her arm. "Let her be."

"I should go to her and explain."

"Explain what? That you've been lying to her all these years?" Stefan asked.

Margarete sighed and shook her head. "Perhaps not."

"She'll come around in time. Many people had to do awful things to stay alive. Lying probably is the least grave of crimes."

Margarete wasn't so sure, nevertheless she relaxed in Stefan's hold. "You can't imagine my devastation when two women in town told me the Nazis had executed you."

Stefan's face turned into a grimace of grief. "That was my grandfather. Something went wrong while we were in Berlin and he got caught hiding an enemy airman."

"I'm so sorry for your grandfather, I know how much you loved him." She snuggled against his broad chest, relishing in the sensation of belonging it gave her. After a while she asked, "Have you heard from my uncle Ernst?"

"No. News is still trickling in on a daily basis. We hadn't heard from you before today, either."

"Uncle Ernst and I met in Berlin. We stayed together in a work detail sweeping the streets after every bombing raid, but got separated in Auschwitz."

"You were... there?" Stefan's voice wobbled with emotion.

"Yes and no. I got evacuated with the rest of the healthier prisoners on the day of our arrival there, but Uncle Ernst was too frail, so he stayed behind. I've been riddled with guilt that I haven't taken better care of him."

Stefan stroked her lifeless hair and murmured, "It's not your fault, my darling. You did all you could."

"My mind knows that, but my heart doesn't." She soaked up the warmth, the energy and the love radiating off his body. "I shall write a letter to Aunt Heidi, maybe she has heard something from him. If he survived, he'll return to Leipzig to search for his wife."

"That's a good idea."

Just then, the door opened once more and Ladislaus entered with a worried expression on his face. "Frau Mertens seems pretty upset, what—" He looked at Stefan and Margarete standing entwined in each other's arms. "And you are?"

"Margarete, I mean..." She looked at the man, recognizing him as one of the foreign workers.

Stefan jumped in to explain, "This is Ladislaus, you may remember him. He's one of the Polish prisoners who used to work in the stables. The Soviets made him the new estate manager."

Suddenly Ladislaus' opened his eyes wide with surprise. "Fräulein Annegret, please forgive me for not recognizing you. It's an honor to have you back at Gut Plaun."

She stopped him with a wave of her hand. "Except that I'm not really Annegret Huber. When I had the chance, I took on her identity to save my own life. My real name is Margarete Rosenbaum and I'm a Jew."

Ladislaus' mouth hung agape at the revelation. For at least thirty seconds no sound was heard in the kitchen, until he recovered his composure. "Well, that certainly explains a lot. In any case, you can stay at Gut Plaun for as long as you wish and live as if you were the lady of the manor. And don't you worry, I'll make sure the Russians know you're off limits."

"Thank you so very much." Margarete gave him a relieved smile. "It's feels so good to be back with friends."

"You deserve it, because you treated the prisoners under your charge so exceedingly well."

"What happened to them?" she asked.

"I believe only a handful died after you were gone. Some have decided to stay as farmhands, but most of them have chosen to return to their homes."

"That makes me so happy to hear." Margarete remembered Lena, the escaped prisoner who'd set her on the path to help thousands in the factory. She hadn't been able to save Lena, but so many others. *Wherever you are now, Lena, I hope you know the war—and the Jewish suffering— is over.*

"So you don't mind that you're no longer in charge of Gut Plaun?" Ladislaus asked.

"Not at all. It was never mine to begin with. I was simply using it to help bolster my false identity. Trust me, I'm much happier being myself again."

EPILOGUE

Weeks passed and summer came to an end when Margarete finally received a letter from Ernst and Heidi. Frau Mertens was the one who accepted it. She still held a grudge against Margarete for lying to her all this time, although she'd come to understand that people had done worse things to survive.

"This is for you, from Oberscharführer your uncle," she said, holding out the letter.

Overjoyed, Margarete settled on the porch with a glass of water, opened the envelope and took her time to savor every word.

My dear Gretchen,

You can't imagine my joy when your letter reached us. To know you survived the ordeal after we were separated took a huge burden from my shoulders.

I know you felt guilty for having to leave me behind, but after everything I heard, I was handed the easier fate. By some providence the Nazis couldn't expedite their plan to kill all the sick patients. They hurriedly fled the Russian advance, leaving the camp unguarded. You will understand that I won't go into detail, since you certainly endured your own share of hardships and it's best to observe silence over the past so as not to relive it again.

Suffice to say, one man took it upon himself to care for me and thanks to him I survived the ten days in limbo until the Russians liberated us. Isn't it an irony that the very soldiers Goebbels had taught every German to fear and loathe were the ones to rescue me in the end?

Shortly after the war I returned to Leipzig and, oh glorious miracle, found my beloved Heidi there. Much thinner than I remembered her, with more gray streaks and deep creases of sorrow, but as lovable, if not more, than when I first met her almost thirty years ago.

She sends you her best regards, by the way, and is equally delighted that you survived.

Unfortunately this letter must also bring you sad news. With the help of the Red Cross we found out that my dear brother, your father, along with the entire rest of your family perished in the same camp that you and I miraculously survived.

Our sister is still missing but there is not much hope to find her again, her husband and children are all confirmed dead, save for one niece who returned from Bergen-Belsen just a few weeks ago and has moved in with us until she gets her bearings.

I wrote before, let's not dwell on the past. Now is the time to look forward and embrace our future. Heidi and I have discussed at length whether we should emigrate to a place not riddled with these awful memories, but have finally come to the conclusion that you cannot shift old trees like us. We have survived the worst, Hitler has taken everything from us, yet he couldn't take our dignity and our longing for home.

Thus, we are determined to stay in Germany. We'd love to

wrap you into our arms again, perhaps next summer, when traveling has become easier?

Meanwhile, please stay in touch and let us know where you go, since I don't expect you to stay at a manor that doesn't belong to you.

Love,

Uncle Ernst and Aunt Heidi

Stefan found her beaming from ear to ear. In spite of being happy for her, she sensed a deep sadness in him. Since she knew how much being near the water helped him to work through his emotions, she suggested, "Let's go down to the lake, shall we?"

Half an hour later, they arrived at the cliff where Horst Richter had forced her to jump into the icy water so many months earlier. She suppressed a shudder as the memories threatened to overwhelm her, took Stefan's hand and led him onto the small pebble beach next to the cliff.

"What's wrong?" she asked.

Stefan gave her a forlorn gaze, before he averted his eyes across the water to the other side. "I used to love this place, especially the lake. Now, everywhere I look I see my grandfather, but it's not his smiling face, it's his corpse hanging in the town square. It's almost as if he's trying to scare me away."

"Your grandfather was a wise man. Perhaps he's right and your time here has come to an end."

"Hmm." He nodded slowly. "I've been thinking about this a lot. I moved here and became a fisherman because the Nazis sacked me from my job, but deep in my heart I always wanted to be a chemical engineer. I'd love to return to Cologne and help build up our country's industry again."

She smiled. "What's keeping you from fulfilling your dream?"

He turned around, squinting his eyes at her. "You don't know?"

"No."

"You."

"Me?" Margarete asked surprised.

"Is that so strange? I love you so much. I almost lost you, now I never want to be separated from you again. Not even for a single night. How can I move to Cologne without you?"

She shook her head, unable to grasp his failed logic. "But... you wouldn't have to go alone."

"What?" His mouth hung agape and it took him several seconds to process her answer. "Does that mean you'd come with me?"

"Oh, Stefan, how can you be so daft?" she scolded him. "Gut Plaun gave me a home when I needed one, but I don't *belong* here. You are my home and I'll be happy anywhere, as long as it is with you."

"Really? You'd give up your comfortable life here and venture with me into an unknown future in an unknown city?"

"I certainly would," she said, just to find herself swept up in his arms, his lips feverishly pressing kisses all over her face. Then he sat her down and said, "Let's make this right. Will you, Margarete Rosenbaum, loveliest woman on earth, agree to become my wife?"

"Actually I already answered that question, don't you remember?"

He took her hand. "I do remember, but back then it was a hypothetical question, since we couldn't actually get married. In any case, last time the woman I asked to marry me called herself Annegret, today I ask Margarete. What is her answer?"

"Yes. Yes. Yes. I do." Then she fell into his arms, kissing him as if she never wanted to stop again.

———

They got married in Plau am See in a small ceremony at the town hall with just their closest friends, wearing Stefan's grandparents' rings once again. After the reception at the manor, Margarete took Dora aside. "If you want to move with us to Cologne, Stefan and I will help you get on your feet."

"That is so kind of you, but I want to return to Ukraine. Without Oliver, there's nothing to keep me here. My parents will be delighted to meet their grandchildren and can help raise them."

"I can understand this. Have you already thought about when to leave?"

"Not really, since I wanted to save up some funds first. I don't want to arrive home empty-handed," Dora said.

"If that's the only thing holding you back, it can be solved quickly. Come with me." Margarete climbed the stairs to the suite that belonged to her when she posed as Fräulein Annegret and where she now resided together with Stefan. Once there she crawled into the space where she'd hidden Lena during her stay at the manor and returned with a package wrapped in a soft cloth.

"What's this?" Dora marveled.

Margarete unwrapped it and looked at the precious jewels. She took the pearl studs she'd worn so often during her time as Annegret, and wrapped the rest again into the cloth, before she handed it to Dora.

"No, I... I can't possibly accept this."

"Yes, you can. They belonged to Frau Huber and I don't want any of it. They were never mine to begin with."

"But you..." Dora protested.

"Without you I wouldn't be here. You could have turned me in to the Gestapo when you found Lena in my rooms."

"I would never have."

"I know. You're the most loyal and honest person I know. You were kind to me when everyone else hated me. You loved Oliver with all your heart, you kept my secret, assisted me in helping the prisoners, you carried food to Olga, you did so much. Now it's time to think of yourself and your children. Take the jewelry." Margarete closed Dora's hand around the silken cloth. "I insist."

"Thank you, that is incredibly generous of you. Olga is returning home too and with this," she pointed at the pouch, "we can travel together most of the journey."

"What happened to the girl she and Frau Gusen were hiding? Did she survive?"

"Lili? Yes, she made it through." Dora beamed with joy, although seconds later a shadow darkened her expression. "Sadly none of Lili's family survived."

"Where will she live?"

"Frau Gusen agreed that Lili can stay with her for as long as she wants. I believe the old woman needs Lili as much as the girl needs her. The two of them will be fine."

"That's a relief," Margarete said, nostalgia washing over her. In an unusual expression of emotions, she wrapped her arms around Dora. "Wishing you all the best for your future."

Dora's voice was hoarse as she replied, "You are a true friend, Margarete. I'll never forget you, or my life at Gut Plaun."

———

Two weeks later another letter arrived at Gut Plaun, and this time it was addressed to Dora. It was the first time she'd ever received a letter, so she turned it in her hands, wondering who it was from. Since it didn't show a sender's address, she finally opened the envelope with curiosity.

When she finished reading, tears streamed down her cheeks. Soon though, she began to smile at the memory of her beloved Oliver. The letter had been written by one of his comrades, a young man called Kalle, who not only attributed his own survival to being taken under Oliver's wing, but also told her the story of her husband's heroic death.

Dora imagined the scene of Oliver giving these two women a chance at survival so vividly it was as though she'd been right there next to him, because it captured the essence of the man he'd been. He had died the same way he had lived: spreading kindness and protecting those who needed it most.

Although she would grieve for him the rest of her life, this letter gave her the much-needed peace of mind that Oliver's death had not been in vain.

Several days later Dora and the two children boarded a train headed for Ukraine. That same day, Margarete and Stefan left as well, heading in the opposite direction. Ladislaus wished them luck and announced that he and the maid, Gloria, were getting married and would return to Poland by the end of the year. Frau Mertens retired from working and settled into a small cottage in town.

For Margarete it was a bittersweet moment, because leaving Gut Plaun was the final line underneath her existence as Annegret Huber. In the train, she looked at the landscape that had become so familiar, reflecting on the events of the past years. So many things had happened since the serendipitous bombing of the Huber villa in Berlin, which had resulted in her assuming Annegret's identity. She'd been incredibly naïve when first arriving at Aunt Heidi's house in Leipzig; it was a wonder that she'd even survived those first weeks until settling down in Paris with Wilhelm. She still fondly remembered him, despite all his flaws. In the end he'd proven himself to been a good-hearted man, sacrificing himself for her and the greater good.

"I am such a lucky woman," she said to Stefan.

"That does sound strange coming from someone who recently returned from the horrific camps." He took her hand into his, as she leaned against him.

"I know, but apart from all the terrible things that have happened, I have received so much goodness from individuals, especially from Oliver and Dora. They not only helped me, but they also supported my quest of helping the prisoners every step of the way, despite the high risk for them personally. Without them, I couldn't have done it." She looked at Stefan, her eyes shining with love. "But most of all, I'm lucky because I met you."

He gave her his irresistible smile. "Actually, I'm the lucky one to have found you. I just wish I could have told my grandfather who you really are. He'd be so proud."

"I'm sure he'll be watching us from wherever he is now."

———

Once they arrived in Cologne, Stefan easily found a job with the British occupiers, since he could prove he'd been considered politically unreliable by the Nazis. They rented a beautiful newly constructed apartment on the outskirts of Cologne, and half a year later Margarete fell pregnant.

Within the year, Ernst and Heidi decided to join them in Cologne. They were both getting older and with the damage Ernst had sustained from his years in the prisons and camps, they both felt safer having family nearby. The apartment became rather cramped, but Margarete was happy nonetheless. She especially welcomed Heidi's help with her newborn daughter.

"I'm so happy," Stefan said as he pulled Margarete close and nuzzled her neck.

"Me too. We survived so many things and yet no matter

what tried to knock us down, we were able to get back up again. Thank you for believing in me and for always doing what is best, even when it's the hard thing to do."

"That's what love does. Love stands firm in the midst of adversity and I'm so grateful that I met you. You are my life."

A LETTER FROM MARION

Dear Reader,

Thank you so much for reading *Daughter of the Dawn*. If you did enjoy it, and want to keep up to date with all my latest releases, just sign up at the following link. Your email address will never be shared and you can unsubscribe at any time.

www.bookouture.com/marion-kummerow

Sadly, this is the last book in the Margarete's Journey series, but I'm already working on a new series about mixed couples with one them being Jewish and the other one Christian/Aryan. As always the initial idea expanded into so much more. It'll need a lot of research, since the first book will take us back to the year 1923 to the Beer Hall Putsch, Hitler's failed attempt to overthrow the government.

You will encounter some people from Margarete's Journey in the new series, and in the later books I plan to explore the path why Thea (the catcher) has turned against her own people, which I find absolutely fascinating in a terrible way.

Anyhow, back to *Daughter of the Dawn*. After Stefan rescued her, things seemed to float along much too easily for Margarete, so I had to give her a new challenge.

What better reason to do risky things than desperately needing money? Without Katze's blackmail there wouldn't have been a reason to leave her comparatively safe location at Gut

Plaun and travel to Berlin, where she was captured. I imagine that corrupt and cruel Katze was put into prison, where some of his former victims served as guards and made him pay for his sins.

Thea Blume is an intriguing character who was inspired by the real person Stella Goldschlag, a notorious catcher who worked for the Gestapo and was nicknamed by her fellow Jews "the blonde poison" or "the horror from Kürfürstendamm"; Kurfürstendamm being the main shopping street in Berlin.

I'm planning to dig much deeper into her life and her motivation to become a collaborator with the Gestapo in later books of the new series.

About the sabotage: the nitropenta factory is modeled after the one that actually existed in the nearby town of Malchow, just across the lake. There is no evidence of sabotage in that factory. My grandfather, though, worked as chemical engineer at Loewe Radio, which produced radio equipment for the Wehrmacht. He was arrested by the Gestapo for, amongst other charges, sabotaging the production, which you can read about in the trilogy, Love and Resistance in WW2 Germany. I have a witness report from one of his co-conspirators, which he made during the denazification process after the war on how a small group at Loewe sabotaged the production while always blaming bad quality of raw materials, or normal wear and tear of production machines.

As for Ladislaus, I wanted to show how far a little bit of kindness goes. Poland has changed hands so many times during the past centuries that many citizens learned to speak two or three languages, which proved very useful both being a German prisoner and later with the Soviet army. So it often happened that the former prisoners helped those who had treated them well and protected the local women from being raped or otherwise harmed. Although the opposite is true as well, and many former forced workers, presumedly those who had been treated badly by their "employers", joined the occupying powers in the looting, lynching and torturing.

Throughout the three prior books my editor repeatedly hinted that she wanted a happy end for Ernst and Heidi. Poor Uncle Ernst has suffered enough, so I happily obliged and let him and his wife spend the rest of their days near their niece Margarete and hopefully many grandnieces and grandnephews. You will meet the young Ernst Rosenbaum again in my next series.

The SS Hauptscharführer Dobberke is a real person, whose penchant for beating the prisoners in his care unfortunately was true. He became Stella Goldschlag's handler (the Jewish catcher who inspired Thea Blume). Despite his obvious anti-Semitism he apparently had a long-term relationship with a Jewish nurse, who also was a prisoner in the transit camp at Schulstrasse.

As for the short time Ernst and Margarete spent in Auschwitz, Primo Levi's memoir *If This Is a Man* gave me a clear idea of what transpired in the ten "days of limbo" between January 17th 1945, when the SS left the camp, and January 27th when the Red Army liberated it. Btw. Primo Levi was an Italian Jew and resister who when captured by the Nazis wrongly believed that admitting to being a Jew was the lesser crime than belonging to the resistance.

In reality the last transport to Auschwitz left Berlin much earlier than in *Daughter of the Dawn*. The exact date is not clear, it must have been around November or December 1944. Yet, I didn't want Ernst and Margarete to spend much time in Auschwitz, because I dreaded going into details about their experiences there. Perhaps one day I'll be courageous enough to write a book dedicated to a prisoner inside this epitome of evil.

As for Margarete's experiences on the death march, I have written about this topic more extensively in the book *Uncommon Sacrifice* in my War Girl series. If you're interested in a non-fiction book by a survivor of the death march leaving Auschwitz I can recommend *The Brothers of Auschwitz* by Malka Adler. Some of the scenes Margarete lives through have been inspired by his true experiences.

The Russian army arrived between April 30th and May 2nd in the area around Plau am See to occupy the villages without much resistance. In time they appropriated most of the bigger estates such as Gut Plaun. They usually requisitioned the buildings for their officers and later seized the entire property along with the fortune attached to it, if there was any left. So, after Margarete and Stefan left, they might have moved in their administrative people, or, since the manor was rather far away from town, they might have kept it as a state-owned farm to produce food under a manager like Ladislaus. Most probably they would have later installed a German communist to run it.

As for the factory, it was dismantled, like most every factory in the Soviet occupied zone and shipped to Russia as part of the war reparations. The Soviets even dismantled rail tracks and sent them home, just to find out later that you cannot transport so many or such huge cargoes on the streets.

If you're wondering what happened to Thomas Kallfass after he was sent to Mauthausen, I might one day in the future write a book set in that camp which I visited on a research trip with a group of like-minded people from the Bergen-Belsen study group. For the moment, I imagine that he suffered greatly, because SS men who ended up in the camps were disliked by prisoners and guards alike. He finally died there of starvation coupled with exhaustion from working in the quarry.

I want to end this book on an uplifting note though, reminding you that even in the most evil of times, goodness exists; we just have to find it. We may not be able to change the world, our governments, or the grand scheme of things, but we can make a difference in the lives of the people around us.

Again, thank you so much for reading *Daughter of the*

Dawn. I hope you loved it, and if you did I would be very grateful if you could write a review. I'd love to hear what you think, and it makes such a difference helping new readers to discover one of my books for the first time.

I love hearing from my readers—you can get in touch on my Facebook page, through Twitter, Goodreads or my website.

Marion Kummerow

https://kummerow.info

 facebook.com/AutorinKummerow
twitter.com/MarionKummerow

Made in United States
Orlando, FL
18 April 2023

32206115R00157